Dark Overlord's Wife

THE CHILDREN OF THE GODS
BOOK THIRTY-NINE

I. T. LUCAS

Dark Overlord's Wife is a work of fiction! Names, characters, places and incidents are products of the author's imagination or are used fictitiously and are not to be construed as real. Any similarity to actual persons, organizations and/or events is purely coincidental.

Copyright © 2020 by I. T. Lucas

All rights reserved.

No part of this book may be reproduced in any form or by any electronic or mechanical means, including information storage and retrieval systems, without written permission from the author, except for the use of brief quotations in a book review.

Published by Evening Star Press

Jacki

Previously.

"What's wrong?" Kalugal frowned. "Why are you crying? Talk to me, Jacki. I need to know what's happened."

It was the damn kiss's fault.

One passionate moment shouldn't have affected her like that, clouding her judgment and weakening her convictions. She was supposed to be stronger and smarter than that.

"I can't do it. I can't be the new toy that you play with until you get bored with it. I wouldn't survive that."

She should have left when she'd had the chance. Agreeing to stay in Kalugal's home had been a colossal mistake, and now she was freaking out because she wasn't sure she could survive it.

But how could she have said no?

For every day she stayed with him, Kalugal made a twenty-five-grand contribution to Kian's charity. At that rate, in just thirty days, the sanctuary for rescued trafficking victims would have received three quarters of a million in donations.

Except, lasting a month without succumbing to temptation or falling for Kalugal was impossible.

In fact, it was already too late.

She hadn't lasted even a week.

Jacki had tried to deny it, refusing to let herself admit how much she wanted him, but the incredible kiss they'd shared just a few moments ago had blasted that thin layer of denial into oblivion.

He was perfect, the kiss had been better than anything she could've imagined, and Jacki realized that forgetting Kalugal would be impossible, and that was after spending only five days with him.

An entire month would destroy her.

She needed to run, find a cave to crawl into, and lick her wounds for a decade or two.

Instead, she was sitting on Kalugal's lap and crying her eyes out while he was still waiting for an explanation. He must be thinking that she was having a nervous breakdown, and he wasn't far wrong.

Except, he wasn't looking at her as if she was crazy. Frowning, he seemed offended. "What the hell are you talking about? Do you think that this is a game for me?"

Why was he playing dumb? Did he enjoy hurting her? Or maybe he just didn't understand?

By his own admission, Kalugal had very little contact with humans, and his hookups didn't count as relationships. He probably knew less about women's emotions, fears, and insecurities than the average teenage boy, and she had no choice but to spell it out for him.

"What else could it be? You are you, and I am me, and we are not in the same league on any level. There could never be something long-lasting between us, and I don't do hookups or flings or whatever you want to call them. It's all or nothing for me."

He shook his head. "This is not a casual fling for me, Jacki. I have feelings for you, and I think we could have something beautiful together. But it's not going to happen unless we take the first step." He started rubbing small circles on her back. "What are you so afraid of?"

"I've just spelled it out for you. You are an intelligent guy. It shouldn't be so hard for you to understand."

"You think that we are too different to make it work?"

She nodded. "You are the immortal son of a goddess. I'm a human. I could never be more than a plaything for you, and I refuse to be anyone's toy. Even yours."

"What can I do to prove to you that I am serious?"

Evidently, she hadn't been clear enough. "You can't be. What I want is love, respect, devotion, and loyalty. Nothing less will do. Can you give me that?"

"You have my respect, and as long as we are together, you have my loyalty as well. Love and devotion will take more time, but they need a starting point. They can't happen if you are not willing to take the first step."

Smooth.

All that talk about respect and loyalty and the supposed feelings Kalugal had for her had been a prelude to convincing her to have sex with him.

Why was it so important to him, though? Was he one of those guys who couldn't tolerate losing or accept no for an answer?

Except, that was usually a sign of insecurity, which wasn't something that Kalugal suffered from. He was full of himself and for a good reason. Not only was he a freaking demigod, but he was also smart, incredibly handsome, and charming. Nevertheless, even if he meant what he said, he'd said it with one motive in mind.

"And what is that? Having sex with you?"

"To be frank, yes. I'm not an expert on relationships, but I believe that intimacy and sexual compatibility are vitally important. Those are the building blocks of love."

Jacki had heard a similar speech from most of the guys she'd dated and refused to have sex with.

Her answer to that was well-rehearsed. "Well, I'm not an expert on any of that, but for me, love and commitment are vitally important, and without them, there will be no intimacy and no sex."

That should have been the end of that, but Kalugal persisted. "Have you ever been in love, Jacki?"

She shook her head.

"Have you ever had sex?"

For some reason, that was more difficult to admit than never having been in love. People assumed that there was something wrong with her, and Jacki had learned that it was best to give evasive answers and leave them guessing.

Except, Kalugal had asked a direct question, and the only way she could answer it was with a yes or no.

Jacki shook her head again.

"That explains it."

Finally, he was getting it. Maybe she should have opened with that. "Have you ever been in love?"

"No, but I've had plenty of sex."

She chuckled. "I believe that."

"I don't know if I can fall in love without experiencing intimacy first."

The guy was relentless, but it wasn't going to work. "And I can't allow myself the intimacy without having the love first."

He sighed. "Then we have a problem. Any idea how we can solve this?"

Yeah, he could fall in love with her, propose to her, and then she might consider it for about five seconds before saying no. There was no future for them.

Perhaps she should suggest marriage.

In her experience, when every other argument failed, mentioning that scared off even the most persistent guys.

"You could marry me. That would at least fulfill the commitment and devotion requirements, and you wouldn't even have to lie and tell me that you love me."

Holding her breath, Jacki waited to hear Kalugal back out gracefully. He would probably do a better job than other guys who'd just told her to have a nice life and left. And those were the polite ones. Those who hadn't believed her, thinking that she'd used marriage as a way to reject them, had been much worse.

"I will never lie to you, Jacki. I might keep things from you, things I can't reveal before I have your love and loyalty, but I promise never to deceive you."

He seemed sincere.

Was he just an incredible actor, or had he meant everything he'd said?

There was only one way to find out. Her previous marriage proposal had been intended as a jibe, but if she could convince Kalugal that she was serious, he might realize how much he was hurting her by playing games with her feelings, and if he had a heart, he would stop.

"It seems that we are not that different after all. You can't tell me your secrets before you are sure of my love and loyalty, and I can't be intimate with you before I'm sure of your love and devotion. Perhaps marriage is not such a crazy idea. It might be the best solution for both of us."

Kalugal

Marriage could be a solution. A human ceremony that would mean nothing to Kalugal.

They could get a license and be married three days later. If things didn't work out, and Jacki didn't transition, they could get a divorce.

Naturally, he would have her sign a prenup so she wouldn't walk away with half of his fortune, but he would take care of her. The agreement would provide Jacki with enough money to live comfortably for the rest of her natural life, but it would be a reasonable amount. A couple of million should suffice.

The only downside he could foresee was the emotional impact a divorce would have on Jacki, and probably on him as well.

Despite his best efforts to keep an emotional detachment, he was getting used to her company, and losing it would have a significant impact on him. But that would have happened with or without a marriage ceremony, so why not humor Jacki and give her what she wanted?

Should he go down on one knee and propose?

Given that she was sitting on his lap, it would be difficult to do.

Besides, if he was going to do it properly, he needed a ring. Or maybe not? Damn, he should have paid better attention to human customs.

Perhaps it was better to wait until he had everything ready. Also, he should at least pretend that he'd given it some thought. If he popped the question right now, Jacki might not take him seriously.

"I didn't think for a moment that marrying you was a crazy idea. In fact, I was excited about your proposal. But I know that you weren't serious. Besides, you seem to value old-fashioned traditions, and I want to propose to you properly."

Jacki arched a brow. "Are you serious?"

"Very. But since this is all very sudden, I suggest that both of us sleep on it."

Jacki narrowed her eyes. "Not in the same bed."

"Of course not." He stifled a chuckle. "You must have encountered very persistent suitors to be so cautious. Or is it still about my pretend attack on you?"

He'd thought that Jacki had forgiven him, but maybe some residual resentment lingered, and that was why she didn't trust him.

Jacki might think that he was tricking her once again, which in a way he was. Their marriage would be real, but it would be short-lived if Jacki didn't transition, a fact that he was still keeping from her.

"It didn't feel fake when you forced a kiss on me, or when you pushed me down on the couch and got on top of me."

"I know, and I'm sorry. But I explained why it was necessary."

She waved a hand. "I get it, and I even understand that you had no other way of proving that Jin's tethers to you and me were gone, but it wasn't a pleasant experience."

He smiled. "It was for a little bit. You were excited when I started kissing you."

Jacki blushed and looked away. "I'm attracted to you. There, I admitted it. And I was semi-okay with a kiss. But when you pushed me down, I got scared."

He arched a brow. "Only semi-okay?"

"Fine. I liked the kiss. But I knew that there could be nothing between us, which, by the way, hasn't changed. There is nothing really for us to sleep on. We can't get married."

"Because of my immortality?"

She nodded. "Even if you eventually fall in love with me, I only have two or three decades until I get too old to still be attractive to you."

"First of all, I'm already half in love with you. You have your reasons for holding back, and I have mine. But just so you know, I like everything about you. I love spending time with you, and when I don't see you for more than a couple of hours, I miss you." He rubbed his chest. "An ache starts right here, and the only way to alleviate it is to go to you."

"Oh, Kalugal." Her eyes softening, she lifted her hand to his cheek. "That's so sweet, and I feel the same. But all it means is that we are setting ourselves up for a major heartache. There is no solution to the disparity in our lifespans."

"I'll take whatever time I can have with you. Let's enjoy each other one day at a time while it lasts."

It wasn't a lie, but it wasn't the whole truth either. If Jacki didn't transition, he would have to let her go to prevent precisely the heartache she was talking about.

The longer they stayed together, the more difficult the separation would be.

In fact, he was already in trouble.

Since Jacki had moved into his old office, the first thought that entered his mind upon waking up each morning was that she was right there, and it made him happier and more excited to start his day than anything in recent or distant memory.

Waking up with Jacki in his bed would be a hundred times better and losing that would be a thousand times worse.

She shifted and leaned her head against his shoulder. "I asked Jin how she's dealing with Arwel being an immortal, and she said the same thing. Her motto is live for today and don't think about yesterday or tomorrow."

"Smart advice."

Jacki shrugged. "For some. I'm not like Jin."

"In what way?"

She chuckled. "It took her no time at all to get intimate with Arwel. She saw something she liked, and she took it. Case closed. She wasn't thinking about forever, or about love and devotion."

"Good for her."

"I bet you wish that I was more like Jin."

It was a trick question, and despite his limited relationship experience, even he knew not to fall for it.

"I don't want to change anything about you. You are perfect the way you are."

Except for her mortality, the statement was true.

"Are you referring to my looks or to my personality?"

"Everything."

He liked that Jacki was reserved, and that she didn't flirt with every eligible male, and he also liked that she was honest about her feelings. He loved that she was brave, loyal, and devoted to her friends, and he loved her curiosity and her eagerness to learn.

"Are you saying that I'm perfect?" she asked mockingly.

"Absolutely."

"No way. There must be something that I'm missing."

Smirking, he looked at her bare earlobe. "Diamond earrings. You are definitely missing those." He lifted her hand and examined her fingers. "A diamond engagement ring and a professional manicure. You're missing those as well."

Simmons

"Jin and Jacki's signals disappeared again." Elijah walked into the Director's office.

With his sparse hair sticking out in odd directions and his dress shirt unbuttoned at the neck, the esteemed Doctor Roberts looked frazzled. Had he fallen asleep on his office couch again?

"I know." Simmons lifted a finger, signaling for his friend to remain quiet until he activated the loud fan that functioned as a noise machine to keep their conversation private.

His office was clear of surveillance, he had enough clout for that, but the adjoining offices were not, and the walls had ears.

With that done, he sat across from Roberts and braced his elbows on his knees. "They must have returned to the underground facility they've been hiding in."

The signal from the trackers was weak, and it came and went. Nine days ago, Jacki and Jin had started broadcasting, then Jacki's signal winked out for a couple of days before coming back up. Wendy and Richard had started broadcasting only about a week ago, and after Wendy's phone call, they had stopped again.

Simmons figured that Richard and Wendy had been hiding in an underground facility for some reason. Then they had been taken to a cabin in Big Bear, and after Wendy's call, they had been returned to the underground.

But Jacki and Jin hadn't been with them. Last night, Jin's signal had disappeared, and this morning Jacki's had as well. But unlike Wendy and Richard's, their signals had snuffed out of existence abruptly without them changing locations first, which was more troublesome.

There was no way for their hosts, or rather captors as he suspected, to locate the trackers and remove them, so that left only two other possibilities.

The first and more probable cause was interference, but then why had it been absent before?

Also, it was not likely to happen in two separate locations only several hours apart.

Jacki's signal had been coming from an affluent town in the Bay Area, and Jin's had been transmitting from somewhere in the Malibu mountains, but his operative had reported that there was nothing there. Jin must have been camping in the outdoors, but the operative had been too lazy to go searching on foot, saying that the area was too large and too inaccessible for one man to cover.

The other possibility was death. The nanos needed a live host to form the grid and broadcast. But that didn't make sense. Why help the group escape and then get rid of them?

Except, it might have been done in retaliation for Wendy's call. Their captors might have concluded that the trainees were not worth the risk of keeping. Which, with the exception of Jin, was true. Her talent was priceless.

"They could be dead," Roberts echoed his thoughts. "Perhaps the people who helped them escape realized that they'd let a Trojan horse into their community, and they decided to destroy it before it did that to them."

"I doubt it. Jin is too valuable. They might have gotten rid of the other three, but not her."

She was the only one he actually wanted to get back. The others had interesting talents, but they were all pretty useless. Wendy's empathic ability had limited applications, Richard's object telepathy was weak, and Jacki's visions were unpredictable and of little importance. The girl was a knockout, but she was either a lesbian or asexual, so she was of no use to him as a plaything either.

The three were good for only one thing, and that was combining their genetic material to produce more talented offspring.

"I need to make the damn trackers transmit a stronger signal." Roberts smoothed a hand over his sparse hair, trying to force it to behave. "When we send the trainees on missions overseas, they will be useless."

"Can you do that and still keep the trackers undetectable?"

Elijah shook his head. "That's the problem. But science is advancing at breakneck speed, and miniaturization is at the forefront of that. In a year, I might be able to do that."

"That's too far off. Our current group of trainees will be ready for deployment beforehand, and we might need to send some of the graduates overseas." Simmons crossed his arms over his chest. "What about the miniature drones that you've been working on? The drones would follow the weak signal closely, and they could broadcast a much stronger one that we can pick up from anywhere."

"The problem with the small ones is their limited flight range. I'm trying to work out a solution where they attach themselves to moving vehicles, but that's not going to work with aircraft."

Simmons nodded. "We would have to send another operative with each of them to handle the drone and monitor them closely."

Roberts snorted. "As if that's going to prevent them from running away."

Simmons leaned back in his chair. "Our four escapees are a special case that I don't expect to encounter again in the future. To run, they must have had the help of someone with the ability to remove Marisol's compulsion. Not only is it an incredibly rare talent, but to bring him or her along on the mission, their abductors also had to know about the compulsion beforehand."

"The organization captured Marisol. That's how they knew about it."

"That's not going to happen again. After the incident, Marisol agreed to report in every couple of hours and to be implanted with a proper tracker. If she gets abducted again, we will know about it much sooner and retrieve her before she reveals what she knows."

"My trackers are proper. They are just not strong enough." Roberts crossed his arms over his chest. "I wish we could compel our recruiter to keep her mouth shut about the program the way she compels the trainees."

"That would be great, but unfortunately, we don't have another compeller. Besides, Marisol is probably immune to compulsion like she is to every other kind of mind manipulation."

Roberts grimaced. "I really don't like that woman. But that's neither here nor there. Now that we've lost their signals, what are we going to do about our missing trainees?"

"I think they moved all four into an underground facility, where they are probably incarcerated. Except, Jacki and Jin's signal just stopped without first moving to another location, and since one was in the Bay Area and the other in Malibu, I have to assume that the organization has several underground facilities. When they move them again, the trackers will resume broadcasting."

"And if they don't?"

"We only have Jacki's precise location, but my guy reported that the place was an impenetrable fortress with security cameras all over the place. He later changed his report saying that the first address he'd given me was the wrong one, but I suspect that he's been compromised, and that someone either paid him to lie or got into his head. In any case, we could check out both addresses."

"How are you going to pull that off? It's not like we have a massive backup."

Simmons chuckled. "I came up with a good cover story. While collecting information on paranormally talented people, we stumbled upon a suspected terrorist organization that plans to use paranormal abilities to sabotage our government. I'll just forward it to Homeland Security and let them take care of the problem for us."

"I like it. But then what?"

"Then I'll offer to use those damn paranormally talented terrorists in our program. Naturally, they will enjoy none of the privileges our regular trainees do because they are dangerous, and we have to keep them locked up. We can't send them out on missions, but we can use them as test subjects."

Roberts smirked. "In our breeding experiment."

"Bingo."

Vlad

As Vlad drove into the parking garage of the building across the street from the keep, he had the urge to turn around and go home.

He wasn't ready to face Wendy. What was he supposed to say to her? How should he act around her?

Why the hell had he agreed to spend an entire week with her in the remote mountain cabin?

Because he still had feelings for the traitor. That's why. And because he was a fool.

Except, it was too late to chicken out.

So instead of turning around, he navigated the narrow lane spiraling down through the building's many parking levels until he reached the lowest one, which was reserved for the clan.

Bowen and Richard were meeting him there, and he was going to hitch a ride with them to the cabin. That way, he wouldn't have to see Wendy before or during the drive.

Perhaps inspiration would come on the way.

Vanessa should have given him some pointers, but apparently therapists were only good at talking the big talk but useless at giving actionable advice.

"Be patient," she'd said. "Don't keep your anger bottled up inside you," she'd advised. "Be a good listener."

How was he supposed to be patient and at the same time not keep the lid on his anger? It was either one or the other. And what did she mean by being patient? Should he say nothing and just listen?

What if Wendy didn't say anything either?

He could have called Bhathian, who was much better at giving useful advice, but Vlad was sick of everyone butting into his personal life.

Besides, he needed to figure things out for himself, and if things got really awkward between him and Wendy he could just spend his days hiking and not come back until nightfall.

The problem with that was his mother, who was joining them on Sunday. In case things didn't work out between her and Richard either, she might need him there as a buffer.

Watching his mother with the guy, or any man for that matter, would be difficult and would add an additional layer of discomfort. If the jerk misbehaved or wasn't taken with her right away, Vlad was going to blow.

There was a limit to how much he could keep boiling inside of him.

He had suggested that they introduce Stella as his sister, but she and Vanessa had come up with a different story to explain his mom's youthful looks. She was thirty-five years old, had Vlad at sixteen, and looked young because she took good care of her skin.

It was a lame story, but it wasn't up to him.

As the door marked storage opened, Bowen came out with Richard in tow, and Vlad popped the trunk. After taking his duffel bag and guitar case out, he walked over to the two.

"Vlad, my man." Richard pulled him into a bro hug. "I'm glad that you're coming with us, but I'm surprised that you're willing to give Wendy another chance. If it were me, I doubt I would be able to forgive her after the stunt she pulled. You are a better man than me."

Bowen nodded in agreement. "Vanessa must have forced your hand."

Ignoring their remarks, Vlad walked over to Bowen's car. "Can you open the trunk?"

The Guardian clicked the remote, the thing opened, and Vlad dropped his things inside.

Once the three of them were seated, Richard turned around and lifted his arm. "I got a shiny new bracelet. Apparently, my friends and I are emitting transmissions. Bridget thinks that we were implanted with miniature trackers that didn't activate until recently. That's why she didn't detect them."

"I didn't know that was even possible." Vlad pushed his hair out of his face. "When and how was it discovered?"

Backing out from the parking spot, Bowen glanced at him. "The security guys noticed a truck making rounds near our community, and Kalugal's men noticed the same thing next to his place. William tested Jin again, and this time she was emitting a signal, so he made cuffs for all of them to disrupt it."

"Why not just remove the trackers?"

"Because Bridget doesn't know where they are in our bodies, and she doesn't want to cut us up." Richard put his arm down and turned to face the front.

Bowen pulled up to the gate and waited for it to retract. "What it means, though, is that Wendy took a risk for nothing. They knew where she and the others were the entire time."

"But she didn't know that." Vlad crossed his arms over his chest. "So, it doesn't lessen her betrayal."

"I'm with you on that," Richard said. "I don't understand why she would do such a thing, though. Maybe they were holding something over her?"

"Perhaps she didn't like being a fugitive," Bowen suggested. "It's not an easy life, and she is just a young girl. Not everyone is brave."

Richard cast the guardian an incredulous look. "Don't tell me that you are softening toward her."

Bowen shrugged. "Following Vanessa's advice, I'm choosing to reserve judgment."

Wendy

Wendy lifted her hand and looked at the metal cuff that Bowen had slapped on her wrist.

It wasn't ugly. It kind of looked like a bracelet, and it wasn't heavy either. But she didn't believe Bowen's story about the supposed trackers she and Richard had in their bodies.

First of all, there was no way the CT scan and the ultrasound hadn't discovered them, and secondly, she would have known if she had gone through a surgical procedure to put them in.

There would have been a scar or a tenderness in the incision area.

Obviously, the cuffs themselves contained trackers, and the reason she and Richard had them on was so they could be located if they tried to run.

It wasn't a coincidence that they'd gotten them right before leaving for the cabin. Also, the cuffs were impossible to remove. She would even have to shower with it on.

It didn't take a genius to figure out what they were for. Those were prisoner cuffs, similar to the ones used for house arrests.

Whatever. It wasn't as if she could do anything about it, and she couldn't blame Kian for not trusting her. Richard was innocent, but he was deemed guilty by association.

"Does the cabin have a hot tub?" she asked just to break the silence.

Leon shook his head. "I don't think so. But Kian keeps upgrading the place, so who knows, maybe he added one since the last time I was there."

"What is there to do?"

"Nothing much other than hiking and spending time with friends."

As if she had any.

Everyone hated her.

Why was Vlad even coming? Had the therapist bribed him or coerced him somehow?

What had she offered him to convince him to come?

It was going to be a nightmare.

Whatever. She could always tune the world out by watching anime.

"Does the cabin have a television?"

"It does, but there is no internet connection, so no streaming services. But the server has thousands of movies and shows on it, so you will have plenty to choose from."

She grimaced. "I bet there is no anime."

"I'm not sure." Leon cast her a sidelong glance. "Why do you like it so much? Aren't you too old to watch cartoons?"

"Anime is not cartoons, and some of the shows are very grownup. I prefer animation to real actors. No matter how bad things get, I know that it's not real, so I don't get sad or angry."

"How about regular shows that are more funny than sad? Like *Scrubs*, or *Friends*, or *How I Met Your Mother*?"

"Those are old. And besides, they annoy me."

"Why?"

"Because they pretend to be real but are not. People are never as nice to each other in real life, or as happy, or as hopeful."

"I don't know about that. People in our community are usually kind to each other, and I know that if I need help with anything, I can count on my friends to do their best to provide it."

She snorted. "Until you put it to the test. Then you'll see how quickly they will scatter. People are selfish."

"That's not my experience. I've put it to the test many times and was never disappointed."

"Oh yeah? Give me one example."

Leon frowned. "Do you know that our organization is involved in rescuing trafficking victims?"

Wendy had heard Mey and Jin talk about it, but she hadn't paid much attention. At the time, she'd been more interested in keeping her distance and plotting how to get her hands on a phone.

"I heard something, but I'm not sure what exactly you do for them. Besides, what does that have to do with your friends having your back?"

"My friends and I raid places that buy trafficked individuals who are then forced to sell their sex services. We rescue the victims, destroy the houses so they can no longer be used for that purpose, and deliver the scum who run those places to the police. Those raids are not without risk, and my friends and I have to work as a team and watch each other's backs."

"Why do you do that? Isn't that something the police should do?"

He cast her an indulgent look. "As disillusioned as you are with society, I'm surprised that you believe that. If the authorities could handle it, trafficking wouldn't be the worldwide plague that it is."

He had a point. "What do you do with the people that you rescue?"

"We take them to a sanctuary for rehabilitation. Vanessa is in charge of that. Once they are better, we move them to a halfway house and help them find jobs or get training or both. When they're capable of taking care of themselves and think that they are ready, they can leave. We never kick anyone out. But if they try to live independently and it doesn't work out, they are welcome to come back."

"Sounds very altruistic. Who pays for all that?"

"We have many donors."

So that was why they were doing it. It was a neat way to fund their organization by pretending that it was all about helping the victims of trafficking.

"I bet that you keep a hefty chunk of those donations to cover so-called administrative costs and pay the directors' salaries. All those charity organizations are just another way for the people running them to get rich."

Leon shook his head. "When we started, we covered all the costs from our own pockets. It put a tremendous strain on our resources, but we all voted to do it anyway because we believed that it was the right thing to do. Later, we started to receive donations, but we still cover the lion's share of the expenses."

"I don't believe you."

He arched a brow. "You're an empath. If I were lying, you would have sensed it."

"You might be a good actor. As long as you convince yourself that what you are saying is true, you can fool the best of empaths."

"Was that how you fooled Edna?"

"More or less." It was more, not less, and her method was not something anyone could emulate.

"I see. Well, I'm not a good actor or a good liar, and everything that I told you was true. People are a mixed bag, good and bad, but there are many more who are good than those who are bad."

"Not in my experience."

He grimaced. "I bet."

Jacki

Jacki had spent most of the night thinking about Kalugal's marriage proposal, or rather her joke of a proposal which he'd accepted, saying that the idea wasn't crazy and that they should sleep on it.

What had he meant by that?

Was she supposed to give him an answer this morning? Or was he supposed to give her his?

Damn. It was all very confusing.

But assuming that he'd meant it and that she was supposed to give him an answer after sleeping on it, what would it be?

Her heart and her soul had already said yes, but her mind knew that it would be a mistake. Nothing had changed, Kalugal was still a demigod, and she was still a human.

Except, Kalugal's admission that he liked everything about her and wouldn't change a thing was almost as good as a declaration of love, and it pretty much obliterated her determination to say no.

Why keep fighting it?

Why give up a chance for something amazing because it would only last a couple of decades at most?

Half of all marriages ended in divorce anyway, so no one had a guaranteed happily ever after. And perhaps a couple of decades with Kalugal were worth more than a lifetime with a human.

A demigod wanted to marry her, and she was still thinking whether she should say yes?

Anyone else in her position would have jumped on it without hesitation, and the only reason she was still undecided was because of her stubborn all-or-nothing attitude.

She needed to compromise and accept a little bit less than all but much more than nothing.

As the realization settled upon her, Jacki felt a tremendous weight lift off her chest. She was going to say yes, marry Kalugal, and have the best twenty years any woman could dream of.

And if it was less than that? It was still worth it.

Flinging the comforter off, Jacki swung her legs over the side of the bed. Without bothering with slippers, she padded to the bathroom door and put her ear to it. When she could hear no sounds from the other side, she pushed it open and ran across to lock the other door.

Was Kalugal still asleep?

She hadn't heard him in the bathroom, but he might have used it while she'd dozed off.

In total, she hadn't slept for more than five hours, but after her decision to say yes had been made, Jacki was too hyped up to stay in bed, and she no longer felt tired.

Except, the mirror told a different story. Jacki had dark circles under her eyes, and if she wanted to look good while giving Kalugal her answer, she needed to apply a bit of concealer.

But that was the last step. First, she had to shower and then blow dry her hair.

That part was done in fifteen minutes flat, mainly thanks to the Dyson hairdryer that had arrived the day before, along with several brushes and a makeup kit she'd ordered. But then Jacki spent another half an hour deciding on the right outfit.

She couldn't show up for breakfast in a cocktail dress, but she wasn't going to wear jeans either.

After trying on and discarding at least ten outfits, she settled on a pair of skinny black pants and a yellow blouse embroidered with a pink thread. It was a little sheer and had a deep neckline, but it was sexy without being slutty, and the color looked great on her.

The last decision was whether to wear pumps or flats, and the pumps won. Jacki was tall, and most of the time she wore flats, but today she wanted to look sophisticated and well put together.

As the fiancée of a demigod, she needed to show some class.

Checking herself in the mirror, she was reminded of Kalugal's perfume-container analogy. He'd said that an expensive perfume shouldn't be put inside a cheap plastic bottle.

Funny how that remark had changed the way Jacki thought about herself. Whenever she was gripped by insecurities, all she had to do was remember Kalugal's cultured voice comparing her to an exquisite fragrance, and it made her stand a little taller.

Taking a deep breath, she flipped her long hair back, squared her shoulders, and headed out.

Hopefully, Kalugal was waiting for her in the library. If she had to start looking for him all over the house, she would probably lose her nerve.

Kalugal

As Jacki opened the library doors, Kalugal got up and walked up to her.

"Good morning, beautiful." He took her hand and kissed her cheek.

"Good morning. Did you sleep well?"

Hearing her tossing and turning all night, Kalugal had been wondering what was going through Jacki's head, and those thoughts had kept him awake.

Luckily, he didn't need much sleep to recharge, and the few times he'd dozed off had been enough.

"Thoughts of you kept me awake," he admitted as he led her to the table. "Coffee?"

"Yes, please."

He poured her a cup. "Given that you haven't slept much either, I assume that you've been thinking about my marriage proposal."

She narrowed her eyes at him. "Do you have a hidden camera in my room?"

He tapped his ears. "I don't need one. When the rest of the house is quiet, I can hear you moving around."

"Oh, boy." She cringed. "That could be embarrassing. I don't want you to hear every sound I make."

Leaning in, he covered her hand with his and smirked. "Nothing is embarrassing between a husband and wife. You can make any sounds you like, and I will cherish every one."

"Right." She pulled her hand from under his. "Does that cover the smells too?"

Kalugal stifled a laugh. "Naturally."

She chuckled. "I like your attitude, but we are not there yet. And as for the proposal, I was the one who popped the question. Not you."

He nodded. "You brought it up, but you weren't serious. I was."

"It doesn't really matter."

As she lifted the cup to her lips and took a sip, her hair spilled forward, framing her face in a golden halo.

So beautiful, and that was just the cherry on top of all of Jacki's other attributes. He counted himself incredibly lucky for having her fall into his lap, and that was worth the entire mess with Kian and the damn tether that Jin had attached to him. Otherwise, he would have never met this amazing woman.

"I agree." He leaned closer. "So, what's the verdict?"

Jacki hid behind the curtain of her hair. "I've given it a lot of thought."

"And?"

"You go first. You said that both of us needed to sleep on it, meaning that you've been undecided as well."

"I wasn't. I just didn't want to pressure you. As far as I'm concerned, we can apply for a marriage license on Monday."

She swallowed. "So soon?"

"Why wait?"

"To make sure that we make the right decision. This is crazy, Kalugal. I know that I suggested it, but it was really meant as a tease. I didn't expect you to take me seriously."

He sighed. "I want to move to the next stage of our relationship. And you won't do that unless we are married. I'm fine with that, even though it's putting the carriage in front of the horse. You are perfect for me, and I think that I'm perfect for you, but if it doesn't work for some reason, and you don't get what you want from me, we don't have to stay married."

She shook her head. "I don't want to enter a marriage with divorce as a contingency."

Damn. The woman was confusing. What else could he offer her? Maybe he could give her a little more time.

"Do you want one more night to think it over?"

"It's not going to help."

"What are you scared of, Jacki?"

She lifted her head and looked at him. "Of not being loved. You are promising me everything but that."

"Would you believe me if I did?"

"I don't know. Yesterday, you sounded as if you were halfway there."

"That's because I am. But I will not allow myself to fall in love completely unless I have your love and loyalty first. I know it's unfair to you, and I know that I'm asking you to trust me before I trust you, but I have much more to lose than my heart."

That was as much as he was willing to reveal, and if that was not enough, so be it. Kalugal was a patient man, but in the end, it was a leap of faith that Jacki either took or didn't. He couldn't tell her more.

"Okay," she whispered.

"Okay, what?"

"I'll marry you."

Kalugal let out a relieved breath. "Wonderful." He lifted her hand to his lips and kissed the back of it. "On

Monday, I'm going to send Rufsur to pull a marriage license for us."

"He can't do that. You and I have to be there in person, and we need to show proof of who we are. I'll have to ask Kian to mail my fake documents to me."

"I forgot about your fugitive status. I can ask Kian to bring them to the summit. It's still early, so he probably hasn't left yet for our meeting later this afternoon. But I still think that it would be better for Rufsur to thrall the clerk to think that you and I are there in person. It would save us the trip and be safer for you." He gave her hand a little squeeze. "I can keep you safe, and no one is going to take you away from me."

Jacki

Jacki hadn't been born yesterday, and Kalugal's insistence on sending Rufsur to pull the marriage license was awfully suspicious.

Was he planning to trick her?

He could print a fake certificate, show it to her, and then compel someone to officiate over their wedding without checking that the certificate was valid.

Great. She was marrying someone she didn't trust with the most basic stuff.

Except, what if the reasons he'd given her were legitimate concerns?

Furthermore, she couldn't even get married using her real name. She wasn't pulling the certificate as Jacqueline Radford, and she would have to use the fake identification that Kian had supplied her with, which could be just a simple forgery and not the kind that would pass scrutiny.

The marriage idea seemed stupider by the minute.

Jacki let out an exasperated breath. "Let's forget about the whole thing."

Kalugal tensed. "If it's so important to you, we can go to the city hall in person."

"It is important, but it's not only that. I would have to use a fake identity, and so would you. You'll probably shroud yourself in one of your many disguises, and I will have to put the wig and glasses on. So, no matter what, the two of us are not really going to be legally married."

"What about a religious wedding? We can have a priest marry us."

"Are you a Christian?"

"No. Does it matter?"

"Yeah, it does. If you are not a believer, having a priest marry us will be meaningless to you."

He snorted. "And you think that a state-issued marriage license will mean anything to me? I'm doing this for you."

Closing her eyes, Jacki slumped in Kalugal's arms. "None of this is real. You should just let me go. Kian's people will pick me up, and that will be the end of the story."

His arms tightened around her. "I'm not letting you go. There must be another solution."

"How do immortals get married? All of you have fake identities, and if you have no religious authority, then who officiates over your weddings?"

"There were no weddings where I came from, but I can ask Kian how the clan handles that." He started rubbing her back again. "In the past, human marriages used to be simple. Two people would pledge to love and cherish each other in front of witnesses, and that was it. Their community knew that they were husband and wife, and that was enough."

"Are you suggesting that we do the same?"

"Why not? It will be more real than anything else. No fake names, no disguises, just you and me and our witnesses."

Sounded good in theory, but if their witnesses were exclusively Kalugal's men, it would be like having no witnesses at all. They would always side with their boss.

"I might consider this on one condition."

"Shoot."

"I want my new friends to be at the ceremony."

"You mean Kian's people?"

She nodded.

"He will never agree to that. Did you forget how cautious he is around me? He will think it's a trick, and that I want to compel his people and turn them against him."

"They can all wear earplugs."

"Then how are they going to hear us pledge our commitment to each other?"

"We can learn to say it in sign language."

Kalugal laughed. "Of all the silly ideas, this one takes the cake."

"Why? What's wrong with sign language? It can't be too hard to learn a few sentences."

He eyed her with a raised brow. "You're serious."

"It's a legitimate solution. I don't want to get married with only your men as our witnesses."

"I'll try to persuade Kian to do this for us. He might agree to let a couple of civilians who are not privy to any strategic secrets join our ceremony, but I sincerely doubt that he would allow any of his warriors to come."

"I would love for Arwel to be there, but I'll settle for the civilians."

Kalugal let out a breath. "I'm glad that we found a solution that works for both of us."

"Yeah, me too."

"Are you still excited?"

Was she?

Their wedding plans hadn't been romantic to start with, and the discussion about practicalities had kind of ruined it for her entirely. Did she even want to go through with it?

Perhaps she needed another kiss to remind her how it had all started and why it was still a good idea.

Kalugal

Jacki sighed. "Not as much as I was this morning. I don't know why I didn't think about the identity issues before. I don't like feeling stupid."

"It didn't occur to me either, and I never feel stupid." He winked before tightening his arms around her. "After the epic kiss that we shared yesterday, we got carried away and didn't think things through. But because we are both smart, we found a solution."

Kalugal didn't like Jacki's defeated mood, and he didn't like that she was second-guessing her decision. He wanted her to be excited and happy about marrying him.

She waved a hand. "Practicality is the antidote to romance."

"True. Perhaps we need a repeat performance to remind ourselves why we wanted to get married in the first place."

Smiling, Jacki wound her arms around his neck. "Best idea I've heard so far. You must have read my mind."

Now, that was a welcome mood change.

Cupping the back of her head, he coaxed her lips to part, and when she moaned softly, he slid his tongue into her welcoming mouth. Licking, savoring, tasting.

Exquisite.

Jacki shivered, her body softening against his as she surrendered to the kiss. Not for long, though. She enjoyed his dominance, but she wasn't passive. Clutching his shoulders, she tentatively kissed him back.

It went against his nature to let her take over, but it was also erotic as hell. For the first time, he could allow a woman to kiss him back despite his elongated fangs.

Still, as her tongue slipped into his mouth, he had to fight the instinct to deny her entry. Sliding his hands over her back, he caressed her softly, encouraging her to keep going.

Unafraid, Jacki swirled her tongue around one fang, sending an unexpected jolt straight to his groin. It felt as if she was licking his manhood instead, and just like what was happening down below, his fangs punched out to their full length, protruding over his lower lip.

Maybe it was the novelty of it, or perhaps it was an immortal male's natural response to his fangs being licked, but the stimulation was overpowering.

With his dormant predatory instincts coming dangerously close to the surface, Kalugal was afraid that he might accidentally nick Jacki just by taking over the kiss.

Applying a little force to the back of her head, he pulled it back.

Thankfully, her eyes were closed, and she didn't see the complete transformation.

When fully elongated, his fangs were quite terrifying. Could he get them to retract before she looked at him?

Or perhaps it would be better for her to see them in their full elongated glory now, and not on her wedding night. It could be a nasty surprise that might ruin the mood for her.

Caressing Jacki's gorgeous golden hair, he gently kissed her forehead. "Open your eyes."

She shook her head. "I don't want to."

"You need to see me the way I am. You need to internalize that the man you are marrying isn't human."

"I know that." She smiled without opening her eyes. "I'm marrying a demigod."

It seemed that he'd discovered the one thing he didn't like about Jacki. She was stubborn, and she liked to argue about everything.

"Open your eyes." He infused his tone with command. Not compulsion, since she was immune, just authority.

This time Jacki obeyed, and the smile slid off her face, but she didn't stiffen in his arms, which was a good sign. She wasn't scared.

"Your eyes are glowing. They are so beautiful."

Was she trying to be polite and not mention his fangs?

"What about these?" He pointed.

"They are bigger than I thought. They didn't feel as big when I kissed you."

"They grew even more. When you licked my fang, I discovered that they are highly responsive to stimulation."

Her eyes widened. "You didn't know that until now?"

"You are the first woman I've ever let kiss me back."

Jacki's entire face softened. "I love that I'm your first in something. It makes me feel special."

Okay, he could expand on that.

"You are also the first woman who remembers my real face after I've kissed her."

Except, he had to qualify that claim by adding in recent years. When he was much younger, Kalugal often hadn't shrouded himself, only erasing his face from the females' memory later.

For some reason, though, that hadn't worked on Eva, and she still remembered him.

Then again, after discovering that he'd taken her virginity, Kalugal had been more concerned with erasing that from her mind than the memory of his face.

"You seem unsure of that," Jacki said.

"There was one exception, but it wasn't intentional. It was a mistake."

"Tell me about it."

He arched a brow. "I don't think we should discuss my prior partners. You might get jealous. I know I would be if you told me about yours."

"Except, I don't have any, and now that you've mentioned that one incident of a woman who remembered your real face, you have to tell me the rest, or I'll keep obsessing about it."

Argumentative wench.

"I don't like it when you argue with me."

Glaring at him, Jacki straightened in his arms. "Tough. Get used to it. If you want a wife who will always answer with a 'yes, dear,' you shouldn't marry me."

"But I want to marry you, and not someone who says 'yes, dear' to everything I ask of her. I would just appreciate a little less arguing."

She narrowed her eyes at him. "Are you trying to get away with not telling me about that woman?"

"Not at all. The story is simple. It happened about fifty years ago, and things were different back then. She was a college student, and she wasn't shy. In fact, she acted so boldly that I was sure she was experienced. But she was a virgin, and when I discovered it, I tried to save the situation by erasing the entire thing from her mind. Normally, I would leave the memory of the sex intact except for the biting part but muddle the memory of my face. In Eva's case, however, I did it the other way around. I figured that if she didn't remember losing her virginity, she wouldn't have to tell that to her future husband. Back then, it was a big deal."

"Why didn't you erase your face from her memory as well?"

"I intended to, but apparently I failed to do so, because she remembered me."

Jacki

It was strange that the most important part of Kalugal's story had escaped Jacki's notice, reaching her awareness only a few seconds later.

She'd known that his fangs were not for decoration, but she'd assumed that they were a weapon to be used in a fight with other males or for hunting.

But Kalugal had just said that he'd bitten his sex partners with those monsters and then erased the memory of the bites.

"I thought that the fangs were a weapon. Why were you biting women?"

"Arwel didn't tell you?"

She shook her head. "He only said that immortal males had fangs, but that they didn't drink blood like vampires. He didn't explain what they were used for, and I just assumed that they were like wolf fangs, used for fighting or hunting."

He smirked, looking like a smiling tiger. "They have another function. During sex, the venom acts as an aphrodisiac and a euphoric. It delivers the best orgasms, and many of them. You are in for a treat."

She swallowed. "But first comes the bite." She reached with her finger and touched one pointy fang. "Ouch." Blood beaded from the small incision.

Grabbing her finger, Kalugal licked the blood off. "Our saliva has healing properties." He brought the finger closer to her eyes. "Look. It's not bleeding anymore. Does it still hurt?"

Jacki shook her head. "It's amazing. But that was only a tiny nick. I bet the bite hurts like hell."

"It does, but only for a second. Then the saliva together with the euphoric and the aphrodisiac obliterate the pain and turn it into the most intense pleasure a woman could ever experience."

She sincerely doubted it. "If you say so."

"Do you think I'm lying?"

"Have you ever been bitten?"

"No."

"So how would you know?"

"I've been with enough women to know what the effect is."

Jacki rolled her eyes. "Maybe you are just an exceptional lover, and they orgasmed so many times because of your incredible lovemaking skills?"

He chuckled. "I wish. In fact, I try to delay the bite for as long as I can because using it feels like cheating. I like it when a woman orgasms because of my incredible lovemaking skills first."

Damn. Talking about orgasms was starting to have an effect on her, and with Kalugal's sensitive nose, he would sniff it right away. Before, it had been just embarrassing, but now she had his fangs to consider.

She should have realized that there was a connection between fangs and sex because they elongated when he got excited. It was truly amazing how the mind ignored the most obvious things because it didn't want to acknowledge them.

A change of subject might throttle her arousal. "When you meet with Kian, are you going to talk about the government's paranormal talent program?"

Kalugal shook his head as if to realign the gears in his brain to the sudden change of topic.

"Are you trying to make my fangs retract?"

That was a good excuse. "Is it working?"

He grinned. "What do you think?"

"They are definitely getting smaller. Where do they go?" She dipped her head and peeked into his mouth.

"Up into the maxilla."

She chuckled. "Talking to you, I'm learning a lot of new terms. I need to start writing them down. What were the terms you used for the Sumerian writing? Was it phonographic?"

He smiled like a proud teacher. "You remember correctly."

"And what was the other one?"

"Logographic."

"I'll remember that it sounds like logo, which is a picture that represents a name."

"Perfect. Mnemonics are a great memorization device. Our brains are good at arranging things in patterns."

Jacki nodded. "Doctor Roberts talked about it. He said that there were two ways to make memorization easier. One is word association, and the other is to turn things into pictures in your head. Take making a grocery list for an example. Instead of memorizing the individual items, it is easier to remember by imagining a meal made from them, or a fruit bowl with all the fruit that you need to buy."

"Was he an actual medical doctor?"

"That's how he presented himself, but at this point, I don't believe anything they told us." She lifted her cuff and rubbed her arm. "Like giving us so-called immunization shots, but instead injecting us with undetectable trackers."

"Tell me more about him and the other main operators of the program."

"Director Simmons was in charge, Marisol was the recruiter, and Doctor Roberts was the one with all the freaky experiments. He injected us with drugs to see if that would enhance our abilities, and I'm pretty sure that he was behind the breeding super-babies idea too. Marisol was in on it as well because she compelled people to hook up with each other. The others were just regular teachers and instructors, and I don't think they knew what was going on."

"Do you know Doctor Roberts' full name? We might be able to find information on him, like where he went to school and with whom. It might provide us with important clues."

"Doctor Elijah Roberts, and the director's first name is Edgar. He is a doctor too, but not medical. I think his field is neuroscience. Although the guy is so old that he must have graduated fifty years ago. I don't know if Harvard or any other university even had a neuroscience department back then."

"How old is Roberts?"

"Same age as Simmons, more or less. Why?"

"They might have gone to school together." Kalugal lifted her off his lap and put her back in her chair. "Wait here. I'll get my laptop."

Kalugal

When Kalugal returned to the library, he found Jacki nibbling on a piece of dry toast.

"I'll ask Shamash to make us a fresh breakfast."

She waved a dismissive hand. "I'm okay with eating it like that. But if you want, you can ask him to heat it up for you. You shouldn't throw perfectly good food away."

"I feel bad about keeping you from eating it when it was fresh."

"We had important things to discuss, and I'm happy with the solution we arrived at. Cold eggs are a small price to pay."

"You make me sound pampered and frivolous." He pulled out a chair, sat down, and put the laptop on the other side of the table.

Jacki smiled. "That's because you are pampered, but you are not frivolous."

"My days of eating field rations are long gone." Stifling a grimace, Kalugal scooped cold eggs and fingerling potatoes onto his plate.

"I don't know what they serve in those, but I'm sure it's nothing like this." She dipped her knife into the blueberry preserve, spread it over another piece of dry toast, and took a bite. "Yum."

Jacki might be stubborn and argumentative, but she was far from demanding, and it extended to grander things than breakfast.

Even for an important event like their wedding, all she'd asked for was to have a few of her friends witness the ceremony. She hadn't asked for a fancy party, or a beautiful gown, or even for a diamond engagement ring.

But she should have all that. Kalugal wanted to give Jacki a day to remember.

The problem was that neither of them wanted to wait, and a big party meant preparations that would take a long time. And besides, a grand event required a grand attendance, and he couldn't give her that.

It would have to be a modest affair, but he would do his best to make it memorable.

Forking one tiny potato, he put it in his mouth and forced himself to chew and swallow. But that was it. He was unwilling to suffer just to prove that he wasn't a pampered prince.

Kalugal pushed his plate aside and replaced it with his laptop. "Let's check on Simmons and Roberts."

"Don't you want to eat first?"

"I'm not hungry. But if you want to pour me a fresh cup of coffee, I would appreciate it."

"Coming right up."

His fingers flew over the keyboard as he searched the two names.

"They went to Harvard together, and Simmons was in its first neurobiology graduating class, which was also the first department dedicated to the subject in the world." Kalugal looked up. "He was a pioneer."

"What about Roberts?"

"Graduated Harvard Medical School a couple of years later."

"I wonder when he discovered that he was an immune."

Kalugal lifted his head. "Who? Simmons or Roberts, or both?"

"Simmons. Marisol is immune too. I don't know about Roberts."

"That complicates things."

Jacki put her mug down. "Why? What did you have in mind?"

"I thought that I could walk in there and get the other trainees out. But an immune could sound the alarm. The question is whether he is immune to shrouding as well. I could make myself look like one of his supervisors, or his wife." He batted his eyelashes.

"He wears a wedding ring and talks about the missus, but I've never seen her. Is she really married?"

"Let's check." Kalugal did another search. "He's been married to the same woman for forty-some years. Maybe we can gain access to him through her."

"How?"

"I don't have a plan yet, but the more we know about the key players, the better. I want to shut that damn program down and make sure that no one resurrects it."

"You'll need a big stink for that."

He smirked. "No doubt. Either that or arrange a fatal accident for both esteemed doctors."

Casting Jacki a sidelong glance, he wondered what her response would be, but she didn't seem appalled by his murderous suggestion.

"Are you okay with that?"

"Killing them? I don't know. What they are doing is wrong, but as far as I know, they didn't murder or rape anyone. The death penalty seems too severe for their crimes. Besides, I don't want you to play executioner. Especially without giving them a fair trial first."

"It might be the most effective way to get rid of the program, the danger to you, to Jin, and to your other friends."

She looked at her cuff again. "I want to get rid of the damn trackers they put inside my body. The cuff is like putting a Band-Aid on a skin rash. It doesn't solve the problem, only hides it."

"True. Maybe we need to capture Roberts and get him to explain how to do that."

"Maybe Simmons is the one who invented those undetectable trackers?"

"I doubt it." Kalugal closed his laptop. "In any case, my superficial search is just the beginning. When we dig deeper, I'm sure we will find much more."

"Kian's tech people can do that. William and Roni."

"I have hackers that I can use too, but I prefer to use Kian's people because they are immortals." He looked at his watch. "I would love to stay and chat some more, but I have to get ready for the summit. Will you be okay here on your own?"

Jacki nodded. "Who are you leaving in charge?"

"Rufsur. I'm taking Phinas with me."

She arched a brow. "Aren't you afraid to leave him alone with me?"

He leaned and planted a kiss on her lips. "I trust you, and I trust him. We are about to get married. Even a thick-headed block like Rufsur will realize that the competition is over."

"I hope you are right. I like him, and I hate hurting his feelings." She cringed. "Not that I'm doing such a great job of it. I told him that there could be nothing between us because he is an immortal, and I'm a human, but I agreed to marry you despite that."

Kalugal shrugged. "A lady is allowed to change her mind, right? You don't owe him anything."

"I know. But it's going to be uncomfortable."

"I'll talk to him."

"No, don't. It will make it even worse. I'll handle it."

"Are you sure?"

Jacki nodded. "Positive. When are you leaving?"

He glanced at his watch again. "The meeting is scheduled for noon. I'll probably leave in an hour."

"If you have any questions about the program, call me." She grimaced. "I forgot that I don't have a phone."

"I'll text you. You can get texts on the tablet I gave you."

"Okay."

She didn't look okay. "What's wrong?"

"I don't have a cell phone, and the landlines are code blocked. We are about to be married, but you can't even trust me with a freaking phone?"

She had a point. "I'll get you a cellphone."

Naturally, he would screen her calls.

Kalugal wanted to trust Jacki, but he couldn't risk it. What if she was a mole, like her friend? It was unlikely, but not impossible.

On the other hand, there was little she could reveal that wasn't already known. His location had been compromised, so she had nothing new to report in that regard. If federal agents came knocking on his door, he would just send them away dazed and confused.

The problem was that Jacki also knew about immortals, and if anyone believed her, that would require a big-time cleanup job. Memories would have to be scrubbed, computer databases erased, and the immune director and his immune recruiter would have to be eliminated.

Jin

Jin was packing for the trip to the cabin when her phone pinged with an incoming email.

In her previous life as Jin Levine, the oblivious human, she would have ignored it. Back then, her inbox had been full of updates from school, promotions, invitations, and emails from the various bloggers she used to follow.

Now she lived in isolation and had a new email address, and the only ones who had it were her sister, Kian, Arwel, and Jacki.

Except, the only one actually using it to communicate was her friend. The others texted or called.

Dropping the stack of clothes into the suitcase, Jin lifted her phone and opened the email.

Hi Bestie,

I have exciting news, and you are the only one I can share it with. Kalugal and I are getting married. At first, the idea was to just pull a marriage license and then invite someone to Kalugal's house to officiate. But then I realized that it didn't make sense for us to get married using our fake names. Then Kalugal suggested that we have a private ceremony and pledge ourselves to each other in front of witnesses. That way, we would do it as us, and not the fake personalities that we use.

Anyway, I told him that his men wouldn't do as witnesses, and that I want at least some of my new friends to be at the ceremony. He said that he would ask Kian about it when he meets him at the summit, but he doubted that Kian would agree to come to his house or let anyone else attend. What do you think?

Is there a chance he would? Because I would really like you to come. I know Kian would veto Arwel's attendance, but maybe he will let you come. I don't have a date yet, but it's going to happen soon, so be ready to fly over or drive.

Love,

Jacki.

Plopping on the bed, Jin read the email again. Had Jacki lost her mind? And whose crazy idea was it to get married after knowing each other for less than a week?

She typed a response.

> *All I want to say is, wow! Congratulations!*
> *But I can't. This is nuts!*
> *Why the hell are you getting married?*
> *And whose idea was it?*
> *What's the rush?*
> *Did he get you pregnant?*
> *Are you even in love?*

Hitting send, Jin waited for Jacki's response. This was such an annoying way to talk. If she had Jacki on the phone, she could have yelled at her to come to her senses.

The only reason Kalugal wanted to marry Jacki was because of her possible dormancy, but Jin wasn't allowed to tell her that.

Except, why not?

She'd kept it a secret because Kalugal asked Kian not to tell Jacki, and Kian asked her.

But Jacki's future was more important than the promise. What would Kian do if she told Jacki the truth? Yell at her?

Let him try. Jin would yell back just as loudly.

First, though, she needed to know how and why this had happened, and why Jacki had said yes.

As the return email came in, Jin opened it with trepidation. Hopefully, Jacki wasn't pregnant. But then maybe she wanted to be?

> *We are not in love, not yet, but we are in serious like and lust. The problem is that I won't have sex with Kalugal unless I have his love and devotion first, and for reasons Kalugal can't reveal, he can't give me that until he is sure of my love and loyalty to him.*
>
> *I suggested marriage as a joke, but then we both realized that it might be the solution to our problem. Our marriage vows will be about commitment and devotion, but not love because we are not there yet.*
>
> *I know that you believe in living for today, but I'm not like you. My motto was ALL or NOTHING, meaning no casual flings. I realize that Kalugal and I can't promise each other forever, but I figured that a little less than ALL with a demigod is a lot better than NOTHING.*
>
> *Does that make sense to you?*

After reading the email twice, Jin figured it out.

Just as she'd suspected. Jacki was a freaking virgin, and she'd lied when Jin had asked her about it. She didn't do flings, and she didn't do hookups, but Kalugal was irresistible and she wanted him, but not without him marrying her first.

Actually, it wasn't such a bad plan, given that Jacki had no idea how valuable she was to him.

Still, it was hard to believe that a knockout like Jacki was a twenty-two-year-old virgin.

Damn. Jin had lost her virginity on her seventeenth birthday, and she'd been one of the last girls in her friend group to finally get her v-card punched. No wonder Jacki had been embarrassed to admit that.

It was kind of sweet. It seemed that Jacki was an old-fashioned soul who clung to old values, like saving her v-card for her husband. And she also had a point about marrying a demigod being worth a little compromise.

It would be an experience, that was for sure.

The question was what would happen if she didn't transition.

Poor Jacki would be devastated.

Even if Kalugal fell in love with her, he wouldn't keep her. Every immortal's dream was to find his true-love mate, or at least an immortal one who could give him immortal children.

The thing was, Jacki's transition was not guaranteed like Jin's, and her chances of being a Dormant were not great. Jin wasn't sure that immunity counted as a paranormal talent, and Jacki's clairvoyance was unimpressive.

If she didn't transition, Kalugal would divorce her.

Should Jin warn her?

It was a tough call. On the one hand, Jacki deserved to know, but on the other hand, the knowledge could rob her of the little happiness she would have until Kalugal realized that she was not about to transition.

Except, Kalugal was the one who should tell Jacki about it, not Jin. Perhaps she could ask Kian to give him some solid cousinly advice?

Marrying Jacki without telling her about her possible dormancy was deceitful, and she would never forgive him for keeping it from her.

Yeah, Kian should warn him. As a married man, he had experience which Kalugal lacked, and his advice carried weight. Kalugal might listen to him.

Smiling, Jin typed her answer.

> *Now that you finally admit to being a freaking virgin, it does make sense. You were saving your V-card for your husband, but Kalugal is so hot that you can't wait. I don't blame you for wanting him so badly that you are willing to marry the stuck-up, gorgeous, charming, demigod after knowing him for less than a week.*
>
> *There is no way I'm missing your wedding, and if Kian objects, I'll just do it without asking his permission.*

Wendy

Wendy had been surprised when ten minutes into the drive Leon had removed her blindfold, but she had a good idea why.

Once they arrived at the cabin, Bowen would probably get into her head once again, check recent memories, and erase what he didn't want her to remember.

He'd done it with the location of the underground that she and the others had stayed in. She had known it before, more or less, but now the memory was gone, and whenever she tried to bring it up, her head started hurting.

Eventually she'd stopped trying.

What was the point?

There was none, but finding what she felt was hidden just beneath the surface of her consciousness was a compulsive need. Cringing, she tried again, but as always all she got for her efforts was a headache.

Wendy closed her eyes, and after a few moments the damn stabbing needles let up and she dozed off.

"We are almost there." Leon turned into a dirt road and stopped in front of a rickety gate.

The rusted combination padlock keeping it closed looked old, but Wendy was sure it operated just as smoothly as everything else the paranormal organization owned.

Obviously, it was backed by big money, and Wendy wondered whether the story about its members making a killing on the stock market was true.

Probably not.

Maybe the backer was a foreign country. Russia or China or any of the others who would love to undermine the American superpower.

Having a bunch of paranormals working for them would make spying on the United States so much easier. They could get Jin into the White House as a reporter, or an aide, or any other job that would get her close enough to the President to shake hands with him.

Jin didn't seem like the traitor type, but then she hadn't been raised in the States, so who knew where her loyalty lay. And even if she refused to spy on her country, they could force her to do it by threatening Mey.

That was probably what was going on.

Wendy should stop thinking of herself as a traitor. She was a patriot, whose loyalty belonged to her country and not a bunch of people with questionable motives.

Contacting her uncle had been the right thing to do. Unfortunately, it hadn't achieved a damn thing.

After Leon opened the gate, he drove the car through, got out again, and closed it.

Wendy crossed her arms over her chest. "Why bother with the stupid gate? It's not going to keep out anyone who wants in. They could just ram a car through it, and the chain would break."

"True, but we would know that someone is trespassing, and we have countermeasures."

"Oh, yeah? Like what?"

"The trail is full of land mines. We can activate them remotely."

Wendy gasped. "And you are driving over that? Let me out!" She reached for the handle.

"Relax." He chuckled. "I was just joking. There are no explosives."

"Really?" She narrowed her eyes at him. "Or are you just saying that so I don't freak out."

"No explosives." He put a hand over his heart. "I swear."

Wendy let out a breath. "You shouldn't make jokes like that."

"I'm sorry. But I couldn't help myself. You were so serious."

"It's pretty out here," she said as he parked the car next to the cabin. "Can I take a walk?"

The last house she'd seen had been miles away, so it wasn't as if she could run.

"Let's unload, and then I'll come with you." Leon turned the engine off and got out. "There are wild animals out here."

"Really? Or is that another one of your jokes?"

"Look around you. Why wouldn't this place be teeming with wildlife?"

Doing as he asked, Wendy finally noticed the serenity of the place. Everywhere she looked there were trees and shrubs, and the sounds she heard were mostly of birds chirping, leaves rustling, and branches groaning. There was no traffic on the narrow mountain road below, and other than the soft whooshing of the huge wind turbine's blades, all sounds of civilization were absent.

It was windy and a little cold, but the air was so fresh that she didn't mind taking in cold gulps of it.

"Yeah, you're probably right." She zipped up her coat.

Leon opened the trunk and pulled out the suitcase he'd lent her. Thanks to him, this time her things weren't bundled in a bedsheet, making her feel a little less of a vagabond.

As she reached for the handle, he cast her a look that said *back off, little girl, and let the big man handle this*. "It's okay. I've got it."

Whatever. She had more important things to argue about. "I would really like to take a walk by myself. I'll stay near the cabin." She lifted her cuffed wrist. "Besides, I have this. I'm sure it does more than run interference with the tracking signal I'm supposedly emitting. You can find me anytime you want."

Carrying her overstuffed suitcase as if it weighed no more than a shopping bag, Leon walked up to the cabin's front door, entered a code into the lock, and opened the way. "You are emitting a signal, and the cuff can't locate you because its job is to interfere with signals, not emit them. But if you run away, I can remotely activate the release of a poison that will incapacitate you until I find you."

Wendy rolled her eyes. "Is that another one of your morbid jokes?"

"Not this time. If you plan on running, you should be aware of that." He opened the door to one of the bedrooms and put her suitcase on the bed. "But if you still want to go for a walk by yourself, I'll give you an emergency whistle."

"What for?"

"It's so loud that the noise itself will scare the animals off, at least for a little while. It will also notify me that you are in trouble and give me enough time to get to you."

"And what will you do once you get to me?" She looked at his jeans and tight T-shirt. The only place he could be hiding anything was in his boots. "Do you have any weapons on you?"

Leon grinned. "I don't need any. I am a weapon."

"Right." Wendy rolled her eyes. "Are you going to hypnotize the wild beasts or tear them apart with your bare hands?"

"Depends on the beasts. I can hypnotize a bear, but coyotes run in packs, so that's trickier. I would have to fight them off." He said it with a perfectly straight face.

"Right. You're such a comedian. Can you get me the whistle now?"

Vlad

"Leon and Wendy are already here." Bowen parked the car next to Leon's.

Richard was the first to open the door and get out. "It's a nice cabin." He stretched his arms over his head, sucked in a deep breath, and then released it in a long whoosh. "The air here is so crisp."

Right now, Vlad didn't care about how nice the cabin was or whether the mountain air was fresh.

The only one on his mind was Wendy.

After learning about the new virus that was rapidly spreading throughout the world, he was glad that she was safe and isolated from other humans. Except for Richard, but he'd been isolated for a long time too, so he wasn't carrying anything that might endanger her.

Normally, immortals weren't concerned with seasonal influenza or other viruses that affected humans, and Vlad wouldn't have even known about it if not for the notification he'd gotten from his college. Classes were canceled, and from now until further notice, they were going to be held online.

His first reaction had been to shrug it off as mass hysteria that had nothing to do with him or the people he cared for, but while listening to the news on the way he'd realized that the situation was worse than he'd thought.

Wendy was still human, and he cared about her despite her betrayal.

Bowen popped the trunk and pulled out Vlad's guitar case and duffle bag. "Here you go, buddy." He handed him both. "Cheer up. It's going to be okay."

Vlad nodded. "One way or another." If things got too awkward between him and Wendy, he could spend his days hiking.

Slinging the strap of his bag over his shoulder, Bowen closed the trunk and then climbed the steps to the front porch.

"The door is open," Leon called from the inside.

Like a chicken, Vlad waited for Richard and Bowen to go in, and then followed, hiding behind the Guardian's broad back.

When a quick glance around revealed no Wendy, he let out a relieved breath. She was probably in her room, watching her damn anime.

"Wendy is taking a walk outside," Leon said.

Vlad frowned. "Is it safe? I mean, there are animals out there."

Leon shrugged. "I told her to stay close, and I gave her an emergency whistle."

"That can scare coyotes away. But what if she encounters a bear? Or a mountain lion? What if she gets attacked before she can blow the whistle?" Imagining those worst-case scenarios, Vlad started hyperventilating.

"If you are so worried, go after her." Bowen clapped him on the back. "I'll take your things up to the loft."

"Thank you." Vlad handed the Guardian his guitar case and duffle bag.

"We have perimeter cameras," Leon said. "You can check on Wendy using my laptop."

"I'd rather find her and bring her back. How long ago did she leave?"

"Less than ten minutes." Leon walked into the kitchen. "I'm heating up lunch." He opened the fridge and grinned. "Thank the Fates for Okidu. He made enough to last us the entire week."

Even though Vlad was hungry, the urgency quickening his steps had nothing to do with lunch. Wendy was all alone out there, and she might get attacked by a pack of coyotes before he got to her.

What had possessed Leon to let her go out by herself?

After completing one circle around the cabin, Vlad realized that he was wasting precious time. Sighting Wendy was not the only way to find her. He could use his hearing and sense of smell as well.

He stopped and listened, and after a few moments of intense concentration, he heard what he hoped was Wendy stepping over twigs and fallen leaves.

It could also be a bear.

Sprinting toward the sound, he didn't care about the noise he was making. On the contrary, if he was heading toward a bear, the sound of his boots crushing everything in their path might scare the animal.

Less than a minute later, he found Wendy.

Rooted on the spot, doe eyes peeled wide, she gaped at him. "You scared the shit out of me. What are you doing here?"

"Making sure that you don't get eaten by coyotes or a bear or whatever else is lurking in these woods." Relieved to find Wendy unharmed, Vlad wanted to pull her into his arms and never let go.

Instead, he tucked his hands into his pockets.

"That's nice of you." She lowered her eyes. "But why do you care about what happens to me?"

"I don't know. But I care."

She shook her head. "You are too nice for your own good. Besides, what can you do to protect me? Do you have a gun?"

"I don't need one."

Damn. He wanted to tell her who and what he was and be done with the charades. If they were going to erase her memories anyway, why continue with the story?

Despite the way he looked, he was a powerful immortal, physically and mentally. Maybe if he showed Wendy what he could really do, she would realize that by pushing him away, she was giving up a fierce protector.

"Right." Wendy rolled her eyes. "Leon said the same thing. What are you going to do? Hypnotize the beasts?"

"I could do that."

She started walking. "I know that I said it many times before, but I'm really sorry for deceiving you. You are a good person, Vlad, and you didn't deserve it."

He fell into step with her. "Was any of it real? Did you even like me?"

She looked up at him. "I still like you, and I don't blame you for being mad at me."

"What about...?" He hesitated, the question lodging in his throat like a lump of coal. "You know. Was it more than like?"

Letting out a tormented sigh, Wendy nodded. "It scared me. I vowed to never enter into a relationship with a guy, and when things between us moved from friendship to more, I knew that I had to put a stop to it before it was too late. I couldn't allow myself to get attached to you."

"Why? Because you wanted to go back to the program?"

"That was the main reason. My future is secure there. I don't need to depend on anyone. I don't need to settle on a guy, get married, and then discover that I made a huge mistake. I can have friends who have paranormal talents like me, and it can be a good, quiet life."

Wendy was so naive.

"You might be safe during the training period, but after that, you'd get sent out on spying missions, and there is nothing safe or peaceful about that. Why do you think the government is collecting paranormal talents?"

"My talent is not that useful for spying. At best, I might be part of a team of spies."

"You're an empath. You can feel intentions and warn your teammates when you sense danger."

"That's why I said that I could be part of a team. On my own, I'm quite useless."

Wendy

Wendy's heart was beating so fast that she was sure Vlad could hear it.

Since arriving back at her underground jail, she'd thought about him constantly, but her memory didn't do him justice. He was so much more handsome in person.

Perhaps it was the puffer jacket he was wearing. It made him look less skinny.

She was happy to see that he still kept his hair combed back instead of draping his bangs over one eye to hide the fact that it wasn't the same color as the other. They were both beautiful, and the black lashes framing them were so long that they looked fake, and because they were also thick, they created a dark outline around his eyes that looked like he'd put on eyeliner.

If he weren't still so angry at her, she would have pulled him into her arms and never let go.

"You are not useless. You can study psychology and become a great therapist, and if you don't want to deal with adults, you can specialize in helping children. Wouldn't that be a worthier career than spying?"

"It wouldn't pay nearly as much."

"So what? I'm sure it will pay enough to cover your expenses. If you never have a family, what are you going to spend all that money they are paying you on?"

Wendy shrugged. "I can travel to interesting places, stay at fancy hotels, and eat at the best restaurants."

He snorted. "As if they would let you do that. The only travel you are going to do is for all-expenses-paid spying missions."

Spoken like someone who had never lacked for anything. Vlad might have been raised by a single mother, but she loved him and bought him stuff and paid for music lessons and everything else he needed.

He'd never experienced what she had.

Not having the same privileges as her friends wouldn't have bothered Wendy half as much if her father was poor and couldn't afford it. But he wasn't. He just hated her and didn't want to spend a cent more than what he deemed necessary to maintain the façade of a loving father.

"Who is going to pay for my school? And who will support me while I go to school?"

Vlad hesitated for a moment. "Our organization."

"Why?"

"Because we need more people like us. We are building a community."

"Of paranormals?"

He nodded. "It's not easy for people like us on the outside. We need to hide who we are and what we can do. Being part of a community of only paranormals is liberating." He hesitated again. "There aren't many of us, and since marrying an untalented outsider is problematic, we prefer to form relationships within our community. The more people who join, the more variety there is."

Wendy snorted. "Vanessa and Jin both tried to persuade me that I'd be better off with your people because Director Simmons wants to use me for breeding. But it looks like your organization wants me for the same reason. So, what's the difference?"

"Freedom of choice. From what I was told, you were compelled to do things that you didn't want. That wouldn't happen with us. You'll be free to choose whoever you want or not choose at all. If you want to remain single, that's fine too."

"That's what you are saying now. The reality might be different. When I joined the program, no one told me that I would be used as a broodmare, or that I would be compelled to do exactly as I was told."

Wendy still couldn't get over that betrayal, and as much as she wanted to dismiss what Jacki and Jin had said, she had proof that it was all true. She'd felt the difference once Lokan removed the compulsion from her, and Richard hadn't faked his outrage over being compelled to leave his fiancée. Jin and he had hooked up in the program, but as soon as Marisol's compulsion was removed from them, they'd parted as friends.

Vlad let out a breath. "If you would stop being so stubborn, open your heart, and use your paranormal senses, you would know that everything I said was true."

He wasn't entirely wrong. In fact, he might be right.

She was desperately clinging to the only safety net she'd ever had, even after learning that it was full of holes.

But even a torn net was better than none, and what loomed underneath was a bottomless abyss.

"I want to believe you, but I'm too scared to do that."

He nodded. "I understand."

"You do?"

"The organization is my home, and if I was forced to leave it behind, I would be terrified. There is no place for a weirdo like me among normal humans."

Vlad

Wendy released an indignant huff. "You are not a weirdo. You are a sweet, talented guy, who happens to look a little different."

"Thank you. But there is no need to cheer me up. I see the way people look away when I get close. Even guys, but mostly the girls."

"Superficial jerks."

It felt so good to hear Wendy say those things, but Vlad couldn't allow himself to lower his guard. What if she was using him again? Buttering him up so he would soften toward her?

"We should head back. Leon is heating up lunch."

"Oh, yeah? Who cooked it?"

"Okidu."

She grimaced. "That guy freaks me out. He's like a store mannequin. He has no emotions at all."

Vlad stifled a chuckle. "Some people are immune to mind manipulation, like Jacki, and others can shield their emotions. Both are useful talents. I know a guy who has both. Or maybe he lacks both? I don't know. Anyway, I've heard people say that Turner is better than a computer. He takes into account variables no one would have thought to program the computer with."

He was rambling on, trying to keep the conversation on things that had nothing to do with him and Wendy.

When they reached the cabin, Wendy smiled up at him. "Thank you for coming to save me from all the wild beasts."

He opened the door. "You're welcome."

Inside, Richard and the two Guardians were already sitting at the table.

"Good, you are back," Leon said. "Wash your hands and sit down."

"Yes, sir." Vlad took his coat off, hung it on one of the pegs by the front door, and walked up to the kitchen sink.

As Wendy ducked into the bedroom, he sat next to Bowen. "What's there to eat?"

The Guardian lifted the lid off a glass container. "Beef with onions and mushrooms."

"Smells good."

Richard eyed him from across the table. "How did it go?"

"I found her before the coyotes did."

"Are you okay?" Bowen whispered.

"Yeah, I'm fine. It went better than I expected."

"Good."

He had to agree with what most of his friends had said about Wendy. She was just a young girl, terrified of an unknown future and clinging to the only safe haven she'd ever known.

Fear was a powerful motivator, and so was self-preservation. When scared, people often did stupid things. Even immortals.

Stepping out of her bedroom, Wendy looked as if she'd brushed her hair. "You shouldn't have waited for me." She sat next to Vlad and tucked a strand of it behind her ear.

Had she done it for him?

"Let's eat." Bowen scooped a large portion onto his plate and then passed the dish to Richard.

Apparently the guy had either never heard of ladies first, or he didn't consider Wendy a lady.

When Richard passed the container to Vlad, he made sure to rectify the situation. "Would you like me to serve you some?"

Wendy rewarded him with a bright smile. "Yes, please."

He put some on her plate. "More?"

"No, that's enough. Thank you."

Vlad filled his own plate and passed the container to Leon.

It seemed that things were going to be okay. He still felt a little awkward with Wendy, but it wasn't as bad as he'd imagined.

Now that he understood her better, the betrayal didn't sting as badly, and he could find it in his heart to forgive her. The question was whether he would ever be able to trust her again.

Perhaps.

But it would probably take a long time, during which he would constantly test her.

Wendy put her fork down and reached for one of the bottles of water. "Leon told me that your mom is going to join us tomorrow. I'm looking forward to meeting her." She looked down at her half-full plate. "I hope she doesn't hate me."

"She doesn't know you."

"You know what I mean. Because I hurt your feelings."

"It's possible. But my mom is different." Vlad chuckled. "As is her son. She often doesn't react the way other people do." He glanced at Richard. "She can get upset over trivial things like forgetting to buy something for the costumes she makes, but she's usually chill."

"What kind of costumes?" Wendy asked.

"For theater productions. The one before last was *Beauty and the Beast*. She won an award for it."

"That's awesome."

"Not really."

Immortals didn't need the attention such events garnered, especially when pictures were taken and published in magazines or online.

"Why not?"

He'd forgotten that Wendy still didn't know about who they were.

"My mom doesn't like the attention."

That was such a lie. Stella lived for it, but she couldn't have it, which was one of the reasons for her occasional outbursts. Her frustrations needed an outlet.

"How old is your mom?" Richard asked.

"She's thirty-six." The lie tumbled out of Vlad's mouth.

The guy grinned. "So young?"

"Yeah, she was a teenage mom."

Wendy shook her head. "And she raised you all alone and has done such a great job of it. It's remarkable."

"My mom didn't do it alone. She had the support of our community."

"Your organization is that old?" Richard asked. "I thought it was new."

"It's hundreds of years old," Bowen said. "It started in Scotland and has grown in numbers ever since."

That was as close to the truth as Bowen could get, and even that was too much. Perhaps someone needed to talk to Kian and ask his permission to reveal the secret.

Except, the usual prerequisite for the reveal was falling in love, and Richard hadn't even met Stella yet.

Vlad cast Wendy a sidelong glance. Was he in love with her?

Considering the panic that had gripped him when he'd heard that she was alone out in the woods, the answer was probably yes.

Kian

Syssi wrapped her arms around Kian's neck. "I'm so glad that you decided to take me along."

He put his hand on her waist and drew her against his body. "I didn't want to spend even one night without you, and flying back and forth didn't appeal to me either."

She smiled. "I just hope Amanda will be okay without me."

"Classes have been canceled, and testing for paranormal abilities doesn't qualify as an essential service."

"I know. She can stay in the village and run her online classes from home. But she wanted me to help her restructure her lectures, and I'm bailing on her."

"She'll manage. What I'm worried about is the café. With Wonder and Callie both gone, and Jackson running around even more than usual, organizing deliveries, there will be no one to manage it."

"Tessa said that she can take time off from the agency and help out. There isn't much activity going on over there either." Syssi chuckled. "Eva has been trying to convince Jin to come work for her after she transitions. She needs someone who speaks Chinese and can blend in, but naturally, that's irrelevant at the moment."

"Jin doesn't want to be a spy, and she doesn't speak Chinese."

"That's what she told Eva." Syssi pulled out of his arms and went back into the closet. "I scheduled spa appointments for all the ladies. I hope the hotel will not cancel them." She came out with several more outfits draped over her arm. "By the way, I checked out the suite that Shai booked for us, and it's enormous. We can hold the summit there."

"I'm not letting Kalugal anywhere near you. This is just so our group can hang out together. I liked having everyone in the same cabin at the ski resort, and I told Shai to find a presidential suite with four bedrooms."

Syssi looked up at him. "You know what's the downside of that, right? No privacy."

Kian smirked. "All four bedrooms have jacuzzi tubs. I checked."

In the chalet they'd shared with the others, only the master bedroom was equipped with a noisy tub, which allowed him and Syssi some measure of privacy. This time, the other three couples would enjoy the same.

"Did William make special earpieces for all of us?"

"He didn't have time. He barely managed to complete the three for me, Anandur and Brundar. Turner, naturally, doesn't need to block Kalugal's voice."

She shook her head. "That's a shame. I was hoping to see Jacki."

"It can still be arranged, just without Kalugal present."

"He's not going to agree to that. Who did you choose to be Lokan's bodyguards?"

"Magnus, Oidche, and Gregor. They are staying at the motel."

"You should let Magnus go home. He and Vivian are probably miserable without each other."

Kian raked his fingers through his hair.

"I don't know why she still refuses to take Parker over there. Turner even checked with his friend that it was okay to bring the dog to the motel. Parker is homeschooled, so it doesn't matter where he stays. And the boy is immortal, so it's not like the damn virus is a concern."

"I understand her perfectly. Kids need a stable environment. Can't you find a substitute for Magnus?"

"I can. But he's been heading the operation in the Bay Area and doing a great job. Once the summit is over, I'll replace him."

Syssi cast him a sidelong glance. "You need to start packing. Or do you want me to do that for you?"

"I can pack my stuff." Except, as he walked into the closet, his phone rang. "On second thought…"

She chuckled. "I'll do it. Answer the call."

"Thanks."

Checking the caller ID, he was surprised to see it was Jin. She and Arwel were heading to the cabin to join Wendy and Richard. Was there a last-minute change of plans?

"Hello, Jin. How is the motor home?"

"Huge. Thank you so much for approving the purchase."

"You're welcome. I'm sure we will put it to good use."

"What about Bowen and Leon? Did they get a motor home?"

"They plan on taking turns on the couch."

"That's not good. We need that couch for watching movies or snuggling in front of the fire. This was supposed to be a romantic getaway."

"If that doesn't work out, we will find a solution. Is that what you were calling about?"

"No. I need to ask you for a favor."

"What is it?"

"When I spoke to Wendy, I told her that the program wasn't the only safe place for her and that our organization can provide her with a real safe haven. But she has severe trust issues, and she wants to get it in writing. I know that if she transitions, she will be taken care of, but I wanted to ask what can be done for her if she doesn't. Will the clan take care of her?"

"I can find her a job. With her empathic ability, she could be a customer service manager in one of our hotels, after she gets some training, of course. But I'm not going to pay her a quarter of a million a year for that."

"I know, and I told her that she can't expect to be paid as well as she'd been in the program, but she won't be exploited either. Can you put the job offer in writing for her?"

"A piece of paper is meaningless."

"I know. But maybe it will help alleviate some of her anxiety."

"I'll have Shai send you an email detailing the help she might expect from us."

"That would be awesome. Thank you."

"Anything else?"

A moment of silence passed before Jin responded. "No, that's it for now. Good luck with the summit."

"Any last minute pointers on Kalugal?"

"I've already told you my impression of him, but I didn't spend long enough with Kalugal to be sure about anything. He seems like a reasonable guy. He's charming, very sharp, and a major snob. He was nice to me, and he took good care of me even though he had no reason to. I was the enemy."

"He was afraid that I'd blame him if anything happened to you."

"That's what he said, but he seemed genuinely concerned. Kalugal is not a bad guy, or at least I don't think he is. But I might be totally wrong about him."

Kalugal

"You don't seem to be worried." Phinas zipped his coat up as Welgost pulled up to the valet station in front of the hotel.

Per the agreement with Kian, they weren't carrying hot weapons, but Phinas, Ruvon, and Welgost had plenty of cold ones hidden inside their jackets and other places on their bodies.

Kalugal had none.

His weapon was his mind, and compared to that, all those crude instruments were useless.

"Kian is afraid of me, but he doesn't wish me harm. As far as I'm concerned, you can leave your arsenals in the car. No one will attack us."

Phinas shrugged. "Perhaps you are right. But our job is to protect you, and we don't have your special talent."

Kalugal nodded. "Noted. But if you are searched, and your weapons are taken away, don't worry too much about it."

Not wanting to attract attention, Kalugal had chosen one of his less flashy cars for the short trip to the hotel.

The Range Rover was red, so not entirely inconspicuous, but it wasn't as bad as the Lamborghini or one of his other beauties. It was also roomier and more appropriate for four passengers.

As the valet opened his door, Kalugal had a twenty-dollar bill ready for him. "Keep it safe, will you?" If it were one of his fancier cars, he would have given the guy a hundred to make sure that he kept an eye on it at all times.

"Of course, sir." The guy took the twenty with a gloved hand.

Looking at the classy hotel, Kalugal approved of Kian's choice. It was very considerate of his cousin to select a location that was close to his house. Leaving Jacki behind had been surprisingly difficult, and he already couldn't wait for the day to be over so he could go home to her.

Given the importance of the summit, the sentiment was quite ridiculous. He was about to see Lokan after more than seventy years, and he was going to meet Kian for the first time. The three of them were about to put their heads together and come up with a plan for shutting down the paranormal talents department.

And if things went well, they would come out of the summit with a draft agreement for future cooperation.

Following the instructions he'd been given, Kalugal exited the elevator on the third floor and headed down the corridor to conference room number five.

He stopped in front of the double doors and took a deep breath. Behind him, he could feel his three guards tense, but Kalugal wasn't going to let the aggression wafting from them affect him.

Still shrouded in one of his disguises, he planted a smile on his face, relaxed his shoulders, and pushed the door open.

Lokan, who wasn't affected by his shroud, was the first one to get up.

Spotting Kian among the seven other men was easy. If anyone deserved the title demigod, it was him. Kalugal could see no familial resemblance, though, and that was somewhat disappointing. But then their mothers were only half-sisters and didn't look alike.

The next one Kalugal spotted was Wonder's redheaded mate, who he remembered from their chance encounter in Egypt. The third one was very obviously the immune, a blond guy with penetrating blue eyes who zeroed in on Kalugal as soon as he and his men had entered, which meant that he was not affected by the shroud any more than Lokan was.

"Kalugal." Lokan walked up to him and offered his hand. "We meet again."

"Indeed." He shook his brother's hand. "Do you even remember me?"

"I have to admit that I didn't pay much attention to you back on the island, but I recognize you from your portrait. Kian sent me a photo."

"I remember you," Kalugal said. "You haven't changed much."

Lokan smiled. "The gift of immortality."

"Drop the shroud, Kalugal." Kian got up and walked over. "There is no need for it here."

"Right." Kalugal let go of Lokan's hand, released the shroud, and turned to Kian. "We meet at last, cousin."

They appraised each other like a couple of bucks. Kian was an inch or two taller than him, his hair was a few shades lighter, and he was paler. Kian's father must have been a big northerner.

"How are the earpieces working?" Kalugal asked.

Kian's shoulder-length hair covered his ears, but Kalugal was sure he was wearing them. Lokan wasn't, and Kalugal wondered whether it was because his brother trusted him, didn't fear him, or was immune to compulsion because he was a compeller himself.

Kalugal suspected that it was the third option.

"Better than expected," Kian said. "Let's get the introductions out of the way first." He turned to the blond guy. "This is Turner, my strategic advisor."

"A pleasure to meet you." Kalugal offered his hand. "We should make time for a game of chess. It's a rare treat for me to meet a worthy opponent."

"By all means." Turner shook his hand.

"And this is Anandur."

The big redhead grinned as he got up. "Finally, we meet."

Kalugal shook his offered hand. "My pleasure."

They'd met before, but Anandur hadn't seen him. Kalugal was surprised that Kian hadn't told the guy about that, or about the figurine that looked like his mate and had triggered Jacki's vision.

"And this is Brundar," Kian introduced his other guard.

The man dipped his head but didn't offer his hand.

Kalugal had a feeling that despite his angelic beauty, the guy was the deadliest of the bunch and the one he needed to be wary of.

When Kian introduced Lokan's supposed men, it was quite obvious that the three were clansmen and not members of the Brotherhood, which made perfect sense.

His brother wouldn't have been stupid enough to bring Brothers to the summit. Members of the Brotherhood were loyal to Navuh first and to their direct commanders second, and Lokan couldn't risk exposing his involvement with the clan.

It was an underhanded trick on Kian's part to bring six of his to only three of Kalugal's, but it didn't really matter.

Kalugal didn't expect any trouble from his cousin.

Kian

As Kalugal and his men entered the hotel's conference room, Kian gave his cousin a quick appraisal. In person, he seemed much less intimidating than Kian had imagined, but he was well aware that the impression was most likely misleading.

Kalugal was a little shorter and slimmer than him, and his expression was far from harsh. He seemed mellow, friendly, and generally good-natured. But even though his eyes were smiling, and the corners of his lips were quick to lift as well, he exuded inner power.

It wasn't as palpable as Annani's, so the source wasn't his godly heritage. Kalugal simply thought himself superior in every way, and maybe he was.

Engaging with him face to face should be interesting, and Kian wondered how his cousin compared to Turner. Hopefully, he wasn't as sharp and as unemotional because that would make him even more dangerous than Kian had estimated.

Once all the introductions were done, Kalugal pulled out a chair and sat down. "Let's first toast this historic meeting." He reached for one of the bottles of whiskey Kian had ordered and poured himself a shot. "I get to sit at the table with my brother, who I haven't seen for over seventy years." Kalugal put his hand on Lokan's shoulder. "And my cousin, who I'm meeting for the first time. Hopefully, this will signal a new era of cooperation between us."

Kalugal waited until everyone else's glasses were full.

"To new horizons." He lifted his drink.

"To family." Kian lifted his.

Kalugal nodded and emptied the shot down his throat. "It's a waste to drink good whiskey like that, but the occasion demands it." Pouring himself another shot, he assumed one of his charming smiles. "I'm going to savor this one."

"I'm glad you approve of my choice of whiskey for this meeting." Kian poured himself another shot as well.

Kalugal reached for the bottle and read the label. "I'm sure you didn't get it from the hotel bar. Even an upscale place like this wouldn't carry more than one or two bottles of Macallan 25."

"I had a case delivered."

Kalugal dipped his head. "You have my thanks. It's one of my favorites."

Clearing his throat, Turner tapped his pen on his yellow pad. "I prepared a list of items for us to discuss. Shall we begin?"

Kalugal lifted his hand. "If you don't mind, I would like to start with the threat the government's new paranormal talents division poses to us, and by us, I mean all immortals."

"That's actually the first item on my list," Turner said. "I gave your concerns some thought, and in the long run, you might be right. I don't think the program poses an immediate threat to immortals everywhere. But if it grows and gains footing as a legitimate operation, as opposed to a fringe pilot program, it certainly could. Especially with further development of artificial intelligence."

Kalugal looked pleased. "I'm glad that we see eye to eye. That program needs to get shut down as soon as possible, and the director and his cronies need to be discredited as frauds. It's in our best interests for the world to go back to thinking that paranormal phenomena do not exist, and that whoever claims that it does is either a charlatan or mentally unstable."

"How do you propose to do that?" Lokan asked.

"We need to dig up dirt on the director or plant it on him. Hopefully, that will result in the program's closure. If not, we will have to take more extreme measures. First of all, the data the program collected on the trainees needs to be erased, which can be achieved with a sophisticated computer virus." He cast Kian a smirking glance. "I know that the clan has access to advanced code that can do that."

Kian frowned. "How do you know that? You said that you were never interested in us or what we do."

Navuh had known about it because his allies had been affected by the virus that the clan helped create, but it wasn't public knowledge.

"It wasn't difficult to figure out. I'm no expert by any means, but I have acquaintances who are. When your virus was deployed, humans didn't have anything even close to that level of sophistication."

"Speaking of viruses," Turner interjected. "Bridget says that it's getting bad out there."

Kian nodded. "Unfortunately, there isn't much we can do to help."

"Bridget discussed it with Julian. If it reaches the stage where there is a shortage of doctors and nurses, they, together with Gertrude and Hildegard, are planning to volunteer."

"California is doing relatively okay," Kian said. "But as much as it pains me, we have to cancel the rescue operations for now. We can't bring new people to the sanctuary until this is over."

No one argued against that, and for a long moment, somber silence stretched across the conference table.

Kalugal cleared his throat. "Can we get back to the computer virus?"

"It will need to be a very precisely targeted attack," Turner said. "We don't want to infect the government's entire infrastructure. Roni will know more about it."

"Your hacker," Kalugal said. "Is he your best expert, or is it William?"

Apparently, Kalugal had been paying attention and collecting information.

"They are experts in different fields. Roni is a hacker, and William is a developer." There was no harm in telling him that.

"That's a good combination. Why don't you present the problem to them and ask their expert advice?"

"I'll do that."

Kalugal rubbed a hand over his jaw. "Jacki told me that you found Jin by capturing the program's recruiter and forcing information out of her. If necessary, could you do that again?"

"What do you have in mind?"

"She might have dirt on the director."

Kian shook his head. "Since the incident, I'm sure that she is being watched closely, and they've probably implanted her with trackers as well. It would be much easier to plant dirt on the director than dig for it."

"Roni can dig around," Turner offered. "Perhaps he can find old female coworkers who we could thrall to accuse

Simmons of sexual harassment. Except, the military is likely to cover it up."

"We could leak it to the newspapers," Kalugal suggested. "Make a big stink out of it." Leaning back in his chair, he took another sip from his glass. "But perhaps with the use of my special talents, I can do better than that. If you capture Simmons and stash him somewhere, I could walk into that facility shrouding myself as him and walk out with the recruits." He smirked. "More potential Dormants for us to share."

Kian and Turner exchanged glances.

That sounded like a doable plan. They knew that none of the other recruits were immune, so that only left the recruiter.

"We will have to capture the recruiter as well," Kian said. "If she is there when you walk in, she will see through your shroud."

"What about the tracker?" Lokan asked.

Kian waved a hand in dismissal. "We can take care of that with another cuff."

"If she is an immune, how did you make her forget the abduction?" Kalugal asked.

"Drugs," Turner said. "Those work on everyone."

Kalugal arched a brow. "Could they work on Jacki?"

Kian wasn't happy with where his cousin was going with that. "The drugs can affect short-term memory and muddle recent events. So, don't think you can make Jacki forget what she knows by using them. By now, her memories are long-term. If you no longer want her to stay with you, I'll take her off your hands."

"It was just a hypothetical question. I have no intention of letting Jacki go. In fact, I would like to discuss with you my future plans for her, in private if you don't mind."

This should be interesting. "We can take a break and stretch our legs. How about a walk around the hotel's grounds?"

"By all means."

Kalugal

As Kian walked over to the conference room's double doors, Kalugal cast a shroud over himself. "Would you like me to shroud you as well?"

"I don't need it, and I rarely use it." Kian glanced at his bodyguards, who had followed him to the door. "You two can come, but you need to turn the volume on your earpieces way down. Kalugal wishes to speak with me privately."

The moment Kian allowed his guards to come along, Kalugal's men rose to their feet as well.

Kalugal rolled his eyes. "Five men following behind us will look ridiculous and attract attention. I don't need you to come with us." He turned to Kian. "You don't need your guards either. We are just going to stroll through the hotel's grounds."

"Anandur and Brundar know how to look inconspicuous."

"Right." Kalugal regarded the two, looking them up and down. "As if a ferocious redheaded Viking and a fallen angel are not going to attract attention."

The redhead grinned, taking Kalugal's comment as a compliment. The blond's expression didn't change, but then Kalugal hadn't expected it to. Throughout the meeting, the Guardian had done a great impersonation of a statue.

But then, he surprised him by actually opening his mouth to speak. "I can make us both invisible," the Guardian offered. "And if you wish, I can make your men invisible as well."

Kalugal waved a hand. "Make it so. And if the rest of you want to join us, you're welcome. It seems that Kian and I will not have our privacy after all."

"I wouldn't mind stretching my legs as well." The immune got up and joined the group. "But I'll keep my distance and not intrude on your conversation.

"I'll stay here," Lokan said. "And so will my men."

"Thank you." Kalugal dipped his head in appreciation.

As the seven of them left the room, Kian cast Kalugal a sidelong glance. "It comes with the job. I'm so used to having Brundar and Anandur with me at all times that I often forget that they are there."

"You don't ever go out alone?"

Kian shook his head. "I'm the regent, and with the position comes responsibility. If I take unnecessary risks, I'm endangering more than myself. My people depend on me."

"Makes sense for you because you are in charge of a community that includes females and children. My men might not like it when I travel alone, and Rufsur gives me the same speech, saying that they would be lost without me, but I do it anyway. If anything happened to me, they could take care of themselves."

Kian nodded. "It's different when you are in charge of only warriors."

Kalugal glanced behind him, making sure that his men were a fair distance behind them. Unlike Kian's guards, they didn't have earpieces that muffled the sounds of his conversation with Kian.

"Things might change for me soon, though. Jacki and I are getting married."

Kian stopped and turned to him. "Married? Why?"

Kalugal took his cousin's elbow and kept walking. "My men don't know about it yet. Jacki is an old-fashioned girl, and she has trust issues. For our relationship to progress to the next level, she needed assurances, and a marriage proposal satisfied that need."

Kian chuckled. "She wouldn't have sex with you without a ring on her finger. Clever girl."

"That she is, but the idea was actually mine." It had been Jacki's, but she hadn't been serious, and Kalugal had run with it, taking it to the next level. Besides, he didn't want Kian to think of Jacki as a manipulative gold-digger. "Because of Jacki's immunity, I need her commitment and loyalty before I can tell her about her dormancy, so marriage works for me as well."

"Jacki can't get married using her real name. We prepared fake documentation for her, but it won't pass closer scrutiny. We can make her better ones, but it will take time."

"Given our special circumstances, we decided to make it a private ceremony without anyone officiating over it. We will pledge ourselves to each other in front of witnesses. The thing is, Jacki wants her friends to be there, and I want her to have a proper wedding, with a beautiful bridal dress and an elegant reception. The celebration could be a great opportunity for our people to mingle."

As he'd expected, Kian immediately assumed that this was a hoax designed to lure him and his people into a trap.

Chuckling, he cast Kalugal an amused look. "With my people wearing earpieces, that would be a very strange party. And since we don't have enough of them, and William is producing the devices one at a time, only a couple of Jacki's friends will be able to attend."

That was better than he'd expected. Kian was willing to allow two of his people to attend, which would fulfill Jacki's minimum requirement for having at least some of her friends witness their pledge, but it wouldn't make her happy.

Kalugal wanted more for her, and to achieve that, he was willing to make unusual sacrifices.

"I have a better solution. You can have William make me a cuff like the one he made for Jacki, but instead of it producing interference, it will be equipped with a zapper. Turner can hold the remote, and if I try to compel your people, he can immobilize me." Kalugal smiled. "Problem solved."

Kian stopped again, turned, and looked into Kalugal's eyes. "You are willing to put your life in my hands to give Jacki a proper wedding?"

Kalugal smirked. "I don't fear you, Kian. I know that you don't harbor malicious intentions toward me." He leaned forward, getting into Kian's face. "I trust you."

"No, you don't."

"Yes, I do. Your main concern is your people, and the only reason you would ever attack me is if I pose a threat to them. I have nothing that you want, and you have nothing that I want, except for your clanswomen, that is. My men would love to have a chance to meet them, but that's up to you. You probably consider former Brotherhood members unworthy of your clan females."

Kian snorted. "That's true, and yet my sister is mated to an ex-Doomer."

That was a piece of shocking news. "How did that happen?"

Kian resumed walking. "He kidnapped her, and when we found them, I wanted to tear his throat out with my bare fangs. My sister attacked me to protect him."

"Unbelievable. What did you do?"

"For many weeks after that, I couldn't even look at her. Our mother got involved, naturally siding with Amanda. Everyone thought that I was the unreasonable one."

Kalugal shook his head. "Why would the goddess encourage your sister's mating to a former Mortdh follower?"

"Because Annani is a romantic, and she believed that Amanda and Dalhu were fated for each other. She was right, of course. They are."

Kalugal shook his head again. "I think of myself as a reasonable guy, but I don't know if I could have accepted a former enemy as a brother-in-law."

"It wasn't easy. But Dalhu submitted to a terrible test to prove his love for Amanda, and after that, I had to accept that he was the right choice for her. I still put him on long probation, but I allowed him to move in with her."

"How is your relationship with him now?"

"Excellent. He's proven himself trustworthy time and again. You can ask Jacki about him. She met him."

"But she didn't know who he was."

"She didn't know who any of us were."

"Perhaps he could attend the ceremony? I would love to meet him."

"I don't know if he'd want to go. Dalhu is a bit of a recluse, spending most of his time with his canvases, painting beautiful landscapes, and occasionally portraits."

"He is the talented artist who provided you with portraits of my brothers?"

"Correct. But he didn't remember you."

"I wasn't part of the Brotherhood's high command. When I escaped, I was only a junior commander."

"That was what I assumed. But the other Doomer that crossed over to our side remembered you."

"I'm sure there is a story there too."

"There is. You can ask your brother about it. He is mated to the woman who that former Doomer rescued from Sharim, Losham's adopted son."

"Fascinating. I will do that as soon as I can."

Kalugal couldn't wait to have a few moments alone with Lokan, and not just because he was curious to hear the story of how his brother came to be mated to a clanswoman. He wanted to know how Lokan managed to infiltrate the harem and deliver a communication device to their mother. But first, he needed to finalize the details of his and Jacki's wedding.

"You didn't give me an answer about the ceremony yet. Will you be okay with letting more of Jacki's friends attend if I wear a cuff? It's very important to her."

"I'll discuss it with Turner in regard to security, and I'll also talk with my sister. Amanda is the queen of organizing parties. If anyone can pull off a beautiful wedding on short notice, it's her."

Kalugal stopped and offered Kian his hand. "Thank you. This ceremony means a lot to Jacki and me, and it also symbolizes a new beginning for all of us."

Nodding, Kian shook Kalugal's hand. "Let's hope it's a good one."

Lokan

As Kalugal left with Kian, Lokan leaned back in his chair and let out a long breath.

Kalugal was difficult to assess. He seemed easygoing, relaxed, and surprisingly charming. His self-confidence was a good indication of the power he wielded.

Surrounded by men who were his potential enemies, he hadn't looked concerned. Kalugal was either a superb actor, an excellent judge of character, or had tricks up his sleeve that none of them were ready for.

Could he trust him?

Lokan's instincts said yes, but they weren't reliable. They were influenced by his desire to have Kalugal as an ally, a true brother who he could count on, and not someone he should be wary of as he had been of his adopted brothers.

Except, wishing it didn't make it so, and he needed to tread carefully with Kalugal.

His brother's agenda wasn't clear. He claimed to have no interest in the island or in Annani's clan, and to wish to be left alone. And yet he'd agreed to participate in the summit and was willing to strike some sort of a cooperation agreement.

When the conference doors opened, and the group walked back in, the first thing Lokan noticed was Kian's upbeat mood. Whatever they had discussed on their walk must have been good news, and he wondered whether they were going to share it with him and the clansmen pretending to be his bodyguards.

Kalugal cast him a quick smile. "I apologize for not including you in the conversation, but it's a personal matter, and I had to get Kian's approval first."

"Did you get it?"

"It's contingent on several things that he needs to check, but it looks good. I'll fill you in as soon as I can."

Damn, the guy was too charming.

Lokan nodded. "We should meet outside of the summit."

"Perhaps after we adjourn for the day, you and I can grab a drink in the hotel's bar?"

"Sounds great, but I can stay only for a short time. My mate is waiting for me."

"I know what you mean. I want to get back to Jacki too." He tilted his head. "She tells me that the two of you have met."

"We did. I was the one who removed the recruiter's compulsion from Jacki's friends." He smiled. "She is one hell of a lady. I heard that she went after you and your second-in-command and tried to take you both on."

"She did." Kalugal looked proud. "And if we were human, she might have succeeded."

Turner cleared his throat. "Shall we get back to our agenda for today?"

"Yes." Kalugal pulled out a chair and sat down. "Let's finalize the tentative plan for rescuing the rest of the trainees and shutting down the program. I think that my plan can work."

"Which one?" Turner asked. "You had several."

"A combination of all of them. You capture the director and his recruiter and keep them away from the facility. I shroud myself to look and sound like him, walk in, and collect the trainees. After that, you can either let the pair of them go or get rid of them. Roni will infect their database with a computer virus, and if he can make it look as if the director did that before disappearing, that would be best. We also need to get rid of Roberts. I have a feeling that he is the real brain behind the operation."

"I'm not going to kill three people over this," Kian said.

Lokan shook his head. Kian's sanctimonious attitude could be a real pain in the ass.

"Why not? They are not good people."

Kalugal lifted a hand. "If you are squeamish about it, my men can do it for you. Those three humans need to be eliminated, and the best way to make sure they don't ever cause trouble again is to end them."

"I don't agree," Kian said. "By solving one problem, we will create another. The director and his cronies have access to an incredible infrastructure that collects information on paranormal talents. Some of those talented humans are potential Dormants, and we need them. Without Simmons and his cohorts, we will lose the only access we have to those Dormants. We don't have the means to identify them on our own."

"How are you going to get the information out of them?" Kalugal asked. "You've said that the recruiter is probably watched closely and has an implanted tracker on her."

"We will follow the recruiter around and keep track of the trainees she brings into the program. Once they are sent out on missions, we will approach them."

Kalugal reached for one of the bottles and refilled his glass. "We can't let the program continue. That's more important than collecting possible Dormants. We will have to find a way to tap into the collected data and deploy our own bots to search for trigger words."

Kian eyed him with both brows raised. "As I said, we don't have the resources. Do you?"

"I might."

"How?"

"The American government is not the only one collecting information. The Chinese do that as well, and it will be easier to hack into their servers."

Kian looked doubtful. "Are you sure about that? They don't have installations spread out all over the world."

"You mean the Western world. But who said that all the possible Dormants are in the West? Jin and her sister are proof that you need to broaden your horizons."

"That's true. Still, perhaps we can come up with a solution that would enable us to take control over the program, giving us access to the information, but not letting it leak to where it shouldn't."

Kalugal shook his head. "I can't pretend to be Simmons indefinitely. I have a business to run."

"Of course not, and I would never suggest it." Kian glanced at Turner. "What do you think? Can that be done?"

"I don't see how, but I'll give it some thought."

"Thank you." Kian poured himself another shot. "This was a very productive meeting. Let's toast our future cooperation."

Kalugal lifted his glass. "To family." He looked at Lokan and then at Kian.

Leaning toward his brother, Lokan clinked his glass. "To family."

Rufsur

Rufsur wondered what had prompted Kalugal to leave him in charge instead of taking him to the summit.

On the one hand, it made sense to leave the most senior officer behind. In case things went wrong, and Kian's intention hadn't been cooperation but capturing Kalugal, Rufsur was the most capable of leading the men and organizing a rescue.

But on the other hand, leaving him alone with Jacki was like putting the cat in charge of guarding the cream.

The boss was well aware of his infatuation with the girl. And even though Rufsur had backed away after Kalugal had made it clear that she belonged to him, it didn't mean that those feelings were gone.

Was it a test of loyalty?

And if it was, what was he going to do about it?

It depended on how Jacki felt. On the face of things, it seemed like she was taken with Kalugal, which wasn't a big surprise, but maybe her feelings didn't run deep, and Rufsur still had a chance.

Then again, was Jacki worth alienating his boss and maybe even losing his position as second-in-command?

Tough question.

Perhaps the best thing to do was talk to the girl and see where both of them stood.

Checking the security feed, he found her in the kitchen, which was a good sign. With Kalugal and Phinas gone, she had no reason to make lunch unless she was cooking for him.

A smile curving his lips, Rufsur pushed away from the desk and headed to the kitchen.

"I thought that you would take the day off." He walked up to her. "What are you making?"

"Mushroom and onion filled crepes."

"Sounds delicious. Who are you making them for?"

"The usual suspects. It's just a snack, not a meal. Atzil has dinner ready for this evening." She gestured at the ovens. "He has a roast in there."

Rufsur glanced around the kitchen, but Atzil wasn't there. "Where is he?"

"Taking a break."

Excellent. He had Jacki all to himself. "I'm a little peckish." He leaned over the platter with folded crepes. "Are those ready?"

"In a moment. I need to add garnish. Take a seat." She pointed at the kitchen table. "It will be done in a moment."

"Thank you." Rufsur walked over to the refrigerator and pulled out a beer. "What would you like to drink?"

She looked at the beer he was holding. "Is that Blue Moon?"

"Yes. Do you want one?"

"Please."

The beer was tasty, which was the only reason to drink it. The alcohol content was negligible for an immortal.

He took the two bottles to the table and sat down. "I hope things are going well at the summit and that it wasn't a trap."

"It wasn't. Kian is a straight shooter." Jacki brought the platter to the table and went back for plates. "He really wants an alliance with you guys." She put the plates and utensils down. "Dig in."

"Don't mind if I do." Rufsur put four crepes on his plate. "How well do you know Kian?"

She shrugged. "Not well, but I'm a good judge of character, and Kian is an honorable guy. Besides, you forget that their mothers are pulling strings in the background, and both goddesses would be majorly pissed if Kian did something underhanded to his cousin."

That was true. Kalugal would have wished to please his mother even if she was only an immortal, but given the shocking revelation that she was a goddess and Annani's sister, he probably was even more inclined to do so.

Other than Phinas, the rest of the men hadn't been told yet, but Kalugal hadn't kept it a well-guarded secret either, so rumors about his godly mother must have already spread.

"I don't know how much talking you do with Atzil, but he and the rest of the men don't know about Kalugal's mother being a goddess. For now, I think it's best to keep it that way."

She narrowed her eyes. "Why? Don't you trust them?"

"I do, and so does Kalugal, but I don't know how he wants to handle it." Rufsur leaned closer and smiled. "With one exception, my job is to look out for Kalugal's interests."

"What's the exception?"

"You. As long as I think that I still have a chance, it's every man for himself."

Jacki

Jacki hated to burst Rufsur's bubble, but he would find out soon enough, and it was better that he heard it from her.

"The game never started. I like you, a lot, but as a brother."

He grimaced. "Ouch."

"I'm sorry." She glanced at the kitchen entrance, making sure that Atzil wasn't coming back, and leaned closer to Rufsur's ear. "Kalugal and I are getting married."

He recoiled. "What?"

"We are getting married."

"I heard you. But why? Do you even love him?"

She did, but she wasn't ready to admit it. "Love will come later."

"What about your conviction that a relationship between an immortal and a human is not possible?"

"I figured that two good decades with Kalugal were worth the compromise." She sighed. "I'm only twenty-two, and if I take good care of myself, I will still look good at forty-two, maybe even a little longer. After that, I doubt that Kalugal will still want me."

This was just empty talk.

Jacki hoped that Kalugal would love her so much that wrinkles and saggy skin would make no difference to him, and that he would keep her until she died. But that wasn't fair to him. In thirty or forty years, he would still look the same, and when she lost her physical appeal, he would crave a young replacement.

Maybe they could remain friends and companions, though. Sex had never been all that important to her anyway.

Rufsur shook his head. "I don't understand. Marriage is just a meaningless piece of paper. Why go through the charade? I don't get what either of you has to gain by it."

He was right, of course, but their marriage wasn't about getting a written certificate. It was about a pledge that would be witnessed and therefore binding at least to some degree.

"We are going to pledge ourselves to each other in front of witnesses, and that's stronger and more binding than a piece of paper. Both Kalugal and I have trust issues, and this pledge will help us overcome them and move our relationship to the next level."

He arched a brow. "Are you referring to sex?"

She was sleeping in Kalugal's old upstairs office, and if the two of them had been getting it on, no one would have been any the wiser. Except, Rufsur had kept his eyes and ears on them, and it seemed as if so far their relationship had remained platonic.

"In part, yes. I made a vow to myself that I would never get intimate with a man who didn't cherish me, respect me, love me, and who would stand by me in sickness and in health. I don't have Kalugal's love yet, but a wedding will ensure that all my other requirements are met."

"How did you arrive at that conclusion?"

"Kalugal wouldn't marry me in front of witnesses if he didn't respect me. He's much too prideful to take a wife he doesn't hold in high regard, especially in front of his men, and hopefully Kian and Lokan as well. And since people he cares about and respects will hear him promise that he will always take care of me, he will lose face if he doesn't fulfill that promise."

Rufsur took a long moment to ponder her response. "Your logic is not totally flawed, but you are basing your assumptions on human behavior, and you don't know Kalugal as well as I do. He's not a bad guy, but he has no problem lying and cheating if it serves his purpose. He can promise you the moon with no intention of ever delivering. And as for the loss of face, he will find a way to excuse his behavior or compensate for it. He will not hang you out to dry, and he will most likely ensure that you lack for nothing for the rest of your life, but that's a far cry from what you expect him to deliver."

Rufsur hadn't told Jacki anything new. Ever since she'd agreed to Kalugal's proposal, she'd been struggling with the same doubts.

But then, Rufsur hadn't been there when Kalugal had convinced her to marry him either. He'd sounded so sincere, and the things he'd told her were as close as it got to telling her he loved her without actually using those precise words. And it hadn't been rehearsed either because it had started as her idea, and she doubted Kalugal could lie so convincingly on the spot.

Besides, why would he go to all that trouble if he didn't believe in a future for them?

It couldn't be just about getting her to have sex with him. Jacki refused to believe that.

"I'm willing to take the risk," she said. "If I don't, I might miss out on the best thing that has ever happened to me. And if eventually I get disappointed, I will at least have something wonderful to remember. The only downside is the heartache I'll suffer once Kalugal lets me go, but I can prepare myself for it."

He arched a brow. "Can you?"

She sighed. "Do I have a choice?"

"Yes, you do. Don't marry him and save yourself the heartache."

"It's already too late. I will be devastated no matter when I leave. But if I marry Kalugal, I will at least get a taste of wonderful, and I'll savor it for as long as it lasts."

Jin

As Arwel turned their new motorhome into the dirt road leading up to the cabin, Jin realized that her idea wasn't as brilliant as she'd thought it was.

It wasn't her fault, though. She hadn't known that to get up there they would need to drive on a goat trail that was barely wide enough for a compact.

The motorhome was the size of a bus, and the entire thing shook and clunked until Arwel stopped in front of a flimsy-looking metal gate.

"I don't think we are going to make it up to the cabin with this thing."

He left the motor running and opened the door. "It will be fine. If William's van made it up there in one piece, this brand new motorhome will climb it no problem. Besides, I'm an excellent driver."

As if any guy who'd ever gotten a license thought of himself as less than that. For some reason, men felt that driving reflected on their masculinity.

She needed another excuse. "We should turn around and drive this thing straight to San Francisco. I want to attend Jacki's wedding."

"She didn't give you a date yet, and Kian didn't green-light your participation either." He shook his head. "I still can't wrap my head around her and Kalugal getting married."

"Why not? It happened just as fast for us, and Jacki is an old-fashioned girl with old-fashioned values."

Jin hadn't told Arwel that her friend was a virgin, but he was smart enough to figure it out.

As a gust of cold wind ruffled Jin's hair, Arwel closed the driver's side door. "If Jacki was about to get married to one of my friends, I would wish the couple best of luck. But I don't trust Kalugal. He is good-looking, smart, charming, manipulative, and he's paying twenty-five thousand dollars per day for the privilege of her company. No wonder that she's fallen for him. But that doesn't mean that he feels the same about her. The only reason he wants her is that she can possibly give him Dormant children who will turn immortal. What will he do with her if she doesn't transition?"

Jin sighed. "I know, and I even thought about warning her or asking Kian to convince Kalugal to tell her before the wedding. But Jacki is not stupid, and she knows that she and Kalugal are not going to last forever. She thinks that she is a plain human, but that she has plenty of time until she gets too old to be attractive. If she is willing to marry him under those assumptions, then learning about her potential dormancy will only reinforce her decision. So, what's the point?"

"Would you have agreed to marry me if you didn't know about your potential to become immortal?"

"I'm not old-fashioned like Jacki, so I wouldn't have married you, but I would still have moved in with you and enjoyed our time together for as long as it lasted. What about you?"

Arwel frowned. "Kian would have never agreed for you to move into the village, but I would have quit my job, said goodbye to my family and friends, and gone to live with you among humans."

"There you go." She waved a hand. "Now you understand why Jacki is marrying Kalugal."

"Yeah, I guess, but that doesn't ease my mind. If she doesn't transition, he might kick her out sooner than she thinks."

Jin put her hand on Arwel's shoulder. "Nothing that's worthwhile in life comes with guarantees, but it's better to take a chance and fail than to give up without trying."

Arwel's lips curled in a smile. "I come with guarantees." Then his smile faded. "That's not entirely true. I'm a Guardian, and there is a small level of risk involved in that."

"Don't remind me." Jin pouted. "That's the only reason I'm not overly eager for my transition to start. As long as we are still working on it, you are not going back to work."

"I shouldn't have said anything. The risk factor is negligible, and we haven't lost a single Guardian in centuries."

Jin let out a breath. "That's good to know."

As Arwel opened the door, Jin grimaced. "I still think that we should head to San Francisco. What if Jacki emails me that she's getting married tomorrow? It's an eight-hour drive, and Kian took the clan's jet. Do you have another one?"

"We do, but I could drive through the night while you sleep. Besides, the whole point of getting this motorhome was so you could join Wendy and Richard in the cabin."

Apparently, using Jacki's upcoming nuptials as an excuse wasn't going to work, and Jin had to admit that she was scared to ride in the huge motorhome up a dirt lane that was way too steep and narrow for it.

"True, but neither you nor Kian told me that the road to the cabin was a goat trail. I'm still a fragile human, and I'm scared that this thing is going to topple over."

Arwel leaned toward her and wrapped his arm around her shoulders. "Do you think I would ever take unnecessary risks with your life?"

She pouted. "Guys have a tendency to get overconfident. Especially immortal Guardians who are practically indestructible."

"Would you feel safer going up there in a car?"

"Yes."

"Then I'll call Bowen and ask him to come get you. You can go up with him, and I'll drive the motorhome by myself." He smirked. "Let's make a bet. When I make it to the cabin without a hitch, you'll owe me a massage."

"Deal. But if you get all banged up because you failed, how are you going to give me one?"

"You'll have to settle for an IOU."

Kalugal

"Walk with me for a few minutes." Kian gestured to Kalugal as they stepped out of the conference room.

"Of course."

Before heading home, Kalugal would have preferred to catch Lokan for a quick private chat, but he couldn't refuse Kian's invitation.

By the disappointed expression on Lokan's face, he'd been hoping for the same. "I will see you tomorrow morning."

Kalugal nodded. "Ten o'clock."

After taking the elevator down to the lobby, Kian and Kalugal crossed it to the back exit and started on the same path that they'd taken only a couple of hours ago. No other guests were enjoying the hotel grounds. The humans were either holed up in their rooms or had left.

"Do you play golf?" Kalugal asked.

"No, do you?"

"I don't, but maybe we should give it a go. A lot of talking can be done on a golf course." Kalugal glanced back at their five bodyguards who were trailing a respectable distance behind them. "That would have looked much more natural."

"If you don't mind talking about Jacki in front of everyone, we could do that in the conference room."

"It doesn't feel right to talk about her even with you, but I have no choice."

"I get it. I wouldn't want to discuss my wife with anyone either. But what I wanted to talk to you about is not your relationship with Jacki. You should bring her along tomorrow."

"It has crossed my mind. But I didn't know whether you'd be okay with addressing the program first. I thought that you would want to focus on our coexistence treaty."

"Us working together on shutting down the program is a good start, and Jacki could shed more light on its inner workings and the facility it's in. But that's not my only reason for wanting her here. Wonder is anxious to meet Jacki and hear all about her vision."

"Can I meet Wonder as well?"

Kian shook his head. "We don't have spare earpieces, and I don't want you anywhere around my people who don't have them."

"Maybe Wonder can borrow her mate's device?"

Kian arched a brow. "Did Jacki tell you about Wonder being Anandur's mate?"

"She confirmed what I already knew. I met Wonder and Anandur in Egypt, but since they didn't see me, maybe met is not the right word. I saw Wonder, and I was intrigued by her resemblance to the figurine, so I shrouded myself and came closer for a better look. She sensed me, so I figured that she must be an immortal. Then her mate joined her, and I knew for sure that he was one."

"Who did you think they were?"

"I assumed that they were Annani's people. I doubted that my father had reformed his ways and allowed females to transition or warriors to take mates. So I knew that they weren't members of the Brotherhood."

"We have a theory about that. We know that he doesn't want the Dormant females to transition because he wants them to produce as many offspring as human females do. But he might have another reason that is just as important. The mated bond is incredibly powerful, and it can override his compulsion."

"Fascinating. How did you arrive at that conclusion?"

"Dalhu, the ex-Doomer who fell in love with my sister, said that the longer he stayed away from the island, the more freely he could think. But the final severing cut was his bond with Amanda. His loyalty to her comes first, and he will do anything to protect her."

Kalugal arched a brow. "And you believe him?"

"I do. That's why I eventually accepted him as a full-fledged member of my clan. Dalhu is a formidable warrior, and my sister has a tendency to rush head-long into trouble. She needs a strong protector, and the Fates found the perfect one for her."

"And you believe in that as well?"

Kian chuckled. "I understand your skepticism. I was a skeptic too, but I couldn't keep denying what was happening right in front of my eyes. After thousands of years of searching, suddenly Dormants started appearing out of nowhere and finding their way to their fated mates." He smiled. "That's why I didn't fight you when you asked to keep Jacki. I think she is fated to be yours."

A weight lifted off Kalugal's chest as Kian's conviction encouraged him to believe in what he already felt in his heart and his gut. It gave him hope. "I have a feeling that she is. But what made you think that?"

"The bizarre circumstances of your meeting. The more convoluted they are, the more I suspect the Fates' involvement. Except, we believe that the Fates reward those who suffer greatly or sacrifice a lot for others, and that doesn't really apply in your case. I think they favored you for another reason. Given your powers and being that you are Navuh's son, you can bring change to the status quo that has existed between our people since before the bombing. You are uniquely positioned to unify us, and that may be the Fates' agenda for you and Jacki."

Kalugal snorted. "I didn't take you for the sort of guy who believes in a utopian future. Some causes are lost no matter what, and Navuh and his island fall into that category. Forget about it. Just make sure that your people are protected the way you've done so far and let it be. I'm not going to take over the island. First of all, because I can't, and even if I could, I wouldn't. The potential loss of life is not worth it. There aren't that many of us left."

Nodding, Kian sighed. "I know. I let myself get carried away on the wings of wistfulness. Maybe someday it will become a realistic possibility, but you are right. We still have a long way to go."

Kian

"I don't know if it will ever be possible, not without bloodshed that would decimate our population." Kalugal tucked his hands into the pockets of his suit jacket. "It could mean extinction even for the Brotherhood, which has more members than your clan by order of magnitude." He shrugged. "Maybe my father's organization will eventually disperse on its own."

Kian wished that he could have heard Kalugal's tone of voice to assess the sincerity of his statement, but the downside of using the earpieces was that no matter who the speaker was, everything was delivered in the same emotionless computer voice.

Perhaps the cuff Kalugal had offered to wear would solve that problem as well, and they could forgo the earpieces.

"We had the same hopes, but that was before we realized that he holds the Brotherhood together by using compulsion. A grassroots revolution is not going to happen. But we digress. I wanted to talk to you about Jacki. If you bring her tomorrow, we can ask her to tell us more about the program, and when she is done, one of my Guardians can escort her to see Wonder."

Kalugal, who up until now had seemed relaxed and unconcerned, tensed. "I'm not comfortable with that. I want to trust you, but I'm not there yet."

"You are willing to put yourself in my hands and allow me to snap a cuff on you, but you are worried that I have nefarious plans for Jacki?"

"I don't worry about myself. I worry about you taking her away from me." Kalugal narrowed his eyes at him. "Was all that talk about Jacki and me being fated for each other a ploy to make me lower my guard?"

The only reason Kian didn't get angry was that he understood. He wouldn't trust Kalugal with Syssi either, even if the guy didn't have the power to compel immortals. "Perhaps it is best that we wait for William to send another cuff over, and then you can come with her. Naturally, Turner will have to accompany you."

"I'd prefer that. But then my men will have to join us as well. Turner could disable me, and then you could snatch Jacki as if I wasn't there."

"I swear on my honor that I will do no such thing." Kian smiled sheepishly. "I wouldn't dare. My mother would depose me in a heartbeat, and she might put Amanda in charge. That terrifies me more than you, your compulsion, and all of your men combined."

Kalugal chuckled. "Is she that bad?"

"No, Amanda is an amazing scientist and a wonderful person, but she is not cut out for this kind of work." Kian sighed. "This position is such a tremendous burden of responsibility that I wouldn't want to drop it on anyone I care about."

Kalugal frowned. "I get it. That's why I wouldn't want my father's job even if he handed it to me on a silver platter. Your mother, on the other hand, has the right idea. She dictates policy but leaves the day-to-day management to you."

Kian didn't correct him. So far, Kalugal didn't know about Sari and the European arm of the clan, and the less Kalugal knew, the better.

Raking his fingers through his hair, Kian cast his cousin a sidelong glance. "We digress again, and I want to go back to discussing Jacki and your upcoming wedding. You need to tell her about her dormancy before the ceremony. If she pledges herself to you before you tell her, she will never forgive you."

Kalugal shook his head. "I have to know that she wants to be mine because of me and not the immortality I can give her."

"You already have the answer to that. She agreed to marry you."

"That's true. But what if she doesn't transition? Jacki is not like the other Dormants that you've dealt with. Her memory can't be erased."

Kian sighed. "Look, Kalugal, we both know that no matter what, neither of us can allow Jacki to go back into the human world knowing what she already knows. If she doesn't transition, and you decide to end the marriage, I'll take her, and she'll be the first human to join my clan. At this point, it really doesn't matter if she learns one more thing about us. Trust me, you will thank me for convincing you to do that."

For a long moment, he and Kalugal walked in silence, but Kian believed that his cousin was smart enough to realize the wisdom of his advice.

And if he didn't, Kian would have to tell Jacki the truth before she went through with the ceremony. He'd humored his cousin's request, but things were getting serious. It wasn't fair to Jacki to let her marry Kalugal without being told what he would gain from it.

Hopefully, Kalugal would do the right thing and spare Kian the need to go back on his promise.

"You are right," Kalugal finally said. "As a married man, you probably have a better insight than I do. Keeping secrets and shrouding myself was a way of life for me, and it's difficult to switch gears." He looked at Kian. "It's even hard for me to drop my shroud when I enter the conference room, which is ridiculous since you all know what I look like. I'm so used to only my men seeing my real face, and now Jacki."

"I can imagine that it's difficult, but it also must be liberating for you to have a woman look upon your face with appreciation and know that she sees you."

Kalugal tilted his head. "Are you speaking from experience?"

"I wasn't shrouded when I met Syssi. It's not something I do. But having her love was the best thing that has ever happened to me. She loves me, the man, not the regent, not Annani's son, just me. And with her, I feel free. I don't feel that way with anyone else, not even with my sisters and my mother. They all expect me to be the leader and the head of the clan's business empire. Syssi just wants my company and my love."

Kalugal nodded. "That's what I want from Jacki." He chuckled. "I wasn't aware that this was what I wanted, or maybe I just didn't know how to verbalize the need, but you nailed it."

"Experience." Kian clapped his cousin on the back. "There were many things I didn't understand before Syssi entered my life. She still teaches me new things every day. Like this conversation that we are having? That wouldn't have happened three years ago. And if I heard two of my Guardians talking about feelings and relationships, I would have rolled my eyes and walked away."

"I'm not that bad. Love doesn't scare me."

Kian frowned. "I wasn't scared of love. I just didn't think that any sane woman could love me. I'm not exactly Prince Charming."

Kalugal laughed. "No, you are not. You're an ogre with a heart of gold."

Kalugal

Regrettably, the drive home was too short for Kalugal to come up with the best way to tell Jacki about her possible dormancy.

Which gave him a splendid idea. He could delay his return by driving to a jewelry store and buying her an extravagant engagement ring. Perhaps a massive diamond would stun her into forgiving him.

He glanced at his watch. It was six in the evening, which might be too late to find an open jewelry store, if any were open at all. Stores were closing all over because of the damn virus. Where could he even find one that carried the quality he was looking for? It wasn't as if he'd ever bought stuff like that before, and he didn't have enough time to educate himself about it.

"Phinas, do you know where I can buy an engagement ring?"

The guy turned to look at him. "A ring? Are congratulations in order?"

"I hope so."

After Jacki learned that he'd been keeping such crucially important information from her, she might rethink her acceptance of his proposal.

"It's not my place to question your decision, boss, but isn't it too sudden? You've only known Jacki for one short week. Besides, she is human, and your stance on the issue has always been that getting attached to a mortal is a bad idea."

"I have my reasons, which at the moment I can't reveal."

He couldn't tell Phinas and the other two before he told Jacki. That would make things even worse. He also wasn't ready to admit that he'd known she was the one from the first moment he'd seen her without the ugly disguise.

The truth was that he'd felt drawn to Jacki even before that, but since he couldn't understand why he felt that way about a stranger who wasn't even attractive, he'd explained it away as a feeling of familiarity. He'd thought that he'd met her before and had forgotten.

Except, now that he thought back to that moment outside the cigar club, he realized that there had been something about her that had appealed to him on a visceral level.

The best way he could describe the feeling was affinity.

Kalugal had only gotten that feeling about a human twice before. One was a professor of philosophy at Stanford, and the other was a lowly laborer in one of his archeological digs in Egypt. Both were males, and both had a rare sort of intelligence, an inner light that shone through their eyes and hinted at knowledge that hadn't been learned but was innate.

Or so he'd thought.

Perhaps both had been Dormants, and that was why he'd felt an affinity toward them? It could be a good idea to get in touch with them again and find out whether either possessed paranormal abilities.

Except, Professor Levinson was in his late thirties or early forties, and Kian had said that transition was dangerous for older Dormants. So he might not be a good candidate. The laborer, on the other hand, was a young man in his mid-twenties. But then the guy was probably married with a bunch of kids. In places that forbade premarital sex, people got hitched at a young age. So Ahmed wasn't a good candidate for induction either.

"I've seen commercials for a place that specializes in engagement rings," Phinas said. "But I doubt they'll have the quality that you're looking for."

"Drive toward the city while I search online."

"Yes, boss."

Kalugal needed to catch someone on the phone and compel them to wait for his arrival.

It took him less than ten minutes to go through his options, and a few minutes later, he had a private appointment with the owner of the most exclusive jewelry store in San Francisco.

After the guy had heard how much Kalugal was willing to fork out on an engagement ring, he'd said he would open the place just for him and wait for his arrival with a selection of the best readymade rings his store had to offer.

Jacki deserved the best, and Kalugal would have loved to order a custom-made ring for her, but if he wanted it right now, he would have to settle for what was there.

The next step was to organize a romantic dinner.

He called Atzil.

"What's up, boss? Are you on your way back?"

"Not yet. Is Jacki next to you?"

"No, she went up to her room."

"Good. I'm ordering dinner delivered from Magonito's, and I need you to set it up in my suite. Get a table and a couple of chairs in there, but try to do it discreetly. I want it to be a surprise for Jacki. Use a tablecloth, get candles and flowers, and your best place settings. I want this to be a romantic dinner to trump all others."

"You don't need to order. I can prepare a nice dinner."

Kalugal rolled his eyes. Atzil was a fine cook for everyday fare, but he wasn't a gourmet chef. Except, he couldn't say that without hurting the guy's feelings. "I'm sure you could, but since I want it to be a surprise and Jacki likes to hang around the kitchen, you can't."

"Got it. When do you need everything to be ready?"

"I'll order delivery for eight." Then it suddenly occurred to him that Jacki might have prepared something, and she might get mad at him for ordering from a restaurant. "Did Jacki cook anything today?"

"She made crepes for an afternoon snack, but most are gone. She barely managed to save a couple for you."

"Excellent. If you can, keep her busy somewhere else while you set things up."

"Yes, boss."

Jacki

Jacki put her new cellphone in the back pocket of her jeans and headed down to the kitchen. She'd been hoping that Kalugal would call her with questions about the program, but her phone had remained silent.

She missed his voice, she missed his perfect lips curving in his signature smirk, and she missed his smiling eyes.

Today, the summit was being held only in the afternoon, so their separation was short, but tomorrow it was scheduled to start in the morning and last all day. How was she going to survive so many hours without seeing him?

There was no point in denying what was obvious.

She was already in love with Kalugal and couldn't fathom life without him. Luckily, they were getting married, and hopefully that meant at least several years with him.

Jacki refused to think about a more distant future. If she did, she would get depressed and start crying, and that wasn't going to do her or anyone else any good. She was strong, a fighter, and she could handle whatever life threw at her.

Entering the kitchen, she scanned for Atzil, but he wasn't there. He was probably serving another round of dinner in the dining room. Since the men ate in shifts, every meal involved several sittings, and the entire thing lasted about two hours. Poor Atzil practically lived in the kitchen.

She peeked through the open door to the dining room, but he wasn't there either.

A moment later, the walk-in pantry door opened, and Atzil emerged. Seeing her, he grinned. "You're right on time to help set up the table."

Jacki grabbed a stack of plates. "Did you hear anything from Kalugal?"

"He called a few minutes earlier and said that he's running an errand in the city."

"Did he say when he'd be back?"

"Around eight, or maybe a little earlier than that."

That was disappointing. She'd hoped that he would be back shortly. "Did he leave a message for me?"

Atzil hesitated for a moment. "He said that he wanted to dine with you, but if you are hungry, you can grab a snack."

"I'm fine." She carried the plates to the dining room. "I can wait until he comes back."

As Jacki started putting the plates down, it occurred to her that it was easy to figure out how many men Kalugal had. Since the table could seat twelve, and Atzil served three rounds of each meal, it meant that he had about thirty-six men.

Except, some of the men supposedly ate at the bunker, and it was also possible that not all twelve seats were occupied at each sitting.

What irked her, though, was that Kalugal still kept the real number of his warriors a secret from her. Evidently, he didn't trust her not to tell Kian. Would that change after the wedding?

Kalugal had said it would. But maybe not right away. He'd admitted to having secrets he couldn't share with her until he was positive that he could trust her.

Damn, that wasn't the right way to start things. If she hadn't been so stubborn about her no sex without commitment rule, they could have let their relationship develop naturally, but she didn't trust him enough to do that either.

Whatever. No couple was perfect, and different people had different issues. Hers and Kalugal's was trust, and hopefully, marriage would help them both over that hurdle.

When she was done with the plates, Jacki went back to the kitchen and collected twelve sets of utensils. "Anything else you need me to do after I'm done?"

He closed the oven and nodded. "I'm getting a large delivery of dry goods supply tomorrow, and I need to organize the pantry. Would you mind doing that for me?"

"Not at all. What do you need me to do?"

"Check the containers and bring out those that are nearly empty. I'll get Shamash to clean them up. Also, check expiration dates on everything that is still in its original packaging. I have a feeling that many items need to be thrown out."

"No problem. Consider it done."

"Thank you. It's a big project, and not everything needs to be done today. You can continue tomorrow."

It was the first time that Atzil had asked her to do more than just set up the table or chop vegetables for him, and Jacki was glad for the opportunity to prove herself helpful.

When she was done with the utensils, she went back into the kitchen and smiled at Atzil before walking into his holy of holies. In her imagination, dramatic harp music started playing, and the two cherubim guarding the entry lowered their swords to allow her passage.

The pantry didn't disappoint.

It was the size of a bedroom, and other than dry goods and paper supplies, it also housed a large freezer. Atzil hadn't said anything about checking the expiration dates on the frozen goods, and Jacki wasn't sure whether she should. But when she stepped out of the pantry to ask, he wasn't there.

He wasn't in the dining room either.

Oh, well, she could ask him later. Going over the dry goods would take her at least a couple of hours, and if Atzil wanted her to check the stuff in the freezer, she could do it the next day.

Except, Jacki had a niggling suspicion that Atzil was up to something. When he'd asked her to organize the pantry, his cheeks had gotten a little ruddy, but that could have been because he'd just peeked into the oven. Except, that didn't explain the goofy grin that had been stuck on his face since she'd entered the kitchen.

What are you plotting, Atzil?

Or maybe it wasn't the cook who was up to something, but his boss?

Kalugal

Kalugal felt ridiculous sneaking into his own house, but he wanted to shower and change before seeing Jacki. She was still a vulnerable human, and he might have picked something up during the day. Immortals couldn't get sick, but they could be carriers during the short time it took their bodies to eradicate pathogens.

He wasn't taking any chances with her.

Kalugal still remembered how helpless he'd felt when Jin had gotten sick, and she wasn't even someone he'd cared about at the time.

Jacki was absolutely precious to him, and if he needed to put her in an isolation chamber until this damn virus's spread was over, he would do that.

That was why he'd also ordered his men to shower and change as soon as they got home.

Perhaps he was going a little nuts with that, but he had to keep Jacki safe.

Kalugal hadn't been aware of how bad it was until he'd met with the jeweler. The guy hadn't stopped talking about all the precautions he and his staff had taken to ensure their clients' safety, and he'd filled Kalugal's head with ideas.

After leaving the store, he'd called Shamash to make sure that no one else had left the house that day. He'd also told him to wipe all surfaces, doorknobs, and light switches with disinfectant wipes.

If Kian and his people decided to come to the wedding, he would have to ask them to refrain from going near humans for at least twenty-four hours prior. Kalugal wasn't a doctor, but that was probably more than enough time for immortal bodies to kill any pathogens.

After parking in the bunker, he called Atzil. "Is everything ready?"

"Everything except for the food. It hasn't been delivered yet."

"When it gets there, make sure to wipe all the containers clean."

"Shamash already told me."

"Does Jacki know what's going on?"

"I don't think so. We didn't tell her, and I kept her busy organizing the pantry. She is still working on it."

"Good. Let me know when the food gets here."

"Yes, boss."

Heading to the house through the tunnel, Kalugal paused by the exit door. "Do me a favor, after you shower and change, go straight to your rooms. I don't want Jacki to see you and figure out that I'm back. I want to surprise her."

Stifling a smile, Phinas nodded. "When can we get out? We haven't had dinner yet."

"At eight, I'll escort Jacki into my suite, and you can head to the kitchen."

"Good luck, boss," Phinas said.

The other two murmured the same.

"Thank you for keeping quiet about it."

"No problem." Phinas opened the door and pretended to scope the territory. "All clear."

The four of them tiptoed in like a bunch of thieves, took the stairs as soundlessly as they could, and then dispersed into their respective rooms.

If sneaking into his own house had felt silly, having his men do the same was even sillier. But wowing Jacki into forgiving him was worth the effort. Besides, it added to the excitement, and Kalugal liked the feeling. For the longest time, the only things that had excited him were new artifacts and successful business acquisitions.

In the master closet, Kalugal pulled the three small boxes out of his jacket pocket and put them on top of the dresser.

One box contained two matching wedding rings, the second box contained a pair of diamond earrings, and the third held a gorgeous engagement ring.

The moment he saw it, he knew it was perfect for Jacki.

It wasn't the most expensive the jeweler had, but it was the most beautiful. A simple, pure stone shaped like a teardrop was encased in unadorned platinum gold. It was unique, precious, and straightforward like the woman he'd bought it for.

As Kalugal selected the clothing items he was going to wear for the occasion, it dawned on him that Jacki wouldn't like it if he sprung a romantic dinner on her without giving her any warning so she could prepare as well.

He pulled out his phone and texted Atzil. *In ten minutes, please release Jacki from her task. I want her to have time to freshen up if she wishes to. When the delivery gets here, arrange everything on a cart and have Shamash ready to serve it.*

The answer came right away. *Yes, boss.*

Five minutes later, Kalugal headed out with a change of clothes draped over his arm and a pair of shoes in his hand. Checking that the coast was clear, he took the back stairs to the underground tunnel.

After showering and changing in his room in the bunker, he walked over to his wine cellar. Quickly scanning his selection, he chose a bottle of excellent wine that hadn't cost a fortune. After the last bottle he'd shared with Jacki, she wouldn't touch it without asking how much it was worth first, and the last thing he wanted was to upset her before delivering the news about her potential dormancy.

Setting the bottle on the table, he pulled out his phone again and texted Jacki.

I'm back home and would love for you to join me for dinner. Can you be ready by eight?

Her answer came in a moment later. *I'm ready now.*

He texted back. *I'll come to get you. Are you in your room?*

Yes.

Hopefully, Jacki had changed into something nice. Not that he cared about what she was wearing, but since this would be his official proposal, he assumed that Jacki would want to look nice for that.

Passing by his suite first, he verified that everything was ready as per his instructions. When he was satisfied that Atzil had done a great job setting up a table for two with all the fanfare the occasion called for, Kalugal walked over to Jacki's door and knocked.

"Just a moment!"

As she opened the door, Kalugal took a step back.

Dressed in the black cocktail dress he'd ordered for her and a matching pair of spiky black pumps, Jacki looked like a cover model.

"You look stunning."

Smiling, she smoothed a hand over her hip, pushing the dress down. "You're not so bad yourself. When did you have time to shower? And where? I've been in your bathroom for the past half an hour."

He smiled sheepishly. "I got here a little earlier and showered in the bunker. I wanted this to be a surprise, but given your attire, you guessed it."

"Guessed what?"

He took her hand and lifted it to his lips for a kiss. "I wanted to take you out to a nice dinner, but since that's not possible, I arranged for it to be delivered here."

"Oh. I thought we would be eating Atzil's roast."

Right. As if she would've put on a cocktail dress and heels for that. But it was nice of her to pretend surprise.

"Not today."

Still holding on to her hand, Kalugal walked over to his suite's double doors and opened them. "My lady." He motioned for her to go in ahead of him.

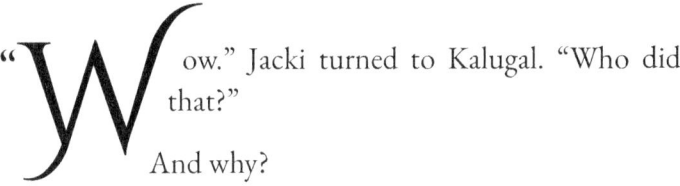

"Wow." Jacki turned to Kalugal. "Who did that?"

And why?

She'd guessed Kalugal was planning something when it had become clear to her that the pantry didn't need organizing. Atzil had just wanted to keep her busy, and the goofy grin that had refused to leave his face had been the other clue. But she hadn't expected such an elaborate setup.

Did Kalugal plan to propose to her again? Or did he plan to break up the engagement and thought to soften the blow by inviting her to a nice dinner?

"As I said, I wanted to take you out on a date, but since I can't, I did the next best thing. I ordered dinner from an excellent restaurant and asked Atzil to prepare a table for us."

He took her elbow, led her to the table, and pulled a chair out for her.

"Now I know why Atzil put me in charge of organizing the pantry when it didn't need any organizing."

"I wanted it to be a surprise." Kalugal pulled out the other chair and sat down.

It was good that she'd guessed something was up and had dressed accordingly, but since it was important to Kalugal, she could play along and pretend like this was a complete surprise. Then again, given his superb sense of smell, maybe a middle ground was better.

"It worked, but I had a feeling that Atzil was up to something, just not this." She waved a hand over the table. "If you ever think of sending him on a spying mission, don't. The guy doesn't have a poker face."

"That's why he is the cook." Kalugal reached for the wine, uncorked it, and poured it into the two flutes.

Jacki eyed the bottle suspiciously. "I hope this is not the other three-hundred-thousand-dollar bottle."

"It's not. I knew you would object to that. This is a reasonably priced wine that is nevertheless superb."

"Thank you." She took the glass. "What are we toasting?"

"Our future together." He lifted his glass and clinked it with hers. "To us."

To cover up the relieved breath that had escaped her throat, Jacki let out a giggle. "To us."

There was a knock on the door, and a moment later, Shamash entered with a rolling cart.

"May I serve dinner, boss?"

"Please do." Kalugal turned to Jacki. "I apologize for not asking you what you would like, but it would have ruined the surprise."

"What did you order for me?"

Hopefully, it wasn't some exotic seafood like clams or oysters or even lobster. Jacki liked simple dishes, and all those sea creatures grossed her out as much as eating grasshoppers or snails would. In her mind, they were the same, with the only difference being the environment in which they lived.

"I've been paying attention, my Jacqueline, and I know that you like salmon. But I bet you've never eaten salmon like this one. It's Magonito's house special. It's such a delicious and filling dish that I decided not to order a first course. I hope that's okay with you."

"It certainly is. I don't like getting full on a salad and then leaving half of the main course on the plate."

When Shamash was done serving, Kalugal thanked him and then promptly dismissed him.

Looking at her plate, Jacki was glad to see that everything on it looked perfectly mundane. A good-sized piece of salmon was smothered in a caper sauce, and next to it was a scoop of creamy pasta, and another scoop of spinach. All were things she enjoyed eating, but spinach was problematic as a date food. There was nothing worse than smiling with green goop stuck between her teeth.

"You're looking at your plate as if it's the enemy. Whatever you don't like, you're welcome to dispose of it onto mine."

"It's not that. I love everything. It's just that spinach is not the best date food. Can you imagine smiling with it stuck on your teeth?"

Kalugal laughed. "Indeed." He forked a generous helping of the spinach, put it in his mouth, chewed, swallowed, and then grinned. "How do I look?"

Jacki shook her head. "You are probably the only man on the planet who can look sexy with spinach stuck on your fangs." She leaned forward. "May I?"

His eyes blazed with an inner light. "Please do."

Jacki got nervous. What if he bit her finger?

His fangs were elongating right in front of her eyes, which meant that Kalugal was aroused, and Jacki remembered too late that his fangs were super sensitive to stimulation. Except, she couldn't back out now without offending him.

Reaching with her finger, Jacki flicked away the piece of spinach stuck on Kalugal's left fang. "All done." She pulled back with a forced smile.

Kalugal's fangs had already started to retract, but his eyes were still glowing, and they were focused on hers. "That was a very intimate gesture. Thank you."

You think?

She felt a blush creep up over her cheeks. "You're welcome."

Kalugal

It had been such a simple thing, but to Kalugal it had felt more intimate than sex because no one had ever reached into his mouth and cleaned his teeth for him before.

What did it mean, though?

Would Jacki have done it for any man she was dining with, or had she done it for him because she thought of him as hers?

Still, the moment had passed, and both of them got busy eating.

"How was it?" he asked when she was done.

"The best salmon I've ever had." She chuckled. "I'm grateful that you didn't order clams or oysters. They gross me out."

"I noticed that you didn't even eat the shrimp-stuffed avocados that you made yourself."

"I just wasn't in the mood for them. For some reason, I'm okay with small shrimps. It's the big ones that gross me out because they look like bugs."

Kalugal nodded, but he wasn't thinking about seafood. He was trying to figure out what to do next. Should he pull out the ring first? Or perhaps he should mention the virus and then steer the conversation to her potential dormancy?

Or maybe he should go down on one knee and ask her to marry him first?

On the one hand, the ring might soften her up, but on the other hand, he remembered Kian's warning to tell Jacki the truth first so she could make up her mind while being aware of all the facts.

Perhaps he should put the box on the table and ask her to wait until he told her the truth?

Damn. He used to think of himself as such an expert on women, but that was only in things he'd practiced, like seduction. When it came to relationship stuff, he was clueless.

The only thing he had to go by was his own preferences, and if he were in Jacki's shoes, he would have wanted the truth first.

Reaching into his pocket, Kalugal held the small box but didn't pull it out. The table needed to be cleared first, but instead of calling Shamash, Kalugal decided to do it himself. Jacki liked it when he waited on her, and right now he needed to earn as many merit points with her as he could.

"Are you done?" He reached for her plate.

She laughed. "I'm too embarrassed to lick the plate, so yeah, I'm done."

"You can go ahead and lick it. I bet you'd look sexy as hell doing that."

"I doubt it but thank you." She started to get up. "Let me help you clear the table."

He put his hand on her shoulder. "Tonight, I'm serving you."

"Okay." She sat back down.

After clearing everything aside from the wine glasses, Kalugal lifted the dessert and coffee tray off the cart and brought it over to the table. "Coffee?"

"Yes, please." He poured them each a cup. "The tiramisu is delicious." He put a piece in front of Jacki. "You should try it."

She eyed the dessert. "I'm so full. I don't know if I can take another bite."

"A moment ago, you wanted to lick the plate."

"It was so good."

"I'll order it again tomorrow."

"You are spoiling me."

He reached for her hand. "It's my pleasure. I want to keep on spoiling you." He kissed the back of it before letting go.

"I want to spoil you too," she murmured. "But I don't know how. I thought I could do that with cooking, but mine can't compare to this." She waved at the cart.

Kalugal had a few ideas, but he was going to save them for later.

Much later.

"You have been doing a great job so far. Every day that I get to spend with you is a pleasure, and I hope for many more." Reaching into his pocket, he pulled out the box and put it on the table. "I want to propose to you properly, but before I do that, there is something I need to tell you. A couple of things, in fact."

As he'd expected, Jacki eyed the box eagerly. "Is that what I think it is?"

"Yes, but I need you to hear me out first."

Dragging her eyes away from the box, she looked up at him. "What is it?"

"The first is just a bit of upsetting news. A very aggressive virus is spreading around the world, but you have nothing to worry about as long as you stay away from other humans. I told my men that if they leave the house for any reason, they have to change their clothes and wash their hands when they come back and to wipe clean any surface they touched. Your safety is my number one priority."

"That's a lot of effort that I'm sure is unnecessary given that you and your men can't transmit diseases."

"We can't get sick, but we can be carriers. I'm not taking any chances with your health."

"Thank you. I just feel bad about causing so much trouble."

"It's only temporary."

Jacki tensed. "I hope that by temporary you mean the virus."

What did she think he meant? That he was going to get rid of her?

He'd better get on with the explanation. "That too." Kalugal rubbed his hand over his jaw. "Do you remember wondering about Jin and Arwel and how they were going to make their relationship work?"

Jacki eyed him suspiciously and then shrugged. "I asked Jin about it, and she said they are taking it one day at a time, enjoying each other without worrying about the future. Her answer was what eventually convinced me to compromise and accept a little less than happily ever after. But what does that have to do with the precautions you are taking to keep from contracting the virus?"

"I'll get to that in a moment." Kalugal took a sip of coffee to give himself a moment to think. "Jin hasn't been entirely truthful with you, but it's my fault. I asked Kian to help me keep a big secret."

Jacki frowned. "I don't understand."

"Jin is a carrier of immortal genes, and those genes can be activated. She can turn immortal. That's why she isn't concerned about her future with Arwel. Once she goes through the transition, she's not going to age either."

Jacki

Jacki hadn't been aware that such a thing was even possible, but then something tickled the back of her mind. Remembering Phinas and Atzil's cryptic comments about their parents, she had a feeling that it was all connected somehow, and that she was missing a crucial piece of the puzzle. Once she uncovered that key piece, everything would make sense.

"How do you know that? Did you compel her to reveal it?"

"Yes. Jin is a Dormant."

"Dormant as in carrying unrealized immortal genes?"

"Precisely." Kalugal smiled proudly. "You are very smart."

"Okay, but what does it have to do with me?"

"You might be a carrier as well."

Jacki snorted. "No way."

Talk about a rabbit hole. Except, compared to the others, this one was a wormhole into a parallel universe.

"Is there a test to check that?"

He shook his head. "There is no test."

"So why do you think that I'm a carrier, and how are you going to prove or disprove it?"

"You're a strong candidate because of your paranormal abilities. Apparently, humans who exhibit them have a higher chance of being Dormants than those who don't. Until Kian told me about it, I thought that the only Dormants in existence lived on my father's island. I didn't know that carriers could be found among the general human population, so I've never searched. But then the Fates decided to reward me with the best gift possible. You."

Jacki's head was starting to hurt.

Kalugal thought that she was a dormant carrier of immortal genes that could be somehow activated, and he'd kept it a secret from her for some reason.

"So you're saying that I could be turned immortal?"

He nodded.

"Why did you keep it a secret from me and even ask my friends to do the same? And why didn't they tell me that I can turn immortal before you asked them to hide it?" She shook her head. "When they took the other trainees and me, they pretended to be an organization of paranormally talented people, and I believed them because it made sense. And then when you told me the truth about Arwel, I thought that they kept it a secret from me because they didn't want to risk exposure, which also made sense. But I should have realized that they had a good reason for going after Jin, and also for agreeing to take me and the other two. If what you are telling me is true, then everyone in the government's paranormal talents program could be a dormant carrier."

Talk about the puzzle pieces falling into place and forming a complete picture.

"It's complicated, especially because you are immune to mind manipulation and can't be made to forget what you've learned. Not every human with paranormal talent is a Dormant, and those who fail to transition have their memories scrubbed. But even those who transition can betray the existence of immortals. That's why the clan doesn't tell the potential Dormants anything until they bond with a clan member, or in human terms fall in love with one. The love bond guarantees the Dormants' loyalty, and when they transition, they become part of the clan. Since by then they are fully devoted to their mates, the former Dormants keep their immortality and the clan's existence secret."

"What happens to those who don't transition?"

"As I said, their memories of encountering immortals are erased."

"What about the immortals they bonded with? Aren't they devastated when they need to make their partners forget them?"

"I don't think it's happened yet. Kian believes that the Fates are responsible for putting Dormants and their fated mates in each other's paths."

That sounded like something a fortuneteller would say, and not the formidable leader of the clan. Kian didn't strike her as someone who believed in superstition. All that talk about fate was ridiculous, and Jacki wondered if it was part of the story that they told potential Dormants and whether the reason for it was sinister.

"Was I the only one kept in the dark, or are my other two friends just as clueless?"

"Kian didn't share that information with me. But unless they fell in love with a clan member, they weren't told."

The gears in Jacki's head had been slow to process the new information, but she was starting to get the big picture. Her potential dormancy was the big secret that Kalugal had said he couldn't reveal until he had her love and loyalty.

Except, she hadn't told him that she loved him yet, and she was glad that she hadn't.

"Are you telling me about it now because of our impending marriage?" She snorted. "Now I know why you were willing to donate insane amounts of money to Kian's charity just so I'd stay with you. Dormants are rare, and you didn't want to let go of the one you had in your hand."

It wasn't about her being smart, or pretty, or even good company. It was all about her genes.

The realization and the disappointment that followed dripped acid down her veins. It was corrosive, destructive, and painful.

Kalugal nodded. "I'm not doing a very good job of explaining." Clearly frustrated, he raked his fingers through his hair, reminding her of Kian.

As the saying went, blood was thicker than water, and even though the cousins had just met, they shared the same nervous tic.

Letting out a breath, Jacki forced herself to calm down and let Kalugal explain. "How about you start from the beginning?"

He smiled. "Yeah, that's a good idea."

As Kalugal took several sips from the coffee, Jacki waited patiently, suspecting that he needed a couple of moments to collect his thoughts.

He put the cup down and leaned toward her, looking straight into her eyes. "I liked you from the first moment that I saw you without the drab disguise. In fact, I felt something even before that, but because it didn't make sense, I tried to explain it away. The first time I met you was outside the cigar lounge, and you were wearing that ugly disguise. Nevertheless, I thought that I must have met you before and that's why I was feeling that strange affinity toward you. Then when you attacked Rufsur and me, I thought that what I felt was admiration for your guts and for your loyalty to Arwel, who I assumed was your boyfriend. And that was way before I knew that you were a possible Dormant, and before I found out how beautiful you really were."

Kalugal looked so sincere that Jacki couldn't help but soften up. The truth was that when she had first seen his picture, she'd felt that same elusive something that he was trying to explain. And she had done the same thing he had, trying to explain it away as a reaction to a hot guy.

Could it be that they were really fated for each other?

"When did you find out that I was a potential Dormant?"

"When Jin was delirious and asked whether she was transitioning, I started to suspect that she was a Dormant and later compelled her to tell me the truth. When she did, I suspected that you were one too and compelled the doctor to confirm it. Naturally, my interest in you intensified, but it was there all along."

"Because I could turn immortal?"

He nodded. "You need to understand. Neither my men nor I have hoped to ever find life-long partners. We didn't know of any immortal females that didn't belong to the clan, and we didn't know that Dormants could be found among the human population. The Dormants on my father's island are the descendants of other Dormants that he had from the very beginning."

"Why are they still dormant? Can some people get activated and some not?"

Kalugal shook his head. "My father doesn't allow the females to get activated because as humans they can produce many more babies. Once a Dormant turns immortal, her fertility rate drops to almost nothing. It's nature doing its best to keep our numbers in check. Otherwise, immortals would have overrun the planet by now."

She remembered that he'd said something about all the children born on the island needing activation to turn immortal. No wonder he'd refused to get into it. Keeping the females from transitioning so they could be used for breeding was atrocious.

"Your father is a truly evil man. I mean immortal."

"I can't argue with that." He looked at her sadly. "Are you still sure you want to marry the son of an evil dictator and the grandson of a mass murderer?"

"What about your mother?"

"She is an angel."

"Then I'll put my faith in you taking after her and not your father and grandfather."

Kalugal

Kalugal felt like dancing a victory dance.

Jacki wasn't mad at him, and she hadn't called off the wedding, but he wasn't in the clear yet.

Should he go down on one knee now? Or should he first explain how the induction worked?

He gripped the box but then put it back. "Is there anything else you want me to explain before I go down on one knee? I want you to enter this marriage with clear knowledge of what you are getting into. I don't want any false assumptions to ruin things for us down the line."

Jacki smiled and reached for his hand. "You have no idea how much what you've just said means to me." She gave it a squeeze. "To me, it indicates that you are serious about it."

"Of course, I am."

She nodded. "When you said that you were keeping secrets from me because you needed to secure my love and loyalty first, was that about the possibility of me being a Dormant?"

"I wanted to be sure that you chose me because of me and not because I can give you immortality."

Jacki frowned. "What do you mean? You've just told me that Kian's people are finding Dormants and activating their genes. I don't need you specifically to activate me, do I?"

So that was why Jacki wasn't mad. She didn't know what was involved and his part in her activation. If she were a male, Jacki would have been right. Any immortal could have done that.

"Remember what I said about the Dormants needing to bond with an immortal before they were told about the possibility of gaining immortality?"

"What about it?"

Kalugal rubbed his jaw. "A female Dormant can only be activated by the immortal who has chosen her as his mate."

"Is it tradition or a necessity?"

"Neither." He sighed. "This requires the birds and the bees talk."

Jacki blushed. "I might be inexperienced, but I'm not ignorant."

"I'm sure you know all about human sexuality, but immortals are a little different."

Leaning back in the chair, Jacki crossed her arms over her chest. "Then let's do it. Give me the birds and the bees talk immortal style."

"You already know that immortal males have fangs and venom and that they bite during sex. You also know that the venom is a euphoric and an aphrodisiac. What you don't know is that the venom also induces transformation in a Dormant. For male Dormants, it's enough to fight an immortal male until he gets aggressive enough to produce venom and bite them. For female Dormants, the venom bite needs to happen together with sexual intercourse. That's why I decided to tell you about it even though you haven't professed your love for me yet. Our wedding night may induce your transformation."

Jacki's eyes widened. "On the first try?"

He smiled. "I don't think it will happen that quickly, but it is possible." He leaned forward. "The transformation is potentially dangerous, especially for older Dormants, but since you are young and healthy, you shouldn't worry too much about it."

"I didn't say yes, yet."

"Of course." He leaned back and lifted his coffee cup. "It's entirely up to you, but I don't see why you would turn down a chance at immortality."

"What happens if I don't transition?"

"We will keep trying until you do. It's like getting pregnant. The fun part comes before."

"Can you get me pregnant if I'm not a carrier of immortal genes? Are immortals and humans even genetically compatible?"

"We are definitely compatible, but the chances of me getting you pregnant are very low, whether you are a Dormant or a human. Immortal males are also much less fertile than humans. Which is fortunate since we can't produce immortal or Dormant offspring. The godly gene passes through the mother, not the father."

Frowning, Jacki reached for her coffee cup and took a sip. "Let's see if I understand it correctly. You can't have immortal children unless you marry an immortal female, or a Dormant who successfully transitions?"

"Dormant females don't need to transition to produce Dormant children, and they don't need an immortal male for that either. If they did, my father's breeding program wouldn't have worked."

"Got it. So, a female Dormant will always have Dormant children, and then her daughters will, and so on."

"Right."

"But Dormant and immortal males can only do that with a Dormant or immortal female."

"Correct."

"Now I understand why you were willing to fork out twenty-five thousand dollars per day to keep me." Jacki put her coffee cup down and pinned him with a hard stare. "It wasn't because of my phenomenal personality, or my clever insights about humanity, or even my looks. My real value to you is my potential as a broodmare for immortal children."

That was precisely the response that Kalugal had feared.

"Naturally, I want to have children at some point, but if that was my prime objective, I would not have offered to induce you. After your transition, your fertility rate will drop to such an extent that children will become a wistful dream. Hundreds or even thousands of years may pass before we are blessed with a child. Do you really think I would want to spend all that time with a woman that is not absolutely perfect for me?"

Jacki

It was hard to stay mad at Kalugal when he said things like that. Jacki was skeptical by nature, especially when it came to things that guys said while trying to seduce her, but what Kalugal had said made a lot of sense.

If producing a child would really take as long as he claimed, he would be an idiot to settle for a woman only because she could one day, maybe, give him one.

And Kalugal was no idiot.

He wasn't impulsive either. He must have given this a lot of thought and decided that she was the one for him.

How would he know, though?

Maybe one of the clan's immortal females would be better for him?

The fact that Kalugal had committed to her before checking out his options spoke volumes.

He really thought that she was perfect for him.

Well, no one was perfect.

Except for Kalugal, but he was a demigod.

But wait, he wasn't perfect either. His fertility rate was low.

That was an unexpected letdown, but maybe there were treatments for that. Jacki really wanted children, and she didn't want to wait thousands of years to have them.

Maybe she should say no?

And what then? Walk away from the best thing that had ever happened to her?

No way.

Kian's wife was pregnant, and they hadn't been together for thousands of years. Perhaps they had gotten lucky, or perhaps the clan had fertility treatments that Kalugal wasn't aware of.

They would find a solution.

"Okay," Jacki murmured.

"Okay what?"

"I accept your explanation." She inhaled a long breath and smiled. "Can I see the ring now?"

He reached for the box but then paused again. "You didn't ask me one important question."

Searching her head, Jacki realized that he was right. She'd asked, but he'd given her an evasive answer, and then their conversation had gone in another direction.

Her stomach squeezing tightly with apprehension, she repeated her question. "What will happen if I don't transition? I mean if we try for a long time and it doesn't happen?"

Leaning toward her, he took both of her hands in his. "I want to be perfectly frank with you. At first, I thought that if it didn't work out and you didn't transition, we would get a divorce, but I've been fooling myself. I've only known you for a week, and already I can't fathom life without you." He chuckled. "And we haven't even had sex yet. Imagine that."

It hurt that he'd thought to get rid of her if she didn't transition, but she could understand it. After all, Kalugal's low fertility rate had caused her a few moments of hesitation as well.

Potentially giving up on having children, or waiting eons to have them, had been difficult, and if she could go back to the human world, the decision would have been even harder. But since she would never have access to human males again, and all immortals had the same problem as Kalugal, choosing him was a no brainer.

Still, she couldn't just gloss over it. "Only yesterday you were thinking about marrying me and then divorcing me if I didn't transition. What has changed today?" She glanced at the little black box. "Let me guess. You bought a really expensive ring, and you don't want me to walk away with it, so you're going to keep me."

She was only half-joking.

Picking up on her humor, Kalugal smirked. "The ring has nothing to do with it. I bought it because it matches your bracelet."

Jacki lifted her hand and looked at the gleaming silver-toned cuff on her wrist. "Am I stuck with this for the rest of my life? Because if I become an immortal, that would be a very long time."

Kalugal's expression turned serious. "Once you transition, your body will most likely expel the trackers, but I'm going to solve that problem for you before that. Kian and I discussed the program today, and we came up with a framework for a plan to extract the remaining trainees and shut it down. In fact, he suggested that I bring you along tomorrow so we can pick your brain about the director and the other players. And after that, we can go to visit Wonder and Syssi and your other friends."

Her heart did a happy flip. "That's wonderful." She leaned back in her chair and put a hand over her heart. "I thought that I would never get to see them again."

"Why would you think that?"

She shrugged. "It was a silly gut feeling. I was scared to be left alone with you, and my mind went in all kinds of crazy directions."

Kalugal looked offended as if she'd just insulted him and also his mother. "I didn't sense fear from you. Before Jin left, you were teasing me mercilessly about my very subtle flirting attempts."

She leaned toward him and took his hand. "It was just a moment of panic because I was suddenly alone. Deep down I knew that you were not going to hurt me. But I also knew that I was never going back to my old life. Not that it had been so great, but I was free. It wasn't easy to make the mental adjustment that living among immortals was my new reality." She sighed. "I always imagined marrying a decent guy and having a bunch of kids. Now I need to mentally adjust to having none for a very long time, if ever."

"I'm sorry." He lifted her hand and kissed it. "I wish I could give you everything your heart desires, but I can promise you that other than having a bunch of kids one after the other you will lack for nothing. I'm going to do my very best to make you happy."

That was the most anyone could promise, and Kalugal sounded sincere.

She squeezed his hand and then covered it with her other one. "No one is perfect, Kalugal, not even a demigod." She smiled. "But I'll marry you anyway."

Kalugal

Kalugal grinned. "Wait, I haven't proposed to you properly yet."

"Okay, I take it back. Ask me to marry you."

It was show time.

"Yes, ma'am." Kalugal pulled his hand out of Jacki's and held out the small box.

Pushing to his feet, he knelt on one knee and took her hand again. "Jacqueline, will you be my wife?" He paused for a moment.

Should he continue with the traditional vows?

Why not. Kalugal was quite sure that he was already in love with Jacki, and if he wasn't there yet, he would be in a very short time. He could promise to love and cherish her, and it wouldn't be a lie.

Except, he hesitated for too long and Jacki thought that he was done.

"Yes, I will marry you."

"I promise that you will never regret this decision."

As he said those words, Kalugal wanted to take them back. How could he promise such a thing?

It was up to Jacki, not him. She might think that his world domination ambitions were ridiculous or find something else that she didn't agree with. They'd known each other for one week, and they still had a lot to learn about each other.

He should have phrased it differently.

"What I meant was that I promise to do everything I can to ensure you don't regret marrying me. But I can't promise that you will find my efforts satisfactory. That's up to you."

Leaning down, Jacki cupped his cheek and kissed him softly. "If I ever regret it, we can have another ceremony, invite the same people who witnessed us pledging ourselves to each other, and revoke our vows. It's not like we will need an official divorce."

She was just teasing him for his previous comment, but it nevertheless affected him, causing his gut to twist.

"Not going to happen." He opened the box.

Holding her breath, Jacki gaped at the ring. "It's beautiful."

"Not nearly as beautiful as the woman it belongs to." He pulled the ring out and slid it onto Jacki's finger.

"It's perfect." She lifted her hand and turned it this way and that so the light from the chandelier above reflected from the diamond. "Thank you."

"I'm the one who should be thanking you for agreeing to marry me." Kalugal pushed to his feet, lifted Jacki off the chair, and carried her to the couch. "Let's seal the deal with a proper kiss."

Winding her arms around his neck, Jacki hesitantly fitted her lips to his.

Sweet, but not what he was after.

Taking over the kiss, he cupped her neck to hold her in place and invaded her mouth.

Jacki moaned, her hands sliding down his back and then up again, growing rougher as she clung to him.

Unable to resist, Kalugal moved his mouth down her neck, and finding the perfect spot for his future bite, he nipped it lightly.

The moaning grew louder, and Jacki's hands on his back slid lower to cup his bottom.

His mate was feisty and not as reserved as he'd thought she was.

Was he a lucky son of a gun or what?

Letting go of her neck, he floated his hand to her breast, stroking the taut nipple over the fabric of her dress.

When she didn't resist, he slid his other hand up her inner thigh, his fingers hovering over the heat of her panty-covered feminine center.

He'd expected Jacki to tense and move his hand away, but instead, her legs parted a little, giving him better access.

If he touched her and found her as wet as he knew she was, he was bound to carry her to bed and finish what they had started.

Jacki wouldn't object, but she would probably regret it later.

Wishing to gift her virginity to her husband, she'd abstained to this day, and he would hate to cheat her out of that fantasy just because they were both impatient.

His mate wanted a proper wedding ceremony, a white wedding dress, and a wedding night to remember for eternity.

And hadn't he just promised her to do everything he could so she would never regret her decision?

It was going to be torturous, but he could wait a few more days.

Easier said than done, though.

The scent of Jacki's arousal was messing with Kalugal's head, melting away the civilized layers and revealing the primitive beast lurking underneath the cultured façade. All he wanted was to throw her down on the couch, tear the dress off her, and impale her with his shaft and his fangs at the same time.

But he was more than his primitive impulses, and he cared about Jacki too much to rob her of her fantasies. With a monumental effort, he pulled his hand away and rearranged her dress.

"Why did you stop?" she murmured into his neck.

"You wanted us to be married first, and I promised to do everything I could to make you happy. We can survive a few more days."

Jacki chuckled, the throaty sound sending another bolt of lightning straight into his groin. "Are you sure about that?"

Jacki

Jacki stood in front of her section of the closet, trying to decide what was the most appropriate outfit for her appearance before the summit members.

She was being silly.

It wasn't as if she was going to testify in front of the Senate, and everyone there knew her.

Maybe that was the problem.

Kian, Lokan, and the Guardians accompanying them had known the Jacki before Kalugal. The Jacki standing in the sprawling master closet of her future husband's mansion was a different woman.

The week she had spent with him had changed her in ways she hadn't realized until this morning.

Last evening all of her insecurities had been flushed out, but later, when she lay in bed reflecting on the week that she'd spent with Kalugal, she realized that she'd never felt better about herself, and that she had him to thank for that.

Slowly but surely, he'd been building up her self-perception, shoring up all the places she hadn't been confident about. By telling her that she was smart and asking her advice, and by spending every free moment he had with her, Kalugal had made her feel precious, beautiful, wanted, needed.

With him, she didn't feel like the foster kid that nobody wanted, but a diamond in the rough who Kalugal had been gently polishing, and the final touch was revealing the truth about her being a possible candidate for transitioning into immortality.

Jacki, the foster kid, might be a descendant of gods.

Why hadn't Jin said anything?

So what if Kalugal had asked her not to. Jin was supposed to be her bestie, and Jacki was still a little peeved at her, which was why she hadn't emailed her with the news yet.

Besides, she needed more time to process it herself. Getting her head wrapped around the possibility of immortal life would take a while.

Heck, getting used to her new wardrobe was difficult enough.

She settled on a pair of wide-legged white slacks and a multi-colored silk blouse. After tucking it in, she tightened the belt that came with the slacks and stepped into a pair of low-heeled white pumps.

Perhaps it was vain, but Jacki wanted her friends to see her the same way Kalugal did. Elegant, sophisticated, and worthy of a prince.

Before meeting Kalugal, she would have thought the outfit too fancy, or too conservative, and totally wrong for a girl like her that worked as a waitress and shared a bedroom with a friend because she couldn't even afford a single room in a shared apartment.

But now, looking at herself in the mirror, she just thought that it was classy and perfect for the occasion.

It reminded her once again of Kalugal's perfume bottle analogy. Before, Jacki would have considered the container too fancy for the common fragrance she'd believed herself to be.

Walking out of the closet, she stopped by the vanity she finally felt comfortable calling hers. A little eyeliner, a brush of mascara, and a dab of lipstick took care of her makeup, and several pins took care of her hair.

She really needed to have a professional stylist do something about it before the wedding, but it would do for now.

Kalugal knocked on the door. "May I come in? Are you dressed?"

"Just a moment."

Jacki smiled. In a few days, he would no longer knock, and it was perfectly fine with her.

Last night, she'd been more than ready and willing to continue their necking session, but Kalugal had pulled away first. It had been a little disappointing, but she was grateful for his restraint.

It showed that he cared.

It must have taken tremendous self-control for him to stop when she'd been doing everything to encourage him to keep going, and he had only done it because he wanted her to have her dream wedding night.

Not that she was still all that adamant about waiting. After all, her insistence on commitment had nothing to do with religious beliefs, and she didn't need anyone's permission and a wedding ceremony to have sex.

Kalugal was a man of his word, and she didn't think even for a moment that he was going to back out after getting what he wanted.

Taking one last look in the mirror, she walked over to the door and opened it. "Good morning."

Kalugal took a step back. "Wow. Suddenly I'm not sure that I want to take you to the summit."

"Why?" Was she dressed all wrong for the occasion? "Is it too much?"

"It's perfect. I just don't want the other men to be looking at you."

Jacki let out a breath. "You scared me. I thought that I had made some horrible fashion mistake."

He took her hand and pulled her against his chest. "You are so beautiful. Every man in that room is going to envy me."

"Don't be silly. Everyone there is married or in a steady relationship."

"So what? They still have eyes and they are men. They are going to look."

Jacki pretended to pout. "You'll have to deal with it because there is no way I'm putting on a burka."

He laughed. "I would never want to hide your beauty from the world. I was just teasing. Ready for breakfast?"

She glanced down at her outfit. "I'll need to be careful. These white slacks are gorgeous, but not very practical."

"I have a solution." He let go of her and walked into the closet.

A moment later he came out with his silk robe draped over his arm. "Put this over your outfit."

"I don't want to stain that either."

Kalugal shook his head. "Do you have to argue about every little thing? The robe is black, and your slacks are white. You can either take the pants off, which I would prefer, or you can put the robe on."

"I'll take the robe." If she took the pants off, chances were that they would never make it to the summit on time.

Kalugal

"Oh, damn." Jacki put her coffee cup down. "I totally forgot that I need my wig and glasses. I hope that you didn't throw them away."

Kalugal grimaced. "I was tempted, but Rufsur stashed them away together with the ugly clothes you had on." He looked at her golden hair and the way the morning light reflected from it, loathing that she had to cover it up with that ugly wig. "I was looking forward to showing you off."

"Really?" She arched a brow. "I thought that you wanted to cover me up so the other men couldn't see me."

"Yeah, but then you pointed out wisely that they were all spoken for." Kalugal scratched his head. "I don't know much about immortal couples, but it seems like they are more loyal to each other than humans are. If my father, the ultimate misogynist, has remained loyal to my mother for thousands of years, there must be a chemical component to it. His morals are questionable at best."

"You should ask Lokan. He seems fully devoted to his girlfriend, who I assume is an immortal."

He nodded. "And she is also a clanswoman. That's another story I can't wait to hear."

Jacki's eyes sparkled with excitement. "You should invite them both over. That would be so nice. When was the last time you talked to your brother? I mean outside of the summit."

"Frankly, I don't remember if we ever exchanged more than a greeting. I was only a junior commander when I escaped, and he was already in the top echelon of the Brotherhood's leadership. He barely acknowledged my existence."

"That's sad. You definitely need to invite him."

"Lokan won't come because he's afraid of me, and if he's brave enough to do it, he surely won't bring his mate along."

Crossing her legs, Jacki adjusted his robe over her white pants. "Maybe it's for the best. Carol is a sexy little thing. Imagine Marilyn Monroe, but shorter, sultrier, with a face of a cherub, and a take-no-prisoners attitude. Men must find her irresistible."

Jacki's jealousy made Kalugal unreasonably happy, but she had nothing to worry about. Leaning toward her, he took her hand and kissed the tip of her pointer. "For me, no other woman but you exists. You are all I want." He kissed another finger. "All I need." He kissed the third. "All I'll ever want." He kissed her pinky. "And all I'll ever need."

"Don't say that." Jacki pulled her hand out of his. "If I don't transition, you will need a woman who can give you immortal children. And when I get old, I won't be attractive to you anymore."

He took hold of her hand again. "What-ifs are the worst mood spoilers. Kian, of all people, thinks that we are fated for each other. That wouldn't have been the case if you weren't a Dormant, right?"

"I don't get it. Kian seems like a logical guy. Why does he believe in fate?"

Kalugal shrugged. "Since the circumstances that brought us together were so bizarre and unlikely, Kian thinks that the Fates had something to do with it. I don't know much about the clan's lore, and usually I wouldn't give much credence to such talk, but coming from Kian I take it more seriously."

Jacki patted his knee. "When I meet my friends later today, I'm going to grill them for details. Now that I know they are immortals, they can finally let go and talk to me. It's a shame that Jin and Mey are not going to be there, though."

"Do you think they would come to the ceremony?"

"I hope so. Jin will come for sure, but I don't know about Mey." She pushed to her feet. "I need to find that damn wig and glasses."

"I'll have Rufsur bring them." He glanced at his watch. "We should get to the car."

Jacki took off his robe and draped it over the couch arm. "I hate having to ruin the look." She waved a hand over herself.

"Me too. You can take the wig and glasses off once we are in the conference room."

"True. I need to put a mirror in my purse. I'll be right back." She hurried into her bedroom.

After exchanging texts with Rufsur about Jacki's wig and the glasses, Kalugal called Kian.

"Good morning, Kalugal." His cousin sounded more gruff than usual.

"Is it safe to bring Jacki to the hotel?"

"Other than the staff, there are barely any humans left here. They might close the place before we are done with the summit."

"We can move it to my house. I can have my men vacate their bedrooms and move into the bunker. I'd be more than happy to host your group and Lokan's."

Kian sighed. "Unfortunately, I don't trust you enough to bring civilians into your house."

That was progress. "Would you have come if you had no civilians with you?"

"I would've considered it."

"Perhaps you should send the civilians home. Then you, Lokan, and Turner and your Guardians can come over here."

"Let's see how it goes. I have an alternative meeting place, but today we are still doing it in the hotel's conference room."

"Can you do me a favor?"

"What is it?"

"Can you tell everyone in your party to be mindful of Jacki's mortality? I need them to wash their hands frequently and keep their distance from humans."

"Of course." Kian's voice softened. "In fact, we already do that. Starting today, we stopped using the elevators and we are taking the stairs instead. Viruses cannot survive in our bodies for more than an hour or two, but they can hitch a ride on our clothes and hands, so we are taking care with those."

"I appreciate it. Jacki is young and healthy, but there is still a small risk, and I'm not willing to take it. Dealing with an invisible enemy that I can do nothing about makes me very uncomfortable."

"Same here. I wish there was more we could do for humanity at a time like this."

"Right now, we can do nothing, but we can invest in research and find a solution for future outbreaks. Would you like to enter a partnership with me?"

"I would love to discuss the possibility."

"Excellent. I'll see you later."

After ending the call, Kalugal crossed his legs and leaned back. He would have preferred for Jacki to stay in the house, and they could have included her in the summit meeting using the internet. But when he'd promised to take her to see her friends, he hadn't thought it through, and he couldn't disappoint her now. He would just have to be careful and remind her not to touch anything.

The truth was that he couldn't imagine his life without her.

Sharing breakfast with Jacki in his master suite felt good. They should do it every morning from now on. In fact, he would love having her all to himself at every meal. But she was about to become the lady of the house, and in that capacity, she needed to interact with his men.

Perhaps they could share dinners with the men only every other day?

He also needed to get her out of the kitchen, but that was going to be one hell of a battle. Jacki wouldn't give that up unless he came up with something very convincing.

If he just told her that it was unbecoming of his wife to toil in the kitchen, she would call him a snob. Maybe

Atzil could say something? Like he didn't like her encroaching on his turf?

Nah, that wouldn't work. The guy was quite fond of Jacki and she would know it was a lie.

Perhaps he could bribe her with more donations to Kian's charity?

"I'm ready." Jacki walked in with a small white purse clutched in her hand.

He got up and offered her his arm. "Then let's go."

She threaded her arm through his. "What about the wig and glasses?"

"Rufsur will bring them to the car."

"Is he coming with us? I don't think he liked being left behind yesterday."

Kalugal nodded. "I'm leaving Phinas in charge today."

Jacki cast him a sidelong glance. "I have a question."

"Ask and I shall answer."

"Did you leave him with me as a test of his or my loyalty?"

He shook his head. "I left Rufsur with you alone as a show of trust, not mistrust."

Jacki

"Can I take the wig and glasses off now?" Jacki glanced up, scanning the ceiling of the hotel's wide corridor. "Do you think there are hidden cameras in here? I can't see any."

Kalugal put a hand on her shoulder. "Wait until we are inside. Kian only took care of the ones inside the conference room."

That was a shame. Her grand entry was going to be a lot less impactful. But then no one in there really cared what she looked like, and she shouldn't care what they thought either. Except, she did, and not only because she wanted to impress them with her new, sophisticated look.

On some level, her appearance reflected on Kalugal, and she wanted her friends to think well of him.

Taking a deep breath, Jacki squared her shoulders and clutched her purse tighter. "Let's go in, then."

Kalugal took her elbow and pushed the door open. "Good morning." He strode into the room as if he owned it.

Jacki knew nearly everyone there, and yet they stared at her as if she was a stranger. "Hi." She waved. "It's me." She pulled the wig and the glasses off.

Kian pushed to his feet and offered her his hand. "Good morning, Jacki. You look well."

Behind him, Anandur chuckled. "That's an understatement. You look like a million bucks."

"Thank you." She glanced at Kalugal and smiled.

Kian shook his head. "I wasn't commenting on your appearance, although you look lovely. These days I'm concerned about the health of every human I know."

"I feel great, and since I haven't left the house in more than a week, I have nothing to worry about."

Kian glanced at Kalugal and lifted a brow.

"Jacki knows." He pulled out a chair for her. "And we are engaged to be married."

Grinning, Kian offered Kalugal his hand. "Congratulations." He offered Jacki his hand as well. "And good luck."

"Thank you." She felt heat creep up her cheeks.

His good luck wish might have been about a number of things, some of them more embarrassing than others.

Lokan was next, pulling his brother into a tight embrace and slapping his back. "I'm happy for you." He offered his hand to Jacki. "If Kalugal and I were normal brothers, I would have said welcome to the family, but I'm not sure whether I'm welcome."

Not to mention that their family was unconventional, to put it mildly, and she had no interest in ever meeting their infamous father.

Jacki forced a smile. "Of course, you are welcome." She clasped his hand. "I told Kalugal that he should invite you and Carol over."

A shadow passed over Lokan's eyes. "Yes, we should."

Apparently, Kalugal was right and Lokan feared to bring Carol to his house.

"Mazel tov." Anandur got up and pulled Jacki into his arms for a bear hug. "When is the happy day?"

Jacki looked at Kian. "I don't know yet." She sat down. "We need to figure out the logistics."

"I've got it covered." Kian pulled a cuff out of his pocket and handed it to Kalugal. "I had it flown in early this morning. I also told Amanda that her party planning services are needed. She's supposed to come back to me with some ideas."

Kalugal dipped his head. "I appreciate it, thank you." He looked at the cuff.

"Who is it for?" Jacki asked.

"For me."

"Why? You don't have a tracker inside of you." She narrowed her eyes at him. "Or do you?"

"My cuff is different from yours. It's a security measure for Kian and his party. If I misbehave, Turner can zap me with whatever is in it and incapacitate me."

"Neurotoxin," Kian said. "It won't kill you, but it's not a pleasant experience."

Were they out of their minds? A freaking neurotoxin?

Jacki glared at Kian. "I thought that everyone except for Turner had earpieces. Why is this thing needed?"

"So I can accompany you on your visit to the rest of Kian's party. I want to meet Carol, and Wonder, and Kian's wife, and the esteemed Doctor Bridget with whom I spoke on the phone when Jin was ill. And since they don't have earpieces, and Kian won't let me near them without that, I offered to wear the cuff instead."

"You suggested it? Just so you can come with me?"

He smiled sheepishly. "Mainly, yes. But I'm also looking forward to meeting the ladies. Other than my mother and Tula, I've never met any immortal females."

"Wonder is going to flip when she hears about this." Anandur sat back down. "Prepare to answer a million questions."

Kalugal pulled a chair out for himself, sat down, and put the cuff on the conference table. "The last time I saw

Tula, I was five years old, and my mother was the only one I wanted to be with. I'm afraid that I don't remember much about Tula, only that she was very pretty and outspoken."

Turner cleared his throat. "Can we start on today's agenda?"

"Let's do it." Kian sat at the head of the table. "I suggest that we start with questioning Jacki. The sooner she's done, the sooner she can join her friends."

"Very well." Turner looked at her. "What can you tell us about the underground facility housing the program?"

"I know a lot about it. Where do you want me to start?"

Vlad

Richard's snoring had kept Vlad awake half of the night, and when the sun finally came up, he gave up and got out of bed.

Richard hadn't felt a thing and just kept on snoring.

Sharing a bed with a grown man was awkward and uncomfortable. Vlad could have spent the night in the room next to Wendy's, but that wouldn't have solved his problem. When his mother arrived, he would have to go back to the loft anyway. His nights were not going to be fun.

The good news was that things with Wendy were not as awkward as Vlad had feared they would be. The pain of betrayal was still there, but it wasn't as sharp as it was before, and having Jin and Arwel there was helping a lot.

Wendy had fun playing the *Harry Potter* trivia game Jin had organized, and Vlad had enjoyed watching her relax and laugh, realizing how melancholy and tense she'd been the entire time he'd known her.

She had laughed even harder at the outrageous combinations they'd all come up with playing *Cards Against Humanity*. She hadn't even been upset when she'd come in last and congratulated Richard who'd won. The guy had a surprisingly twisted sense of humor.

When Vlad emerged from the bathroom, Richard was still asleep. Peeking over the railing, he saw that the sleeper couch was folded back, and the living room was ready for the day, which meant that the Guardians had either never slept or woken up early.

He found them in the kitchen drinking coffee.

"Good morning." Vlad walked over and poured himself a cup. "What's there to eat?"

Bowen pointed at the fridge. "It's self-serve, kid. I'm not your mama."

As if his mother still made him breakfast. He was a grown man, not a kid.

"Did you forget that I work in a bakery? I can out-cook both of you." He opened the fridge and started pulling things out. "I'll make breakfast for everyone."

"Did I hear someone say breakfast?" Rubbing her eyes, Wendy walked into the kitchen.

"Do you want to help me make it?" Vlad handed her a loaf of bread.

"Sure. What do you need me to do?"

"Stuff the toaster."

"Okay."

Vlad pulled out a bag of frozen spinach, two onions, and a box of mushrooms. "I'm going to make omelets." He looked at Bowen, who was leaning against the counter and sipping from his mug. "Can you brew more coffee? Wendy would like some, and I could use another cup."

"No problem, kid."

The smell of cooking must have finally woken Richard up, and he came down to the kitchen. The guy was still wearing the sweats he used for pajamas, and no shoes.

"When is your mother getting here?" He leaned over the frying pan. "That smells good."

"I don't know. Probably later today."

Reaching a hand under his sweatshirt, Richard scratched his hairy belly. "I should change."

"You can eat first," Leon said. "I'll let you know when she's coming. We have surveillance cameras monitoring the drive up here."

"Good to know." Richard took the plate of toast from Wendy and carried it to the table.

Vlad handed Bowen the first omelet. "Can you call Arwel and Jin and tell them that breakfast is almost ready?"

"I'd rather not." The Guardian took the plate. "I don't want to interrupt anything, if you know what I mean." He winked.

Right. Vlad couldn't help the stab of envy that pierced through him. They were so lucky, working on Jin's transition and enjoying mated bliss. Their relationship hadn't hit any snags, and it had been smooth sailing for them ever since the first moment they'd laid eyes on each other.

Well, except for when Arwel had been captured by Kalugal, and then Jin had traded herself for him and had gotten sick. Those had been hard times for the couple, but their relationship hadn't suffered as a result. If anything, it had gotten stronger.

Would he have traded places with either of them, though?

Yeah, he would. Anything was better than the bitterness of disappointment and sense of failure he'd felt after Wendy's betrayal. And even though he understood her better now, it still hurt, and he was far from feeling okay.

As Vlad cracked eggs for another omelet, his phone rang.

Turning the burner off, he pulled it out of his pocket.

"Hi, Mom. Are you almost here? I'm making omelets."

Her answer was a sigh. "I'm afraid I have to cancel. Hildegard, Sharon, and I are heading out to help at a homeless shelter. People are getting sick over there, and they are short on staff because many of them are sick as well. I'm sorry to disappoint you, but this takes precedence."

Damn. This was just one more example of his mother's impulsiveness. He could never predict what she was going to do next. Years ago, before she'd decided to become a costume designer, his mother had worked as a paramedic. She'd even enrolled at a nursing school but had never completed her studies, turning to art instead. It had been just one more fork in the road in a long string of impulsive decisions.

"For how long?" Taking the phone with him, he walked out the front door and sat on the bench.

"As long as it takes. I'm afraid Richard will have to wait."

"Or Vanessa is going to line up another female for him." Rolling his eyes, Vlad couldn't believe what he was about to say next. "You might lose your chance, and who knows when the next male Dormant will show up? It's not like we have many of them."

"If it's meant to be, it's meant to be. I won't be able to enjoy a moment while thinking about the people I could be helping. There are things we can do as immortals that humans cannot, and one of them is taking care of infectious people. We can provide some relief and we might even save lives."

He couldn't argue with that. "Good luck, Mom."

"Thank you. I'm sorry, Vlad. How are things going between you and Wendy?"

"Better than I expected, but it's not easy. Jin and Arwel are here, which makes things a little less awkward."

"I'm glad. I'll call you again tonight."

Wendy

Even without her empathic ability, it wasn't hard to guess what was going on just by looking at Vlad and the guards' faces. Vlad looked annoyed, while Bowen and Leon cast pitying glances at Richard.

Vlad's mother wasn't coming, and Wendy was relieved.

The only reason the mother had decided to join her son in the first place was to protect him from the evil witch who'd hurt him and to make sure that it didn't happen again.

It must be nice to have a parent that actually cared.

Vlad thought of himself as an underdog, when in fact he was a privileged kid who lacked for nothing except maybe a few pounds.

In a couple of years, he would fill out, and that would no longer be a problem either, while she would still be alone in the world with no one who gave a shit about her.

"What's going on?" Richard asked when Vlad came back in.

"My mom isn't coming. She's a paramedic, and her help is needed at a homeless shelter she volunteers at."

Richard looked disappointed. "I hope she's careful. It's always most dangerous for healthcare providers."

Vlad waved a dismissive hand. "Stella hasn't been ill a day in her life. She'll be fine." He turned the burner back on. "Who else is missing an omelet?"

"I am," Leon said.

"Coming right up."

Bowen leaned back and looked at Richard. "What do you think about some target practice today?"

"With what? Do you have guns?"

"We do, but I was thinking about knife throwing. And if you're up to it, we can also make bows and arrows."

Richard smiled. "Sounds like a plan." He chuckled. "You and Leon are going to turn me into a real mountain man." He flexed his arm and looked at his bicep. "The one good thing about this fucking adventure is that I've never been in better shape."

"Here you go." Vlad put a plate in front of Leon. "Count me in for the target practice."

Wendy's heart sank. Now that his mother wasn't coming, Vlad would find other ways to avoid spending time with her.

"Sure thing." Leon cut off a piece of the omelet and put it in his mouth.

"What about you, Wendy?" Bowen asked. "Do you want to practice with us?"

"Do you trust me with a knife?"

Bowen snorted. "Even with a knife in hand you are no threat to me or anyone else here. Except maybe for Richard. He's still slow as heck."

Richard flipped him the finger.

Oddly, Bowen didn't think that she posed a danger to Vlad, who was so skinny it would take two of him to make one Richard. Wendy had seen how strong he was when he'd lifted that popcorn machine off her as if it weighed nothing, and when he'd chased after her, he moved faster than she thought was humanly possible. But as far as she knew, he'd never trained with the guards, so how did they know?

"Well?" Bowen asked. "A yes or no will do."

"I'll gladly practice with you." Wendy assumed one of her innocent-looking smiles. "Have you ever trained with Vlad? He is incredibly strong and fast."

Bowen arched a brow. "I haven't." He looked at Vlad. "I've never seen you in one of the self-defense classes. How come?"

Vlad put the last omelet on a plate and sat at the table. "I don't need it." He tapped his head. "I'm a good shrouder. I can use that as self-defense."

"True, but some people are immune. You can't count on it exclusively. Besides, I would love to see what you can do." Bowen glanced at Wendy. "Your girlfriend seems very impressed with your abilities."

As Vlad's face went red, Wendy froze, expecting him to say something terrible about her.

"My *friend*," Vlad accentuated the word and paused for emphasis, "must be overly impressionable."

Wendy released the breath she'd been holding. At least he still regarded her as a friend. That was much better than being thought of as a hated enemy. Not that he'd treated her as such even though she deserved it. Vlad was a good guy who couldn't muster meanness even if he tried.

Her eyes misting with tears, Wendy lowered her head and got busy with what was left of her omelet.

"What's wrong?" Vlad asked. "Were you offended by what I said?"

Damn. The guy must have some empathic ability. "Not at all. I know what I saw, and you are being too modest. I bet you can beat these two at knife throwing."

"You are giving me too much credit. I've never thrown a knife at a target before. My aim could be lousy."

Blinking the moisture away, Wendy plastered another smile on her face. "Let's place bets, and whoever loses is in charge of making lunch. I bet that Vlad scores better than the three of you."

Bowen snickered. "I bet on myself. I know how good I am."

Leon nodded. "I'm betting on Bowen."

Richard shrugged. "Can I stay out of it?"

"Sure." Wendy looked at Vlad. "What about you? Who are you betting on?"

"Bowen, of course."

Leaning back in her chair she crossed her arms over her chest. "Mark my words. The three of you will be making lunch today." She pinned Vlad with a mock hard stare. "And don't you try to lose on purpose. I will know if you do."

Kalugal

Kalugal had expected Jacki's testimony to take no more than an hour, but it had ended up taking nearly the entire day.

The amount of details she'd provided was staggering.

They now had a map of the entire facility, with each building marked according to purpose, the number of floors, and the estimated number of units. Turner had assigned different colors to housing, offices, classrooms, laboratories, and manufacturing facilities. They also had the location and estimated size of the major equipment operating the facility.

"How come you committed so much to memory?" Turner asked.

"I have an excellent visual memory. I can close my eyes and see the various buildings, including the number of floors and windows. Before Jin's arrival, I was lonely and bored, and since I like jogging, I used to run the entire perimeter of the underground city every day. I was most curious about the machinery running the facility, and since the entire place is under constant surveillance, I figured that the best place for a private talk was next to the noisiest ones. So that's where I took Jin to plan our escape."

"What are we going to do with all this information?" Kalugal asked. "All I need to know is where Simmons's office is."

Jacki looked at him. "Are you still thinking about shrouding yourself to look like him or one of his superiors?"

"We need to capture the director, detain him, and then I can walk in shrouding myself as him. Before I do that, though, I will need to talk to the bastard and learn his mannerisms and inflection."

Jacki frowned. "I just thought of something. Even though we had access cards, we mainly used them to get into our apartments. When getting into the offices or the training facilities, we just walked in. I think they scanned us somehow."

"That complicates things," Turner said. "They are probably using biometric scanners, and there is no way Kalugal's shroud can fool those."

Kalugal turned to Kian. "Can your hackers do something about that?"

Kian shook his head. "Messing with that is a sure way to attract attention. We can't afford it."

It seemed like his clever plan wasn't going to work after all. "Then we need to get rid of Simmons and Roberts and maybe even the recruiter. Without them, the program will fall apart, and the trainees will be sent home. Case closed."

"For now, maybe." Turner tapped his pen on his yellow pad.

Kalugal arched a brow. "Do you have a better plan?"

"Not yet. But we don't have to kill them off." Turner reached for his bottle of water. "Roni dug up some very good dirt on the two of them. Remember my idea to find female subordinates and thrall them to accuse the two of sexual harassment?"

"Is that the dirt Roni found?" Kian asked.

Turner nodded. "Both had complaints filed against them by female coworkers, starting long before the two joined the military and continuing after. The claims were silenced, but we can find the women and have them testify or leak the original complaints to the press."

Kalugal grimaced. "That will take too long. I say let's get rid of the old men. They are nothing but trouble."

"Roni and William are still working on your virus idea. They might come up with something that wouldn't damage the entire infrastructure."

Jacki cringed. "I don't want to talk about viruses, even computer ones."

Kalugal wrapped his arm around her shoulders. "Then we will call it a malignant code instead."

"That's better."

He turned to Kian. "You've just said that hacking into the government computers will call attention to you. How is infecting them with malignant code different?"

Kian chuckled. "Don't ask me. I'm not a computer expert. My guys said that infecting specific sections can be done without leaving a trace. Something about the code destroying its own pathway."

"How soon will they know?"

"It's a very complicated thing. They need to learn the system first, and that in itself can lead back to them. They have to be very careful, and it will take a long time."

Turner put his pen down and leaned back. "There is no real urgency. We shouldn't pressure them into going too fast and triggering an alarm."

Kian nodded. "I agree."

Kalugal didn't, but he couldn't say why. It was more of a gut feeling than rational thought. The program needed to be stopped, and the sooner the better.

Fiddling with the strap of her purse, Jacki shifted in her seat. "I'm not comfortable with where this is going. I don't want Simmons and Roberts dead."

"If they sexually harassed their coworkers, they need to go to jail for it," Kalugal said. "And since both of them are old, that's like a death sentence for them. We can just hasten the end."

She shook her head. "But then their deaths are on you. I don't want that."

"No one is offing anyone," Kian grumbled. "We are not the mafia. We will find another solution." He looked at Turner. "I think it's time to call it a day and join our ladies."

Lokan let out a breath. "I'm with Kian on that." He patted his stomach. "I'm ready for dinner."

"We will order delivery to our suite." Kian glanced at the cuff that was still on the table where Kalugal had put it. "If you want to join us, you need to put that on."

Reluctantly, Kalugal picked it up, put it over his wrist, but didn't lock it in place. "Before I snap this contraption closed, I want your word that you will remove it at the end of the evening."

"You have my word." Kian waved his hand at the gathered men and Jacki. "In front of all these witnesses, I promise to take it off once you are in your car."

"Not good enough. You could prevent me from ever getting into my car. I want you to promise that you'll remove it once I'm not in the presence of your wife and the other ladies."

"How about this. I give you my word that at the end of the evening I will walk you to your car, wait until you get in, and then remove the cuff."

"That will do."

Jacki

Jacki squeezed Kalugal's hand. "I know that you are doing this for me. It's very brave of you."

He'd even dismissed Rufsur and his other two men, telling them to go home and then come pick them up when they were ready to go. In Jacki's opinion, he was much more trusting of Kian than Kian was of him. To the point that it made her uncomfortable.

Not that she really feared that Kian would do something to Kalugal, but she would have preferred to err on the side of caution. In return, Kian also dismissed Lokan's so-called guards. She knew that they were Kian's men, not Lokan's, and so did Kalugal.

His lips curved in a smirk. "I admit that climbing the stairs to the sixth floor is not an easy feat, but it doesn't count as bravery unless we encounter rats in the stairwell." He pretended to shiver. "If we do, you'll have to defend me because I hate rodents."

She elbowed the jokester. "I mean the cuff. It's like walking around with an explosive tied to you."

He glanced over his shoulder at Turner. "How are you doing, buddy? I hope you are not going to trip and press that remote by mistake."

"Don't worry. Just keep going."

They were all taking the stairs because of her, the one human who could get infected. They were good people, all of them. Kian and his men, and Kalugal and his.

She hadn't met all of Kalugal's people, but those she had were decent guys and not at all like what she imagined the island's Doomers were.

Those former members of the Brotherhood were proof that people could change.

On the other hand, they'd had the advantage of Kalugal leading them. Without him, they wouldn't have been able to break free from his father's compulsive influence.

"That's our floor." Kian pushed the emergency staircase door open. "Our suite takes up the entire top level of the hotel, so we have no neighbors."

Jacki adjusted her wig and her glasses. In a moment, she was going to take them off again and meet her friends.

"I can feel your excitement," Kalugal whispered in her ear.

"I won't deny it. I thought that I was never going to see them again. This is such a treat for me."

Kian knocked on the suite's double doors, pushed one open, and headed straight for Syssi, embracing her as if he was returning from a month-long trip.

Jacki pulled the wig off and removed her glasses.

The doctor walked up to them first. "Hello, Kalugal. I'm Bridget."

"A pleasure to meet you." He looked her up and down. "You look nothing like your son."

Bridget narrowed her eyes at him. "How do you know Julian is my son?"

Kalugal tapped his nose. "Familial smell."

"You're good." Bridget looked confused.

Did immortal families even share a scent? Kalugal had never mentioned it. But then there was still a lot Jacki didn't know about immortals, and to cover it all would probably take several months. He might have just not gotten to that item yet.

Kalugal laughed. "Just joking."

"Then how did you know?" Bridget frowned.

"You mentioned it when we were on the phone. You said that your son was coming to take care of Jin."

"If you say so. I don't remember mentioning that Julian was my son."

As the bedroom door opened and Carol rushed out, Bridget stepped aside to avoid getting toppled over by the tiny torpedo.

"Jacki!" Carol shrieked and barreled into her, crushing the much taller Jacki to her ample chest. "You look amazing." She let go and took a step back. "Like a whole new woman."

"Thank you."

Carol turned to Kalugal. "Hello, I'm Carol." She offered him her hand. "I would hug you, but Lokan would get jealous."

"I don't blame him. You are a beautiful woman, Carol."

He was smiling and his tone was polite, but Jacki had a feeling that Carol's exuberance was a bit much for Kalugal.

He would have to get used to her. After all, Carol was family, so it wasn't as if he had a choice.

"Go ahead," Lokan said. "I don't mind."

He'd probably sensed his brother's chill response, and that was why he was okay with it.

Carol glanced at Jacki. "May I?"

"Go for it."

A wide grin split Carol's cherubic face. "Come here, my future brother-in-law." She pulled Kalugal down, put her hands on his shoulders, and kissed him on both cheeks.

"When are you two getting married?" Kalugal asked.

Lokan and Carol exchanged glances, and Carol shrugged. "There is no rush. We are in a precarious situation at the moment."

Untangling herself from her husband's embrace, Syssi turned and smiled. "That's why you should jump ship and cross over."

She walked over and pulled Jacki into a quick hug before offering her hand to Kalugal. "Finally, we meet. I'm Syssi, Kian's wife."

"That wasn't hard to figure out." He took her hand, shook it gently, and then smiled broadly. "Congratulations."

"Thank you. But on what? Kian and I have been married for three years."

He glanced at Syssi's middle. "You are expecting a child."

"How did you know?"

He tapped his nose. "Your scent is different."

Bridget huffed. "I knew that I didn't forget mentioning that Julian was my son. You did smell it."

He lifted his hands in mock defeat. "Guilty. I have a very sensitive nose."

Jacki wanted to find the nearest bathroom and hide. All those times she'd pretended that Kalugal had no effect on her, he'd known perfectly well that she'd been lying.

How mortifying.

But they were getting married, so that was okay. Soon, she would sample all those things she'd secretly fantasized about doing with him.

"Jacki?" Kalugal arched a brow. "Is everything okay?"

"Everything is perfect." She leaned toward him and kissed his cheek. "I'm glad that we are getting married soon."

"Speaking of weddings ..." Syssi took her hand. "We need to plan your party."

Kalugal

As Kalugal smiled, shook hands, and said all the right words, his mind struggled to process and understand the feelings that the experience was evoking in him.

The truth was that he was nearing an emotional overload.

Kian, who was usually gruff and tense, was a completely different man with his wife. The love the two felt and freely expressed for each other was practically palpable.

The same was true for Lokan and his cherubic spitfire, who, apparently, had no sense of personal space.

Kalugal wasn't the type who enjoyed friendly hugs, especially not from attached women.

The doctor and her immune mate were more reserved in their shows of affection, but the bond between them was nonetheless obvious.

Wonder, as well as the blond Guardian's mate, weren't present. It was also possible that the stoic warrior didn't have a mate or that he'd left her home.

Closing his eyes for a moment, Kalugal tried to imagine what that home might be like. He'd heard the word village mentioned several times, which implied trees and trails and couples walking hand in hand, greeting friends, maybe even pushing strollers with babies in them.

An immortal utopia.

"Where is Wonder?" Jacki asked Syssi.

"She and Callie went to get snacks from the hotel's gift shop."

So, Callie was the name of the blond's mate. He wondered what kind of woman found the man-statue worthy of love. Brundar's angelic beauty was almost feminine, but the deadly vibe he emitted was anything but.

"Come sit with Lokan and me." Carol beckoned him to the couch across from where Syssi and Jacki were sitting and chatting animatedly.

Kalugal would have preferred to join his mate on the other couch, but refusing Carol would have been impolite.

When they were seated, he took in the size of the presidential suite Kian had secured for his people. The living room had two couches and four armchairs, and there was also a dining table with twelve chairs around. The place was big enough to host a party, and he wondered whether that was what Kian had in mind when he said he'd got it covered.

Except, Kalugal wanted all of his men to attend his wedding, and there was not enough room for every one of them to join them. He could have, however, invited Rufsur and his two other guards to come up.

He was still surprised at himself for telling them to go home. With the cuff on, he was entirely at Kian's mercy, but he didn't feel unsafe.

Kalugal was a good judge of character, and his cousin took great pride in his people's high morality. He wouldn't have gone back on his word even if he hadn't given it in front of witnesses.

Besides, Kian was working with Lokan, which indicated that he sought cooperation rather than conflict. Lokan might not be as powerful as Kalugal, but he was still part of the Brotherhood's leadership, and he was in a position to do much more damage to the clan than Kalugal ever could.

Except, Lokan had one big advantage over Kalugal. He was bonded to a clanswoman, and Kian considered their bond more powerful and meaningful than Lokan's alliance to the Brotherhood.

Was he right about that?

Kalugal glanced at Jacki. Would he choose her above all others? Above his men who were like brothers to him?

Hopefully, he would never have to make that choice, but he had a feeling he would choose Jacki. And that was even before they were bonded or were officially mated.

Just observing the other couples in the room, Kalugal knew that he craved what they had.

"Who wants what to drink?" Kian asked. "The selection is Snake Venom and Perrier."

Kalugal lifted his hand. "I would love to try that beer I've heard so much about."

Next to him, Carol scrunched her pixy nose. "It's gross. I don't know how the guys can drink it. If you ask me, it's just a show of machismo." She pushed out her chest and lifted her chin. "Look at me," she assumed a deep voice. "I'm a manly man. I can pour engine oil down my throat and pretend to like it."

Syssi laughed. "I second that opinion. I'll take a Perrier."

Maybe there was something to what Carol had said because all the ladies chose the sparkling water, while all the men chose the beer.

"It's an acquired taste," Lokan said.

In a move that surprised Kalugal, Kian didn't send one of his men to bring the drinks. Instead, he opened the door to the suite's full-sized kitchen and went to bring them himself.

"I'll help you," Anandur offered and followed his boss.

Interesting.

Since no one looked surprised, Kalugal deduced that it was something that Kian did often. Apparently, after his workday was done, Kian shed his role as his mother's regent and became more friendly, acting as if they were all one big family.

Except, it was an illusion. Everyone still looked up to him and took their cues from him.

As the suite's front door opened, Kalugal turned to look, expecting his first glimpse of Wonder, aka Gulan, aka Annani's best friend and servant.

She walked in with the one named Callie, a pretty woman with long honey-colored hair gathered in a ponytail.

They were both dressed casually, even simply, and had almost no makeup on. In fact, that was also true of Kian's wife and the doctor. Carol was more stylish, but Jacki was by far the best-dressed woman in the room.

He liked it. But maybe she wasn't comfortable? Humans liked fitting in.

Casting Jacki a quick glance, he saw her showing Syssi her engagement ring and grinning happily.

Good.

Kalugal returned his gaze to Wonder, but she wasn't looking in his direction.

Anandur had just walked in from the kitchen with an armful of Perrier bottles for the ladies, and Wonder gazed at him with the same loving look that Kalugal had seen in the other couples' eyes. Even the blond, who during the summit had worn the expression of a cyborg, lifted his lips in a ghost of a smile, got up, and walked over to his mate.

After taking the bags from both women, he carried the snacks they'd gotten to the kitchen. His mate followed, and Kalugal wondered if the two were going to steal a quick kiss in there.

"Jacki." Wonder smiled happily and rushed to give her a hug. "You look amazing."

Kalugal pushed to his feet and walked over to them.

"Thank you," Jacki said. "Let me introduce you to my fiancé."

Wonder turned around and smiled. "The famous Kalugal. Kian told me that you have an interesting story for me."

He offered her his hand. "Famous or infamous?"

"Both." Her handshake was firm, and her smile was bright.

"I hope nothing too bad." Kalugal liked her, and he also liked her man.

With his light-hearted, almost irreverent attitude and smiling eyes, Anandur reminded him of Rufsur.

Wonder glanced at Carol, who shrugged. "I said nothing bad."

"Let's sit around the table." Kian put a load of beer bottles down.

Behind him, Callie walked in with a bowl of pretzels, and Brundar with another bowl of potato chips.

"The hotel store didn't have much of a selection." She smiled apologetically. "This is all we found."

"It will do until dinner." Kian motioned for her to take a seat and then lifted his beer bottle. "I propose a toast to many more family gatherings like this."

Kalugal purposefully used his left hand to lift his bottle, so everyone would see the cuff on his wrist. "I'll drink to that, but I hope next time will be without unnecessary safety measures."

"To trust." Syssi lifted her Perrier bottle.

"But not blind trust." Kian clinked his beer with his wife's water bottle.

Kalugal did the same, clinking bottles with Jacki to his right and Lokan to his left. He then took his first sip of the beer Carol had described as gross.

The taste was pretty bad, but it was potent.

"How do you like it?" Kian asked.

"I'm not a fan. But it will do." He looked at Wonder, who was sitting across the table from him. "How much did Kian tell you already?"

"Nothing. He only said that you have a story for me."

Kian shrugged. "I didn't want to deliver a second-hand account. I figured that it would be better if Wonder heard it from you and Jacki directly."

Jacki

Jacki looked at Kalugal. "Would you like to start?"

He nodded. "Since my story is chronologically older, it makes sense for me to go first."

Putting his bottle down, Kalugal crossed his legs and leaned back in his chair. "I don't know how many of you are aware of my hobby, which is archeology." He chuckled. "Rufsur calls it an obsession, and he might be right."

He smiled at Wonder. "In one of those digs, I found a figurine of a beautiful woman. Since those kinds of small statuettes were quite popular, it wasn't a rare find, but the workmanship was remarkable, and there was something about the woman that seemed familiar."

He cast Jacki an apologetic glance. "Since I've known many women throughout my life, I dismissed it. I assumed that the figurine bore a resemblance to one of them."

Reaching for the beer, he took a sip, grimaced, and put the bottle back down. "Then a few years later, I stopped by a famous tourist attraction in Egypt and saw a woman who might as well have been the model for the figurine. Since I've visited the Colossi of Memnon many times before, I don't know what prompted me to visit it again." He looked at Kian and smiled. "Maybe it was fated, eh?"

Jacki saw the moment Wonder connected the dots. Her jade eyes glowing, she pointed at Kalugal. "It was you! You were shrouding yourself. I knew that I sensed an immortal." She turned to Anandur. "You sensed him too."

"I did." The Guardian pinned Kalugal with a hard stare. "Why didn't you show yourself? With your power, you had nothing to fear from us."

Kalugal smiled indulgently and reached for the bottle again. "I'm a very careful man. I was traveling alone, and as you are well aware, some immortals and humans are immune to my compulsion ability. Besides, I assumed that you two were Annani's people, and as I said before, I had no wish to engage with the clan. As long as you didn't bother me, I had no reason to bother you."

Wonder crossed her arms over her chest. "You were also the old man at the airport."

He nodded. "Correct."

"How come Anandur didn't get the normal warning sign that immortal males get when they meet an unfamiliar male of their kind? I sensed you, and my alarm mechanism is not as strong as Anandur's." She blushed. "I'm not supposed to have it at all, but then I'm not supposed to be stronger than most immortal males either."

Kian frowned. "Come to think of it, when you entered the conference room yesterday, I didn't feel anything either." He looked at the blond. "How about you, Brundar?"

The Guardian shook his head. "Kalugal must be like Turner, but only in that regard. I can sense his emotions."

Kalugal shrugged. "Maybe it's my non-aggressive nature. I'm competitive, and I enjoy winning in business, but I'm not a fighter."

Kian regarded him coolly. "That's because you've never had anything worth fighting for. Without the compulsive component, your father's propaganda had no effect on you, and since no one has ever threatened the Brotherhood directly, you didn't fear for the safety of the people you cared about. I'm sure your aggression would come out roaring if anyone threatened your mate."

"You might be right." Kalugal clasped Jacki's hand under the table.

"Immortals are born aggressive," Anandur said. "Even the females. We are predators by nature. There must be something wrong with you."

Kalugal smiled. "Perhaps I'm more evolved than other immortals."

Kian snorted. "You are certainly full of yourself. "

"Guilty as charged. I don't believe in false modesty."

"Maybe the reason you don't trigger my alarm or that of my men is that you are my cousin."

"Lokan triggered my alarm," Anandur said. "And he is also your cousin."

Kalugal shrugged. "It's not important." He turned to Jacki. "Would you like to continue the story from here?"

She nodded. "When Kalugal showed me his artifact collection, and I saw the figurine, I noticed the resemblance to Wonder and asked if I could hold it."

"Wait a minute." Wonder lifted her hand and looked at Kalugal. "You said that the figurine seemed familiar to you even before you met Anandur and me in Egypt. Did you figure out why?"

"Yes, but I only connected the puzzle pieces much later." Kalugal looked at Kian. "After Kian heard my and Jacki's stories, he told me about your ancient origins and that Tula is your sister. I've met Tula, and she looks a lot like you."

Wonder's chin started to quiver, and her eyes misted with tears. "She does? She was such a tiny thing. I was sure she would grow up to be petite."

"Oh, she is not nearly as tall as you are, and since I was five years old when I last saw her, I don't remember her clearly, but she has the same high cheekbones as you, the same long, thick hair, and the same smile. She even tilts her head to the left the same way you do when you don't understand something or need clarification."

Wonder swiped a hand over her teary eyes. "I miss her so much. I talk to her once a week for a couple of minutes, but that's not enough. Now that you are talking with your mother as well, my allotted time with Tula has shrunk."

"I apologize for that."

"No, that's okay. Talking to you means the world to Areana."

Jacki shifted in her chair. "You need to get them both out of there, and if Areana refuses, take her by force and then get her a good therapist. The woman is obviously brainwashed."

"She is not," Carol said. "Areana really loves Navuh, and she believes that she has a calming influence on him."

"How do you know that?"

Carol straightened her back and pushed her chin out. "I was the one who infiltrated the harem and actually got to talk to her in person. Areana loves her mate."

Kalugal

Kalugal gaped at Carol in shock. "You infiltrated the harem? How?"

"Magic." She snapped her fingers. "I'll tell you all about it when you invite Lokan and me to dinner at your house. Jacki was just getting to the interesting part of her story, and it's not fair to Wonder to keep her hanging." Carol pushed a lock of hair behind her ear. "Besides, my story is so awesome that it deserves its own evening."

Next to her, Lokan shifted uncomfortably. "I'm sure Kalugal has better things to do than entertain us. He has a summit to attend and a wedding to plan."

"I would love for you two to come over. In fact, Jacki suggested the same thing earlier."

"I did," Jacki said. "We are family, well, almost, and I want us to get to know each other better."

Cornered, Lokan had no choice but to nod in agreement.

If they had not been in the company of Kian and his group, Kalugal would have reassured his brother that he had nothing to fear from him, but to do so in front of the others would mean loss of face for Lokan.

Wonder released an impatient breath. "So, you asked to hold the figurine, and then what happened?"

"A vision," Jacki said. "My immunity is not my only talent. I also get visions sometimes. They are never about big things, like the damn virus, and they are never about me. I get visions about people I know, and mostly they are about future events. Like someone falling in love, or wrecking their car, or getting a new job, things like that. But this vision was unlike any of the others I'd had. It was about a past event."

Jacki shivered and reached for her nearly empty bottle of Perrier. "It was horrible." She twisted the cap off and took a sip. "I saw a caravan, and a guy who looked like your twin brother riding in one of the wagons with an older guy sitting next to him."

"It was me," Wonder whispered. "I was pretending to be a man."

"I know. When I told Kian what I saw, he figured it out. Anyway, there was a massive earthquake and the earth split open. It happened so fast. The crack just kept growing, and the wagons kept tumbling into it. You were so brave and strong, trying to save people and pull them to safety, but then another wagon tumbled down and took you with it. In moments, there was no one left. Everyone in that caravan was dead. Or maybe in stasis, like you were."

Wonder shook her head. "I was the only immortal in that caravan. The others were all human. None of them could have survived that."

For a long moment, everyone remained quiet, paying respect to the dead with their silence.

Jacki's shuddering breath was the first sound. "You must have had a secret admirer, Wonder. Someone who knew you and cared about you carved that figurine of you."

"There was no one." She lowered her eyes.

Kalugal arched a brow. "Are you sure? I had it dated and it's only about two and a half thousand years old. Whoever carved it must be an immortal."

When she lifted her eyes, they were blazing green light. "I had no secret admirers. I was a big girl at a time when everyone else was tiny. Men didn't find me attractive."

"Esag did." Anandur wrapped his arm around her shoulders. "Maybe he was the one who carved it." He pulled her closer and kissed the top of her head. "Wouldn't it make you happy to discover that he was still alive?"

Wonder nodded. "I hope he is. And maybe the two warriors who Annani's mate sent with him are alive as well." She looked at Kalugal. "Where did you find the little statuette?"

"In Egypt."

"That makes sense. Esag was sent to find me, so if he was out in the desert but not in the area of the chasm, he could have survived the earthquake."

Kian drummed his fingers on the table. "If Esag and his companions survived, then other immortals might have survived as well. We've been searching for unaffiliated immortals for centuries and have found none. But with the new technology available to us now, perhaps we can resume the search."

Lokan

"How?" Lokan asked. "I don't see how technology can help us. If there are other immortals scattered around the globe, there aren't many of them, and they are very adept at hiding."

"We are not there yet," Kian said. "But we might be in a few years. As Kalugal pointed out, surveillance equipment will become more and more prevalent all over the globe. With the help of facial recognition software and artificial intelligence to sort it out, it will become nearly impossible to hide."

Lokan shook his head. "That creates a problem, not an opportunity."

Jacki lifted her hand. "What about this?" She pointed at her wrist. "Maybe William can create cuffs that interfere with facial recognition. And even if he can't, what about these?" She pulled a pair of glasses out of her purse. "Supposedly, they can fool the software."

"That's true." Kalugal leaned back. "The thing is, everyone who needs to hide can buy a pair on the internet, and those unaffiliated immortals must be aware of that. Finding them now will not be any easier than it was in the past. Frankly, I don't think locating a few individuals is worth the tremendous effort it would take. It's not like we expect to find entire communities of them."

"We need to grow our numbers." Kian pushed the bowl of pretzels away. "And the only way to do that is to find more immortals."

"There are plenty of immortals on the island." Lokan glanced at Kalugal. "I'm not a geneticist, but I'm sure that we have enough genetic variety. If we can effect change and allow the Dormant females to transition, and the warriors to take them as mates, our problem is solved."

"Not really," Bridget said. "Females hold the genetic key for immortality, and because of your father's breeding program, you don't have enough female Dormants. Even if all of them transitioned tomorrow and immediately found mates, it still might not be enough."

"What if there was peace between the clan and the Brotherhood?" Lokan asked. "Would that provide enough genetic variety?"

Bridget shook her head. "I'm not sure. In human models, a population of ten to forty thousand was estimated as safe to preserve genetic variation. We don't have that even if we were to combine all immortals living today. Then again, the infusion of human genes over the generations was actually a good thing. It saved us and the Brotherhood from extinction." She smiled apologetically at Kian. "Even though Navuh's breeding program is abhorrent, in a way it has benefited all of us. Without it, immortals would have eventually gone the way of the dinosaurs. Our clan's growth is painfully slow in comparison."

The disgusted expression on Kian's face showed his opinion of Bridget's statement. "I'd rather we end as a species than propagate Navuh's way."

Bridget lifted her hands. "I just explained the science. I didn't claim that it was morally right. We've fought long and hard to change humanity's attitudes toward women, and we are still far from achieving our goals. Women are still regarded primarily as breeders and possessions in many parts of the world."

"Yeah, the parts under Navuh's influence," Kian spat.

Bridget smiled a sad smile. "Really, Kian? We fight traffickers in our own back yard. You can't blame Navuh for that."

"Let's change the subject," Kalugal offered. "Despite Kian's valiant efforts, we can't solve all of humanity's ailments. We can't solve the problem of preserving immortals as a species by finding a few additional individuals either. But we can start introducing my men to your clanswomen. You have a group of immortal males right under your nose, Kian."

Kian didn't look too enthusiastic about that proposal, but he nodded. "We will need to figure something out.

After all, that's one of the reasons we are holding this summit."

"What about the Brotherhood?" Lokan asked. "Aren't we going to do anything about that?"

So far, Kalugal had shown no indication that he was interested in the island, which was good news as well as bad. Lokan didn't want his brother to take the future seat of power from him, but he needed Kalugal's help.

"Not in the near future," Kalugal said. "If at all. I'd rather not poke the hornets' nest." He turned to Lokan. "Even if Kian and I combine forces, our numbers are negligible compared to the Brotherhood. Just as we don't want to attract Uncle Sam's attention, we don't want Navuh to zero in on us either."

"I wasn't talking about attacking the island. With your ability, you could take over peacefully. Just compel everyone to stop following Navuh."

Kalugal sighed. "I'm not that powerful yet. Give me a thousand years, and I might be able to do that."

"What about our mother?"

Kalugal looked at Carol and then turned to Lokan. "Your mate said that Areana is happy where she is. If we force her to leave, we would be no better than our father. It should be her decision."

Kian

When dinner was delivered and left by the door per Syssi's instructions, Anandur and Brundar, together with their mates, brought it in.

Kian pulled several more bottles of whiskey from the crate he'd ordered and brought them to the table.

At the rate they were going, he would have to order another one.

Mentally patting himself on the back for thinking to bring quality booze to the summit, he opened a bottle and started pouring it into the glasses of those sitting on his side of the table. Small things like that mattered. The whiskey contributed to the feeling of camaraderie between him and Kalugal, as well as their people.

So far, the summit was going well, and even though they hadn't discussed their future cooperation yet, they were already doing that by planning to take down Director Simmons and release the trainees.

Perhaps this could be the blueprint for future joint endeavors. From time to time, they could meet up in a neutral place and discuss either business or strategic cooperation. The rest of the time they could stay out of each other's way.

Well, except for arranging meetups between his clanswomen and Kalugal's men. But that was a discussion for another time.

"We should toast Jacki and Kalugal's engagement." Kian handed the bottle to Anandur, so he could serve those sitting on the other side of the table.

Brundar opened a bottle of wine and poured for those who didn't want whiskey, meaning all the ladies except for Carol and Syssi.

Cradling her soda water between her palms, Syssi looked wistfully at everyone else's glasses. "I don't even like whiskey, but it feels strange to toast with water."

"Would you like a little wine?" Kian reached for one of the bottles.

"No, it's fine." She glanced at Jacki and then leaned to whisper in Kian's ear, "This is such a nice dinner. We can turn it into an engagement party."

Jacki hadn't heard her, but Kalugal had.

"Thank you, but I wouldn't want to celebrate without my men. They are like brothers to me."

"Celebrate what?" Jacki asked.

"Our engagement." He took her hand and brought it to his lips for a kiss. "Syssi said that we can celebrate it over this beautiful dinner, but as lovely as the sentiment is, I can't do that without my men." He looked at Kian. "I would love to invite you all to our wedding, but how are we going to manage that?"

Kian shook his head. "If you want to celebrate with us, you will have to choose which of your men can participate. I can only allow one of yours for one of mine."

Kalugal arched a brow. "How many men do you still have in the area?"

Holding his glass, Kian leaned back. "How many men do you have?"

As they stared at each other, Syssi waved a hand between them. "Stand down, you two. We were supposed to drink to Jacki and Kalugal's future happiness."

"Of course." Kian pushed to his feet and lifted his glass. "I'm not great at speeches. The best I can wish you two is to be as happy together as Syssi and I are."

"Or Wonder and I," Anandur raised his glass.

Even Brundar lifted his. "Same here."

Pushing to his feet, Lokan turned to his brother. "May the bonds of love hold you two together as snugly and as securely as they hold Carol and me."

That was a nice one. Lokan was a good politician.

Bridget got up and raised her glass. "To eternal love and happiness."

That was a good one too.

Kian made a mental note to remember both for the next time he had to salute someone's upcoming nuptials.

Once the glass clinking and drinking was done, Jacki rose to her feet. "I want to thank you all for being so wonderfully supportive of me. You've taken me under your protective wing even though I came uninvited. Basically, I'm a stowaway, and yet you've shown me kindness and offered me friendship for which I'm grateful. In the short time that I've known you all, you've become like family to me." She choked up a little. "The only one I've ever had. Thank you." Jacki sat back down.

Kian was moved, but he didn't know how to respond. Luckily, Syssi compensated for his shortcomings.

"The moment I saw you, I knew you were one of us." Syssi smiled at Jacki. "I hoped that you would find your fated mate among the clan's single males, but you didn't like any of the men we sent to woo you, and now I know why. You were waiting for Kalugal to snatch you up."

Jacki blushed. "I guess it was meant to be."

Kalugal frowned. "You didn't tell me about the clan males who wooed you. How many tried?"

Jacki waved a dismissive hand. "The three burly bears, and William. But they were all very polite and didn't cross any boundaries, so you can stop frowning."

"I'm frowning because I'm still trying to figure out who the three burly bears are. Am I missing a movie reference?"

Jacki laughed. "Close. Jin said that I was like Goldilocks, and the three Guardians who originally came with us were like the three bears. But since they were all big, muscular men, she called them the burly bears."

Kalugal

Kalugal didn't like thinking about three handsome clansmen chasing after his Jacki, but he was glad to hear that she'd rebuffed them all. Apparently, Rufsur wasn't the only one who'd been disappointed.

Wrapping his arm around Jacki's shoulders, Kalugal kissed the top of her head. "I feel flattered. My future wife has uncompromising taste. She doesn't settle for anything less than the best."

Jacki elbowed him in the side. "Can you not say things like that? Let others sing your praises."

He pretended to pout. "But no one does, so I have no choice but to do it myself."

Syssi chuckled. "You take self-reliance to a whole new level."

He nodded. "I admit to having a tendency for extremes. I don't do anything half-heartedly." He glanced at Kian.

"Which brings me back to the issue of our wedding. I want to have a big party, with tables and food and music, and all the bells and whistles. I know that you are wary of joining with all of my men present, but I have an idea for how you can feel safe doing that."

"Go ahead." Kian waved a hand.

"We can do it the same way that we exchanged Jin for Arwel. I can have my men set up the party outside in the backyard, and you can have drones hovering above, ensuring your safety. And that's in addition to this." He lifted his hand and pointed at the cuff. "I'm sure it can be activated remotely by someone observing the party through the cameras mounted on the drones."

Kian shook his head. "What's in the cuff is not lethal and you know it. You might be okay with suffering a temporary discomfort while your men overcome my people."

The guy was really paranoid, but then if Kalugal's wife and unborn child were at risk, he would have been paranoid as well.

"The drones are armed, correct?"

"Yes."

"So, if my men make an aggressive move you can shoot them down."

"True." Kian crossed his arms over his chest. "And I also have Guardians in the area who can be stationed nearby." He pinned Kalugal with a hard stare. "But I'm not going to tell you how many I have if you don't tell me how many you have."

Letting out a breath, Kalugal reached for the Macallan bottle and poured himself another shot. "It doesn't really matter. I know as well as you do that my men and I are outnumbered. I'm not going to make a move against you, but I understand your wariness. If I was bringing my pregnant wife into the house of a potential adversary, I would be super suspicious and careful too." He paused, letting his words sink in. "And yet, I'm inviting you and your people to my wedding because I trust you." He lifted his cuff again. "And to ease your mind, I'm allowing you to put this thing on me. I'm also agreeing to armed drones hovering overhead during the happiest moment of my life, just so Jacki can have her friends at her wedding. What else do you want me to do?"

Uncrossing his arms, Kian leaned forward and reached for the Macallan. "How many men are we talking about?"

It was pointless to keep resisting. Kian wasn't going to budge until he told him. Eventually he would have to disclose the number anyway for his men to get access to the clan females.

"Forty-seven. How many do you have?"

"In this area, twelve in addition to Brundar and Anandur."

"Including Turner?"

"Turner is not a Guardian. But you are right that he needs to be included. He has plenty of fighting experience, just not with immortals."

"He took me down," Lokan said. "Pulled the trigger and shot me in both knees before I knew what was happening."

"What?" Kalugal frowned. "And why?"

"That's a long story. I'll tell you all about it some other time."

Kalugal shook his head. "The people I'm inviting into my home and to my wedding shot my brother. I need to know why."

"I tried to kidnap two Dormants that were under Kian's protection. I thought that I had the perfect plan in place, but Turner outsmarted me, saved the women, and I ended up in the clan's jail. That's where I met Carol."

Emptying the whiskey down his throat, Kalugal refilled his glass to give himself a moment to think and then glared at Kian. "So, let me get this straight. Lokan tried to kidnap your clanswomen, got shot, spent time in your jail, and yet you trust him more than you trust me?"

Kian glared back. "Who said I do? It's still a work in progress. Besides, Lokan bonded with Carol, which means that he would never do anything to harm her, and that includes her family, meaning the entire clan. Also, he is not nearly as powerful as you are."

"That's where you are mistaken. If Lokan wishes to deploy an army against you, he has the means to do it. He has the Brotherhood at his disposal. I have forty-seven men who haven't seen battle since WWII."

"Kalugal makes a good argument," Syssi said. "We've all gotten sidetracked by suspicion and mistrust. We are talking about a wedding, people. Get real."

That was surprising. Apparently, his first impression of Kian's wife was wrong. She wasn't meek at all, just reserved, and she definitely had Kian's ear.

"When do you want to have the ceremony?" Kian asked.

"As soon as possible." Kalugal took Jacki's hand and gave it a little squeeze. "I can have my men organize everything by Tuesday night. All you have to do is decide whether you and your people attend the celebration."

"Someone is in a hurry," Anandur murmured under his breath.

Kian, who was the only one other than Jacki who knew the real reason for the rush, stifled a smirk and pretended to frown. "Let me sleep on it. I'll give you my answer tomorrow."

Jacki

Jacki's head was spinning with how fast things were moving. It was exciting and a little scary, but she was beyond ready.

Well, that wasn't entirely true.

She had one day to write her pledge to Kalugal, which was the scariest part since she'd never been good with stuff like that. Birthday cards had always been the worst, especially when it was for a close friend. Every time she'd had to write one, Jacki had spent hours searching the internet for something original.

Maybe she could do it this time too.

Except, she'd done pretty well with the thank you speech, and that hadn't been rehearsed. She'd just spoken from the heart. So maybe instead of writing her pledge, she could record it on her phone and then write it down.

"Jacki?" Syssi nudged her.

"What?"

"I asked what you are doing about a wedding dress."

"Oh, I'll order something online."

"You don't have enough time," Bridget said. "You need to tell Kalugal to postpone the party."

Jacki glanced at him through the opened French doors. The presidential suite Kian had rented occupied the entire top floor of the boutique hotel, and it came with a generously sized balcony. After dinner, Kian had gone out to smoke a cigar and all the other guys had followed.

It was nice to see Kalugal chatting with the men, looking at ease and charming the hell out of everyone. Even Kian was starting to soften toward him.

"I don't want to wait. If I can't get a dress in time, I'll wear these white slacks and pair them with a white blouse."

Syssi huffed. "That won't do at all. Maybe Stella can make you a dress."

"Who is Stella?"

"She is a costume designer." Syssi leaned closer. "And also, a new prospect for Richard. Ingrid is out of the picture."

"What happened? The two of them couldn't keep their hands off each other."

Syssi shrugged. "It wasn't meant to be. Anyway, a wedding dress shouldn't be difficult to make for someone who makes elaborate dresses for theatre productions."

"She can't," Bridget said. "And she also bailed out on Richard. Stella, Hildegard, and Sharon are volunteering in a homeless shelter."

"Poor Richard." Jacki sighed. "He has no luck with the ladies. First Jin, then Ingrid, and now the costume designer."

Syssi patted her knee. "Don't worry, we will find someone for him. What's important now is getting you a wedding dress." She pulled out her phone. "Let's see what we can get."

"Maybe I can order a dress from Amazon," Jacki suggested. "They have everything."

Bridget snorted. "Even if they do, it might not get here by Tuesday even with expedited shipping."

"Right." Syssi put her phone on the coffee table and leaned back. "What size do you wear, Jacki?"

"Eight or ten."

"Then maybe my wedding dress will fit you." Syssi lifted her phone off the table. "I'll show you a picture." She scrolled until she found it and handed the phone to Jacki.

"It's gorgeous. Where did you get it?"

"Amanda had a designer friend of hers make it for me. With a few minor alterations, it might fit you."

Jacki looked at the dress wistfully. "Are you sure? It's so beautiful, and it's a precious souvenir."

Syssi smiled. "It's just hanging in my closet and accumulating dust. I'm never getting married again, so it's not like I would ever need it. You will look gorgeous in it."

"Hold on." Bridget pushed to her feet. "I'm going to get my measuring tape."

Syssi laughed. "Why on earth would you have a measuring tape with you?"

"I take my doctor's bag everywhere with me, and it's one of the things I keep in there." She looked at Jacki. "I should take your measurements regardless of the dress. When you transition, there is a chance you'll grow taller."

That was news to Jacki. It made her realize that she didn't know anything about the process and what was going to happen to her.

"Can you explain what the transition involves? Kalugal only knows what happens to men, and I hate going into it without knowing what to expect."

"I'll explain everything. But first, I want to take your measurements."

When a moment later the doctor returned with the tape, it occurred to Jacki that one day might not be enough to make alterations or get the dress to her either. And if it needed dry cleaning, it was a lost cause.

"It's not going to work." She sighed despondently. "There isn't enough time to have it altered, cleaned if necessary, and get it here."

Syssi chuckled. "Leave it to Amanda and me. It will get here on time."

Kian

"What time tomorrow?" Kalugal rubbed his wrist after Kian had removed his cuff.

Instead of escorting them all the way to the car, Kian had opted to do it on the stairwell landing. "Same as today."

"Thank you." Jacki lifted on her toes and kissed his cheek. "I enjoyed myself very much."

"Yes, me too."

"Good night."

Listening to Jacki and Kalugal's footsteps going down the stairs, Kian and the brothers waited until the emergency door opened on the lobby level and then headed back to the suite.

Even though it had been a surprisingly pleasant evening, Kian felt the tension leave his shoulders only after Kalugal had left.

"That was fun," Carol said when they walked in. "Let's repeat it tomorrow." She took Lokan's hand and led him out the door. "Good night, everyone."

When the door closed behind the two, Syssi rose to her feet. "I need to call Amanda. I hope she can cajole Stella into at least altering my wedding dress for Jacki." She cast Kian a sidelong glance. "I hope you don't mind."

He did, but not enough to forbid it. He liked seeing Syssi's wedding dress hanging in their closet next to his tuxedo. Both were encased in see-through protective garment bags, and they made him smile every time he happened to look at them.

"Will she give it back?" He pulled Syssi into his arms. "I think of your wedding dress as a keepsake, just like my tux."

"I know." Smiling, Syssi stretched up on her toes and kissed him softly. "I'm only loaning it to her."

"But it will get altered."

"Probably just the length because Jacki is taller than me. It's not a big deal."

"Fine. I won't say no."

"Good." Syssi's tone implied that she would have loaned the dress with or without his approval, but he'd known that, which was part of the reason he'd agreed.

It was not worth fighting over.

"I'll call her from our bedroom." She pulled out of his arms.

Pouring himself another drink, Kian joined Turner and the brothers at the dining table. "So, what do you think, is he trustworthy?"

"We should test him," Turner said. "He seems genuine, but in my opinion, he is too amicable. When something or someone seems too good to be true, it's usually because it is."

The same thought had crossed Kian's mind once or twice. Kalugal was getting under his skin, and he found himself thinking of his cousin more and more like a family member rather than an adversary.

Except, because he was aware of it, Kian was exercising even more caution, not less.

"How do you suggest we do that?"

"Tomorrow at the meeting, you will ask him to put the cuff back on, and then we will remove the earpieces as a gesture of goodwill. If one of Kalugal's men tries to jump me and take hold of the remote, we will have our answer."

Anandur snorted. "He is not stupid enough to try it. Brundar and I would take his guy down in a blink of an eye."

Turner cast Anandur the kind of look a disappointed teacher gives a slow student. "I'll make it easy for them. I'll put the remote on the table, so all he would need to do is knock it away. Before any of you have time to move, Kalugal could freeze you in place."

"But you and Lokan would not be affected. You could take him down."

"Perhaps. But then it would only be the two of us against two of his men, and Kalugal might count on Lokan not to make a move against him, which would leave only me. If I were in Kalugal's shoes, I would take those odds."

"I agree," Kian said. "The question is how could we prevent it from happening?"

Turner looked at Brundar. "With your hair down, your earpieces will not be visible."

A ghost of a smile lifted one side of Brundar's lips. "I'll have my hand on a throwing knife. Kalugal's guy won't even make it to the remote."

"Amanda is taking care of the dress." Syssi came out of the bedroom. "She can fly in with it tomorrow and also bring the bridesmaids' saris from Eva's wedding. The question is whether we are going to attend the wedding or not." She sat down next to Kian. "Because if we are, then I need to call Jin and Mey. They will want to be there for Jacki."

"Turner suggested that we test Kalugal tomorrow, and if he passes the test, we will attend."

"How are you going to test him?"

As Kian explained, Syssi frowned. "Will you let Lokan in on the plan?"

"Nope. It's an opportunity to test him as well."

"I don't like it, but I get it." Syssi drummed her fingers on the table. "But since we don't have time, I'm not going to wait for the test results to put everything in motion. I'm going to assume that Kalugal will pass it."

"We will need Yamanu here," Anandur said. "If you want to fly drones over the mansion, he'll have to shroud them. Otherwise, the police will show up."

"It can wait for Tuesday morning, but let him know so he and Mey can get ready."

"Yes, boss."

Kalugal

Rufsur got out of the car and opened the back passenger door for Jacki. "How was the evening with the family?" His sarcastic tone indicated that he was still fuming about having been sent away.

He hadn't been happy with Kalugal for going to Kian's suite with Jacki and no protection.

"As you can see, we are well and unharmed." Kalugal slid into the back seat after Jacki. "We had a good time, and I might have convinced Kian to bring his group to our house for the wedding." He wrapped his arm around Jacki's shoulders and pulled her against his body.

For a moment, Rufsur gaped in disbelief, then shook his head and got into the driver's seat. "Are you plotting something?" he asked in their old language.

"I am," Kalugal replied in English. "I told Kian that we will hold the party in the backyard and that he can ensure his people's safety by flying drones overhead. He promised to give me an answer by tomorrow, but I'm betting that it will be a yes."

Glancing at him through the rearview mirror, Rufsur arched a brow.

"I have no other motives," Kalugal said in their old language.

What did Rufsur think they could possibly gain by attacking Kian and his party? Asking for a bunch of females to be delivered in exchange for the hostages?

There was nothing else they needed from the clan, and Kalugal was negotiating for that, which was the safe and proper way to go about his men gaining access to the clan's females.

That was what bugged him most about Kian's continued suspiciousness. The guy wasn't stupid, and he should have figured out by now that Kalugal was a logical man and would never do anything without it benefitting him in some way.

His cousin was either a lousy judge of character or was driven by emotions rather than logic.

"When is the party?" Rufsur asked.

"Tuesday night."

Jacki put her head on Kalugal's shoulder. "What if Kian says that he needs more time?"

"Then we can wait a day or two longer, but I want to start on the preparations. We might only have two days to get everything ready." He kissed the top of her head. "I want you to have a beautiful wedding."

"What about you? Don't you want to have a grand party?"

"Of course, but your happiness is what's important to me. When you're happy, I'm happy."

Unexpectedly, it was true.

Perhaps the bond that Kian had been talking about was already forming. Kalugal still had so many questions he needed answers to, but the best one to provide them might be his own brother and not Kian.

Evidently, Kian trusted Lokan because he had bonded with Carol and that bond was supposedly so strong that it superseded all other loyalties.

The problem was that Jacki wasn't a clanswoman. Even if they bonded, Kalugal's loyalty to her would not necessarily translate to loyalty to the clan. And that meant that Kian wouldn't trust him any more after the wedding than he'd trusted him before, which was not much.

That was a shame, but there was nothing Kalugal could do about it. Jacki was the one for him, and no other female would do. And if she didn't transition, he would enjoy her during her lifetime and mourn her when she died. He wasn't going to give her up for a political marriage to a clanswoman.

The truth was that he would like to have Kian's trust, but he didn't need it. In fact, maybe it was better to keep his cousin at arm's length and out of his business.

Kalugal's men, on the other hand, deserved the truth, and it was time that he leveled with them about Jacki's dormancy. When he made the official announcement, the men would think that he was out of his mind marrying a human.

Rufsur already did.

When they arrived home, Jacki went up to her room to change into something more comfortable, and Kalugal summoned his two lieutenants to his office.

Rufsur pulled a chair out and sat down. "I guess you want to talk about the wedding plans?"

Phinas avoided his eyes as he sat next to Rufsur.

"Not yet. I'll address that tomorrow. I called you in here to explain why I'm marrying Jacki."

"There is nothing to explain," Rufsur said. "You've fallen in love, and you are not thinking straight. Jacki is a human and an immune. As your wife, she'll have access to all your schemes, and you won't be able to make her forget anything."

Phinas nodded.

"Not quite. Jacki might be a Dormant."

Both men looked at him with raised brows, but Rufsur was the one to voice their disbelief. "What on earth makes you think that? Did Kian sell her to you under false claims?"

The guy was starting to annoy him. "I suggest that you refrain from talking until I'm finished."

Rufsur nodded, leaned back in his chair, and crossed his arms over his chest.

Kalugal ignored him, looking at Phinas instead. "We've always assumed that the only adult Dormants in existence were on the island, the descendants of the original females that Navuh had inherited from his father. But we were wrong. Apparently, Dormants can be found in the general human population. The problem is identifying them. One of the indicators is paranormal ability, and Jacki has two. She is immune to mind tricks, even mine that work on most other immortals, and she has visions of the future. That makes her a strong candidate."

"How long have you known?" Rufsur asked.

"From the beginning. I compelled the information out of the doctor they sent to treat the spy."

"Why didn't you say anything before?"

Kalugal smirked. "To prevent even fiercer competition for Jacki's affections."

Phinas was still frowning. "So, let me get this straight. We could have found female Dormants a long time ago but didn't because we didn't know they existed?"

Kalugal shook his head. "The clan knew, and they've been searching from the very beginning and couldn't find any. Then a few years ago they started popping up one after the other."

"Did they develop a method of identifying them?" Phinas asked.

"Kian believes that the Fates have something to do with it."

Rufsur waved a dismissive hand. "That's just some superstitious crap that the clan believes in."

Kalugal leaned forward. "I don't know about that. The circumstances of Jacki popping into my life are so unusual that I'm inclined to agree with Kian."

Jacki

Jacki took off the slacks and blouse she'd worn to the summit and hung them in the closet. She'd been very careful not to stain or dirty them in any way, and the garments were clean, but after a long and exciting day, she would have preferred to launder them. Except, almost everything Kalugal had gotten for her required dry cleaning. She'd heard that some fancy houses had a dry-clean cabinet in the closet, but a thorough search of Kalugal's revealed only a big-ass safe in the back of it.

Wondering whether he was hiding money or weapons in there, she just regretted it wasn't what she'd been looking for. Those clothes wouldn't clean themselves, and they were too pricy to take a risk and hand wash them.

Kalugal must have used dry cleaning on his suits and cashmere sweaters. Heck, he probably sent his silk pajamas and underwear to be dry cleaned as well. There was no way he handled the task himself, though, and must have had Shamash or one of the other men do that. She could just ask him to add hers to the pile.

A simple solution, but not one she was comfortable with.

It seemed like such a trivial thing, but Jacki hated being so dependent. She had Kalugal's credit card but didn't want to spend more money that wasn't hers, and even if she had no problem with that, she couldn't leave the house because she was still a fugitive.

In addition, the director knew where she was. The cuff was interfering with the signals she was emitting, but several days had passed before she'd gotten it, and her location had been discovered.

She was safe inside Kalugal's compound, and she was also safe with his men making sure that no one was following them. But getting out alone was not going to happen in the foreseeable future.

How long would she have to live like that?

A knock on the door interrupted her trip down self-pity lane. "May I come in?"

Jacki opened the door and cast Kalugal an apologetic look. "I'm sorry for hogging your closet. Do you need to change?"

"No. I came looking for you. Have you been in here the entire time?"

She nodded. "I was looking for a dry-cleaning cabinet, but you don't have one."

"If you need anything taken to the cleaners, I'll have Shamash do that."

"I figured that you would say that."

He tilted his head. "Is it bad?"

"No. It's just that I don't feel comfortable with him doing this for me. I would have preferred to go by myself and pay for the service with my own money, but I can't leave the house, and I don't have money."

He frowned. "I gave you a credit card. It's the same as having money."

"Your money. Not mine."

Wrapping an arm around her middle, he pulled her against him. "You are my wife."

"Not yet. And even after the ceremony, I would like to earn my keep." When he smirked, she slapped his chest. "Not on my back."

He pretended offense. "You have a dirty mind, Miss Jacqueline, and very outdated notions about things. Perhaps I would be the one who earns his keep? I'm very talented in certain aspects of the sensual arts."

Jacki laughed. "I'm sure. But how am I going to pay you?"

"In kind."

As the blush that had started as mild warming of her cheeks intensified, Jacki scrambled for something clever and witty to say. But all that came out of her mouth was the truth. "I don't know whether I'm talented or not. So, it won't be an even exchange."

"It doesn't have to be even." His eyes started glowing, which signaled that he was aroused. "I very much enjoy being on the giving side. Providing pleasure is just as satisfying, if not more so than receiving it. And I'm more than ready to pleasure you into oblivion."

His hand started a lazy track down her back until it reached her ass and cupped it. He didn't squeeze, he caressed, and his touch was gentle. When he dipped his head and took her lips, she was ready for him to do more than just kiss her.

As if he'd read her mind, Kalugal's hand on her butt pushed her closer against his straining erection, and as his tongue darted into her mouth, she imagined that hard length doing the same down below. As the tiny muscles of her sheath fluttered and squeezed on empty, she couldn't wait to feel the sensation of having him inside her.

It was going to be a perfect fit, she just knew it. It might hurt a little as he broke through and stretched her virgin passage, but she believed that even her first time with Kalugal would be pleasurable.

Except, he let go of her way too soon. "Let's get out of here before we do something that we will regret later."

"It's only two more days," she whispered.

Kalugal had already committed to marrying her in public, so he wasn't going to back out of it, and there was no reason to wait.

Heck, Jacki didn't know if she could. Right now, she was ready to do it in the closet, on the floor, pushed up against the wall...

Stop it!

The images were only spurring her arousal, and she was getting embarrassingly wet, which Kalugal could no doubt smell.

He misunderstood her meaning. "Precisely. As difficult as it is, we can wait."

Damn. Why did he have to be such a gentleman?

But she was too much of a lady to tell him that she wanted him now. Besides, he probably knew that without her having to say anything.

But if he could hold it in his pants until their wedding night, so could she.

Kalugal

By sheer determination, Kalugal kept his fangs from elongating, but regrettably, he didn't have the same level of control over the lower part of his male anatomy.

Frankly, he couldn't understand his own insistence on waiting. Jacki was not only ready and willing, but she was also disappointed.

She'd wanted him to keep going, but he had a couple of very good reasons to stop. First and foremost, doing it in the damn closet seemed like sacrilege at this point. It would take away from Jacki's wedding fantasy, and she might regret it later.

The other reason was his ability to control his impulses. Jacki's comment about an uneven exchange had evoked images of sexual acts that were out of the question with a virgin. He had to be gentle and patient and minimize her pain.

Power exchange with someone uninitiated required a lot of trust and a slow buildup. It would take a long time until Jacki was ready for that.

"Come on." He took her hand. "Let's go to the library, and I'll pour you a drink."

Taking in a deep breath and then releasing it in a muted whoosh, Jacki nodded. "I need one."

"Did you have a good time today?" He led her out of the closet.

"Yes, thank you." She glanced at his wrist. "I'm still blown away by your willingness to wear a poisonous cuff just so I could visit my friends."

"I didn't do it only for you." It was mainly for her, but he didn't feel that it was a big enough deal to be so impressed with. "I wanted to prove to Kian that I'm a better man than he is, and that I'm willing to take a risk in the name of cooperation, while he's acting like a suspicious ass."

She chuckled. "He is definitely overdoing it."

Kalugal opened the library doors and motioned for her to take a seat on the couch. "Old fashioned?"

"Yes, please."

He poured them both drinks, a whiskey for himself and a cocktail for Jacki, and joined her on the couch. "To us."

Jacki clinked her glass to his. "To my successful transition and our happily-ever-after."

"I like that." Kalugal took a small sip of the exquisite whiskey.

Jacki leaned forward and put her drink on the coffee table. "There are some things we need to talk about."

"Like what?"

Originally, he'd planned on having Jacki sign a prenup agreement, but since their marriage wouldn't be registered anywhere, Jacki couldn't take him to the cleaners even if she wanted to. So, there was no need for that.

"I need a job."

"You already have one."

She rolled her eyes. "Other than being your wife."

"It might not seem so, but that's a lot of work." He waved his hand in an arc. "You are the lady of the house. And since this is a big household, there is a lot that needs to be done."

"Right." Jacki snorted. "This place works like a well-oiled machine. If I butt in, I'm only going to step on people's toes and make enemies. I want a real, paying job, so I can have my own money that I will not feel guilty about spending."

Kalugal let out a long-suffering sigh. "What would you like to do?"

"I can't work outside the house for obvious reasons. But maybe you need help organizing files, or data input, or cataloging your artifacts, or even cleaning your cars. I don't mind what it is, as long as it's a job that's actually needed, not something that you invent for me."

That was a tough one. Most of the time he didn't have enough for his men to do, which had been the main reason some of them had left early on. It was crucial to keep everyone busy to make them feel needed.

"I'm sorry, Jacki, but I can't think of anything that is not taken care of. The only thing I really need is your company. I enjoy talking to you and hearing your perspective. If you want, we can make it a paying job, but that would be silly. You can buy whatever you want, whenever you want it, and it will make me very happy to see you spending money on yourself."

"I was afraid you would say that." Jacki leaned back and rested her head on the couch cushions. "I know that you mean well, but I hate being dependent on anyone, even you."

"How about I establish an allowance for you? Would that make you feel better?" He smiled. "Since you are marrying me, I can stop the donations to Kian's charity and funnel the money into your account."

Her eyes widened. "You can't be serious. That's three-quarters of a million a month."

"I can do the math. You don't have to keep it all for yourself." The gears in his head spinning fast, Kalugal realized that managing a charity was a fantastic solution to the problem of keeping Jacki busy and making her feel needed and useful. "You will be in charge of my new charitable organization. You can donate the money to any charity you want and keep a small portion as the administrator's compensation."

"That's crazy. I will probably just keep sending it all to Kian's charity."

He should have anticipated that Jacki would want to donate every last penny.

"Not all. I will put in a provision for your salary as the administrator, and another one for overhead and other expenses."

She narrowed her eyes at him. "You've just invented a job for me. I wanted to do something that was actually needed."

"It's true that the idea came to me while we were discussing your proposal. But if I'm to continue making contributions, I want to make sure that they go where they are needed the most, and Kian's charity is not the only one out there. I don't have time to research the different options, and besides, I think this is a job better suited for a human who is familiar with human needs."

"If luck will have it, I won't stay human for long."

"A former human would do just as well." He took her hand and brought it to his lips. "Your life hasn't been easy. You know what needs to be done."

"That's a lot of responsibility."

"It is, and I'm sure you'll do splendidly."

"Can you afford to keep donating that much money?"

Good question. He could afford it, but it would be a drain on funds that would be better channeled into the technologies he wanted to promote. On the other hand, donations were tax-deductible, so only half of it was actually coming out of his own pocket. The other half would have gone into the government's coffers anyway, and those bastards spent the taxpayers' money as if it was their own.

"For now, I can keep it up."

Simmons

"Good morning, Elijah." Simmons was surprised to see his friend waiting for him outside his office door.

"I brought coffee." Elijah handed him one of the paper cups.

"Thank you." Simmons opened the door and motioned for Roberts to take a seat.

After activating the noise machine, he pulled out a chair and sat next to his friend. "I thought that you were going to work from home this week."

"And stay cooped up with the wife? No, thank you."

Simmons chuckled. "I hear you. I would go crazy if I had to stay with the old hag."

"I don't know why you stayed with her for all these years. She couldn't even give you a child."

"You know why."

Elijah waved a dismissive hand. "You needed her father at the start of your career, but once you were established, you could have divorced her."

"Not really. Even after he retired, the general could have still made life hell for me if I divorced his precious daughter. And after he died, it was too late for me to father children." He smirked. "Legitimately, that is."

Elijah arched a brow. "You scoundrel, you never told me that you've produced bastards."

Simmons crossed his legs. "I don't know if I did. None of my mistresses came forward. But I might have."

"Is that why you were so interested in Jacki?"

"Immunity is rare, and she was raised in the foster system. She also didn't remember who her mother was, so I had to do a little digging to find out. She was no one I've ever met, but just in case, I took a look at Jacki's bloodwork. I didn't want to accidentally hit on my own daughter."

Elijah snorted. "Much good that would have done you. The girl is pretty, but she's a cold fish."

"Or a lesbian. I don't know why I'm putting so much effort into getting her back. She's useless for our breeding experiment, and her talents are of no real use to us either."

"She might lead us to the others. Especially Jin. We need her back."

"That's the main reason I'm still working on it. The problem is that I can't get approval for a team. Everything has ground to a halt because of the damn virus, and only the most critical missions are getting approved."

Roberts waved a hand. "Forget about it. I've given it a lot of thought, and my conclusion is that an attack force is not the way to go about it. We know that the people who sprung Jacki and the others are paranormals, and given that they managed to override Marisol's compulsion, they have their own arsenal of mind tricks. Regular soldiers might be useless against them."

"I doubt it. Marisol needs to work on people one on one. She can't compel them as a group. So even if they have a compeller, he or she won't be able to order an entire team to stand down."

"They might have someone more powerful than Marisol. We don't know enough about these powers, but I bet some people can compel hundreds. How else can you explain mass hallucinations? Or cult leaders? It's not simple brainwashing. These charlatans have something extra."

Simmons sighed wistfully. "I wish I had that something. Imagine how much easier it would have been for us."

"Yeah, well. Neither of us has that, but we have other talents." Elijah tapped his temple. "I came up with a clever idea. It still requires a team, but the men don't need to be commandos. We can hire an independent contractor that deals with security. I just need several able-bodied men to carry out this mission."

"You've piqued my interest. What do you have in mind?"

"Long-range acoustic device. I'm good friends with the head of the department working on developing a smaller version of it. He is willing to loan me one of the prototypes, no questions asked."

"Those are mainly used by the police for dispersing crowds and issuing warnings." Simmons pushed his glasses up his nose. "I know that they can also be used as a non-lethal weapon, but I've never looked into it. Does it work?"

Roberts nodded. "It has been used, and there is good data about its effectiveness. The device my friend's team developed can fit inside a briefcase, and emit a concentrated, one-hundred-and-fifty-decibel high-energy acoustic wave. The wave is focused within a fifteen- to a thirty-degree beam, so the LRAD can be aimed at a target while the operator and his team are shielded from it. Those in the wave's path, however, would suffer debilitating pain, loss of balance and the ability to move. We can shoot the noise cannon, as it is called, and then walk in, collect everyone, load them into vans, and shoot them with tranquilizers so they don't give us any trouble until we get them back here."

Simmons took his glasses off and rubbed them against his shirt to clean them. "We still need to get into the house, or get them to come out to us, and the paranormals could use their mental tricks on our men."

Roberts smiled. "That's where you come in. Since you are immune, you will carry the LRAD and deploy it. Just in case, our crew of hired guards will have earplugs to protect their hearing. Once the paranormals are incapacitated, any hold they might have had over our team will vanish. Then the men will swoop in and collect them."

Kalugal

Kalugal walked out into his backyard with Rufsur and Atzil in tow.

"We need tables and chairs for sixty-five people." He pointed to the large grassy center. "You can arrange them in a semicircle, facing a podium where Jacki and I will make our vows. Eighteen inches off the ground should do it."

Atzil rubbed the back of his head. "Do you prefer eight large tables or eleven smaller ones?"

"The larger tables. It's a wedding, and people want to sit together."

"I don't like it." Rufsur crossed his arms over his chest. "You are inviting the enemy into our house and showing him the exact number of men you have."

"I already told Kian that I have forty-seven men, so that's not an issue. And if he comes to the party, he will have only six or eight men, including himself. If anyone has anything to worry about, it's Kian."

"Not really since you're allowing him to fly drones overhead to secure his people."

"He wouldn't come otherwise, and it's important to Jacki that her friends attend. Since we are not filing for a marriage certificate, and no one is going to officiate over the wedding, the only way she will feel that it's real is if our pledge is witnessed by her friends, and not just my men."

Atzil nodded. "Makes sense."

Rufsur still didn't look happy. "You shouldn't have told him how many men you have."

Kalugal wasn't sure he had done the right thing either, but second-guessing his decision was pointless.

"Trust needs to start somewhere."

"Why do you need to be the one making all the concessions? Kian was the one who challenged you, not the other way around."

"Because his position is much more precarious than ours. I'm in charge of a group of capable warriors. He is in charge of civilians, women and children, and men who have never held a weapon in their hands. I don't know how many Guardians he has, but my guess would be that it is less than a hundred."

"What are you basing that on?"

"Math and statistics. Only the clan females can provide immortal children to grow the clan, and since they transition early, probably at the same age as the boys, their fertility rate allows for a very low birthrate. The entire clan can't have more than a few hundred members."

"And half of them might be warriors," Rufsur said. "If I were the leader of the clan, I would have mandated that every male receives combat training. It doesn't make sense for Kian not to utilize everyone when there are so few of them. Besides, with Annani's progressive ideals, I'm pretty sure that some of the clanswomen are warriors as well."

"It could be." Kalugal nodded. "But you forget that the clan is involved in a lot of things that have nothing to do with warfare."

"You are both guessing," Atzil said. "And it doesn't matter. What's done is done. Let's focus on making this party happen. We have only today and tomorrow to organize everything."

"Where are we going to get tables and chairs from?" Rufsur asked. "The rental places are probably all closed because no one is having parties at a time like this."

Kalugal clapped him on the back. "I leave it in your capable hands. You can check what they have in the hotel Kian and his party are staying in. I'm sure they have banquet equipment, and you can thrall whoever is in charge to let you borrow what we need."

"Good idea. I'll do that."

"I'll give you a list," Atzil said. "Other than tables and chairs, I also need tablecloths, napkins, place settings, etc."

Kalugal let his imagination conjure a picture of his backyard set up for the wedding. "See if you can get flowers to put on the tables, that would make it look more festive. I want Jacki to have a grand party."

"She will," Atzil said. "I'll cook a feast for her."

Kalugal doubted that. Atzil was used to preparing simple everyday fare, and he'd never done anything fancy.

"Are you sure you can handle it? We can conscript a couple of cooks from the hotel to help you."

Atzil looked offended. "There isn't much difference between preparing a meal for forty-eight people or for sixty-five. I'll get a couple of the men to help in the kitchen, and I'll put up a buffet-style table on the patio."

Kalugal had no choice but to be blunt. "This is a special occasion. It needs a little more flair than your usual."

Atzil squared his massive shoulders. "Don't worry, boss. You'll be happy with the result, and what's more important, Jacki is going to be happy."

Kalugal chuckled. "Knowing her, she will want to help you cook. Good luck trying to keep her out of the kitchen."

"I'll give her something to do." Atzil lifted a finger. "The flowers. I can have Jacki arrange the centerpieces."

"Where are you going to get flowers from?" Rufsur asked. "I doubt florists are considered essential service providers."

"True, but that only means that there is a lot of stock sitting around in florists' shops. You can get a couple of men, load a truck, and leave cash for the proprietor to cover the unauthorized purchase."

Rufsur shook his head. "I never imagined that I would have to resort to thievery again."

Kalugal clapped him on the back. "It's not thievery if you leave money for what you take. In fact, you'd be doing the proprietor a favor."

Vlad

"I think that's enough for today." Wendy handed Leon the bow he'd made for her. "My fingers hurt, my arms hurt, and my back hurts. I'm going to sit out the rest of the training."

"I'll come with you." Vlad slung his bow over his shoulder and took Wendy's from Leon.

"You can stay and train with the guys. I'll watch you from the porch."

As if he was going to leave her alone to do whatever.

There were no phones in the cabin, and he and the Guardians were careful not to leave theirs lying around, but still. He didn't trust Wendy's innocent, friendly act.

That was how she'd gotten him the last time.

"I'm tired too. Do you want something to drink?"

"Yeah, a coke, if there are any left. We are running low."

As Wendy sat on the porch bench, Vlad went inside. He pulled two coke cans and three beers out of the fridge and headed back out.

Bowen and Leon were still at it, showing off like a couple of teenage boys. Richard looked like he was about to drop, but the guy was too competitive to quit.

After handing the cokes to Wendy, Vlad carried the beers to the guys. "Maybe you should take a break too."

Bowen took the beer and popped the top open. "I haven't worked up a sweat yet. Besides, Richard is having fun. Right, buddy?"

"Yeah, I am." Leaning on his bow, Richard popped the cap. "I'm turning into a rugged mountain man."

The guy hadn't shaved in days, but thankfully he was still showering. Despite his lack of care about his appearance, or maybe because of it, Vlad was starting to warm up to the idea of his mother with Richard. He was a decent guy who didn't shy away from hard work, and he got along with others.

It was a shame that she'd decided not to come.

"Bowen and Leon are really nice to Richard." Wendy handed Vlad one of the coke cans.

"They enjoy his company." He sat next to her. "And for some reason, Bowen has decided to take him under his wing."

"Do you like Richard?"

Vlad shrugged. "He's okay."

Cradling her coke can in her hands, Wendy leaned forward. "Do you think your mom would have liked him?"

Wendy wasn't supposed to know why his mother had been invited to join them, but apparently, she'd guessed it.

He cast her a sidelong glance. "I don't know. My mother is unpredictable."

"In what way?"

"She is moody, gets mad at trivial things, but is chill about the big stuff. Don't get me wrong, she's awesome, but not everyone can get along with her."

"I bet you do. You get along with everybody."

He sighed. "That's because I expect nothing, and I appreciate every little thing anyone does for me. I'm self-reliant, and I've been like that since a very young age."

"Me too. But in my case, it wasn't by choice. My mother walked out on me when I was a baby, and my father never gave a damn about me. I had to take care of myself the best I could." She lifted the coke can and took a long sip. "It's not true that you never expected anything, though. You expected your mother to love you."

"I did expect that. But I didn't expect her to remember to make dinner or do the laundry. If she did, great, and if not, I did it. It wasn't that she didn't care. She's just absentminded."

"What's her talent?"

"She's a costume designer."

"Not what she does. I meant her paranormal talent. To be part of the organization, she must have a special ability."

"She's a healer." Vlad said the first thing that popped into his mind.

Stella was a talented artist, but she didn't possess any special abilities other than a bit of thralling, and she wasn't very good at it. But she was a trained paramedic, so there was that.

"How come she no longer works as a paramedic then? Healing is her calling."

"A person can have more than one calling, and my mother is very artistic. Besides, paramedics get paid very little. Making costumes for theater productions is much more lucrative. Doing that, she feels fulfilled and makes enough money to afford a comfortable living."

Especially since their basic needs were covered by her share of the clan's profits, and they didn't have housing or education expenses. The clan provided both.

"Maybe I have another calling as well," Wendy said. "I just have no clue what it might be. I'm not good at anything other than feeling what others feel."

"You could be a great therapist."

She shook her head. "I don't have the stomach for it. I'm barely hanging in there dealing with my own shit. I would drown if I let other people's troubles weigh me down."

"What do you mean? Are you depressed?"

Wendy was so good at hiding her feelings that he hadn't gotten the sense that she was battling sadness.

"I don't let myself get depressed. Whenever my mind goes to places it shouldn't, I distract myself with something. Why do you think I watch so much anime?"

"I thought it was to shut others out."

"That too. But mostly, it's to keep out of my own head."

"Did you talk with Vanessa about it?"

"No. I don't like shrinks."

"Vanessa is cool. I've known her my entire life. Her son is my best friend."

Wendy chuckled. "Are you friends with toddlers? Vanessa can't have a son who is your age. She is what? Twenty-five?"

Damn. He'd painted himself into a corner. "She just looks young. Lots of plastic surgery. She is actually forty years old." Eighty-something was more like it.

"Seriously? Usually, I can tell when someone's had something done. She looks so natural."

Wendy

Vlad was lying, but Wendy didn't know why.

Who cared how old Vanessa was, or whether she'd had plastic surgery or not. But she was glad that the conversation had steered away from where it had been going.

Wendy didn't like to talk about her father. She didn't want to think about him or remember all the nasty things that he had done to her. And she definitely didn't need the pity, or conversely the doubt that those stories were likely to evoke.

She'd learned early on that people didn't want to believe things that made them uncomfortable. It was much easier to think that she was a disturbed teenager than to accept that her charming father had been abusing her.

Keeping her mouth shut was the best strategy. Whenever her father discovered that she'd told someone, the abuse would intensify tenfold. When she had just endured in silence, he'd let her be for long stretches of time.

"I'm not sure about the plastic surgery, I just assumed that Vanessa must have had some to look that young. Maybe she just takes good care of herself." Vlad kept lying like there was no tomorrow. "My mother also looks much younger than thirty-six."

"Why did she leave your father?"

"She was a teenager. She didn't want to get married."

Wendy was getting tired of Vlad's lies. While she was finally opening up to him and telling him things about herself that she hadn't told anyone else, he was making stuff up for no good reason.

"If you don't want to tell me, that's fine. But don't lie to me."

A red hue painted Vlad's pale cheeks. "You are one to talk. Was anything that you've told me true?"

Ouch.

"I've never lied to you. I just didn't tell you the entire truth."

Tilting his head, he glanced at her from under his long bangs. "So, when you told me that I was a great kisser, you actually meant it?"

"Of course. You would have known if I'd lied about it."

"You could be a good actress."

She shrugged. "I am, but I wasn't acting with you. The act that I usually put on is the opposite of that. I try to appear as uninterested as possible even when I am attracted to a guy. I don't want to encourage anyone."

"So why did you encourage me?"

"Because you needed it, and I'm a big softie."

"So, it was a pity kiss?"

"No. Stop twisting my words. I like you, and I think you are a really nice guy who lacks confidence. But usually what I do when I like someone is to push him away because I don't trust men. With you, I just couldn't force myself to do that."

"You didn't push me away because you wanted to use me, not because I was so irresistible."

"That's only partially true. I hated using you like that, but I believed that I had no choice."

"And now you believe differently?"

"I'm not sure about anything anymore."

With a sigh, Wendy looked at the Guardians and Richard, who were goofing around while practicing with their homemade bows and arrows. They had been decent to her even though she'd betrayed them, and nothing in their behavior indicated that they were anything other than what they seemed.

Good men.

She was terrified of letting go of her conviction that evil lurked inside most males, but she just couldn't imagine Bowen or Leon or even Richard hurting a child for any reason.

And Vlad certainly wouldn't hurt a fly.

"Most men are not like your father."

She narrowed her eyes at him. "Vanessa told you?"

"She didn't have to. You made it quite clear that he wasn't a good man."

"He's a monster, but I don't want to talk about him. Tell me the truth about your dad. Was he a deadbeat father?"

"My mother doesn't even know who he was. She hooked up with many different guys."

"At fifteen?"

"No, not at fifteen. She is not thirty-six. She is much older than that, but that's what I'm supposed to say."

"Why? Because Richard is younger than her?"

"Yeah."

"If your mom looks good, what does it matter how old she really is?"

"It doesn't."

Wendy let out a breath. "I'm sorry. This must be difficult for you."

He chuckled. "When Vanessa suggested that my mom should come along to check out Richard, I wasn't too happy about it, but I'm starting to warm up to him. He works his butt off training with the Guardians, and he is a good sport about doing really badly compared to them. I think he and my mom may get along. I just can't think of him as my stepdad, and I never will, but that's okay. I'm an adult, and I don't need a father figure in my life, and if my mother wants to date a guy who is not the wise, mature mentor type I imagined for her, that's fine with me."

"Richard is a bit shallow, but he isn't mean. And that's the most important thing."

Vlad's lips lifted in a sad smile. "You have very low expectations if not being mean is the only quality you appreciate in a life partner."

"It is the most important one. I don't mind if a guy is not the sharpest tool in the shed, or if he is short or tall, or any of the other things people think are so important. All I want is someone who is kind and respectful, but since I have trouble trusting those qualities to be true, I'd rather stay alone."

Vlad

If that was all Wendy wanted in a man, then he was a perfect match for her. Except, Vlad wanted to be more to her than that.

He wanted her to find him desirable and handsome and smart. She'd said all those things to him before, but they might have been lies or exaggerations.

"I'm kind and respectful, and it's not an act. You would have felt it if it was."

Wendy smiled. "You are much more than that."

He wanted her to continue and tell him all the ways he was more, but that would be fishing for compliments. Instead, he just said, "Thank you."

"I don't know why a guy like you is interested in someone like me." She cast him a sidelong glance. "Is it because I was the first one who showed interest in you?"

Ouch. That hurt.

Then again, he'd told her as much, so it wasn't like she was making assumptions because he was so unattractive.

"Of course not. I like you because of you."

"What is there to like? I'm a heartless bitch who doesn't trust anyone. I'm dishonest, manipulative, and disloyal, and I repaid your kindness with betrayal."

The Guardians were practicing a good hundred and fifty feet away, but Vlad could tell that they were listening to the conversation. First of all, because they'd stopped talking and secondly because they were trying very hard not to look in the porch's direction.

Pushing to his feet, he offered Wendy a hand up. "Let's take a walk."

She put the coke can on the wooden floorboards and took his hand. "They are too far away to hear anything, but a walk sounds nice."

As they passed the guys, Vlad waved. "We're going on a short hike."

"Don't go too far," Bowen said.

"We won't."

Vlad waited until he was sure they were out of the Guardians' hearing range. "You know what I've just realized?"

Wendy looked up at him. "What?"

"That I haven't given you enough compliments. I've been so absorbed in my own insecurities, thirsty for every kind word that you've said to me, that I neglected to see that you needed shoring up as much as I did."

Wendy waved a hand in dismissal. "You didn't have to say anything. I saw it in the way you looked at me, and the way you got excited every time we were touching."

"That's not enough. You are very pretty, and any guy would have been attracted to you. But you are also kind and giving even though you don't realize it. You weren't interested in a relationship for reasons that had nothing to do with me, and you gave me compliments despite that. You did it for me, so I would feel better about myself and gain confidence. That's not something a heartless bitch would do."

She shrugged. "You forget that I had an ulterior motive."

"You just said a few moments ago that you meant every word."

"I could have been lying."

"But you weren't."

"How can you be sure of that?"

Vlad stopped, put his hands on Wendy's shoulders, and looked into her eyes. "The question is, what would you rather I believed about you? If you want to keep me away because you still think that a relationship with me will be your doom, you'll do everything to convince me that it was all a game for you and that you didn't mean any of it. But if you no longer think that the program is your only option, and if you are ready to embark on a new journey with me at your side, then you will do everything you can to convince me that you meant it."

As Wendy stared into his eyes for the longest time, he could see in the depths of hers the million and one thoughts racing through her mind.

Finally, she whispered, "Are you asking me to take a chance on you?"

"Yes. But also on my friends and family who are willing to give you another chance. Forget about the program, Wendy. Fate brought you here for a reason. It's time to change your destiny's trajectory and shed the past that has such a crippling hold on your life."

She frowned. "What do you mean?"

It would have been better if Wendy figured it out on her own, but they'd been going round in circles for too long, each one protecting his or her soft, fragile core and afraid to make a move.

If he wanted Wendy to be brave and let go of what she believed was her safety tether, he needed to be brave first and say what was on his mind.

"To avoid pain, you are willing to forgo everything that matters in life and live like a shadow. The bad guys win, and you lose. Don't let that happen. Live your life, figure out what makes you happy, and let yourself fall in love."

"You make it sound so simple."

"It is. You are already halfway there." He smiled. "You found me, and I found you. The only thing standing in your way is fear. Kick it in the ass and send it to hell where it belongs."

Wendy

Could Vlad be right?

Visualizing fear as an ugly black blob that she could kick all the way to hell was so incredibly appealing.

Could she do that, though? Did she have the guts to change the trajectory of her life and embark on a new journey with Vlad at her side?

It sounded so good, so tempting, and Wendy yearned for that bright future with every fiber of her soul, but fear wasn't easy to get rid of. The black, sticky blob clung to her with a ferocious grip, and she wasn't strong enough to shake it off, let alone kick it in the ass and let it fly.

Wendy felt like a shipwrecked mariner who was desperately clinging to a rotten plank to stay afloat. It was cold in the water, and she wasn't sure where the shore was or how long it would take her to get there. And yet she was afraid to let go and swim in the opposite direction, where a luxury yacht was waiting for her. She knew that it was there only temporarily, and it wasn't going to wait forever. She had to decide whether she was willing to take a chance.

If the yacht sailed away, her only option would be to hold on to the rotting piece of wood and hope that she would float to shore before it disintegrated.

Pick the yacht, Wendy, an insistent voice whispered in her ear. *It might be your only chance.*

"How do I kick fear in the ass?"

"You don't cover it up, or hide behind it, or under it. When you let light shine on fear, it will shrink to a manageable size, and then you can kick it."

"You mean, talk about it?"

Vlad nodded. "If you choose to embark on a new journey with me at your side, then you need to convince me that you meant everything you said to me. And the way to do it is to trust me enough to tell me your fears."

"It's hard. I don't like talking about it. It depresses me."

He pulled her gently toward him, wrapped his arms around her, and tucked her head under his chin. "I might not seem like much, but I've got you, and I'll keep you safe. You are not alone."

Letting out a breath, Wendy wrapped her arms around Vlad's slim middle and leaned on him. There was strength in him that was more than physical, and warmth that emanated from his soul as well as his body.

It felt so good to be held, to listen to the strong beat of his heart, and to believe that she was safe with him.

Logically, she knew she was, but with fear embedded into the very fiber of her being, it was difficult to submit to the sensation of safety and accept it as real.

Wendy was going to try, though. The future that Vlad had painted for her was worth fighting for.

"The things I'm going to tell you are ugly. After you hear my story, you might feel differently about me."

"That won't happen."

"I know it will, but in a way, this will be a test for you as well. If you can stomach my story and not think less of me after hearing it, then you are worth taking a chance on." She looked up into his eyes. "I will know how you really feel, so there is no point in trying to hide it."

"I won't."

"Let's walk."

Pulling out of his embrace, Wendy tucked her hands into the pockets of her coat and lowered her head. It was easier to talk without looking at Vlad or touching him. She also decided to block out his emotional responses until she was done.

Otherwise, she wouldn't be able to finish.

"My mother left when I was a baby. She chose her drug addiction over me and left me behind to be raised by a monster."

As Wendy went on to describe her life growing up with her father, she pretended that she was talking about someone else to prevent the tears from choking her.

Thankfully, Vlad didn't ask any questions, and the only sound coming out of him was an occasional growl when she talked about the abuse or the disbelief from the few people she'd dared to tell about it.

"I kept missing homework assignments and failing at tests because the pain, sometimes physical and sometimes mental or both, made it hard to concentrate on school stuff. When the teacher asked what was going on, I told her, and she summoned my father to a meeting. He convinced her that I was a pathological liar. He told her that I was a disturbed kid because my mother left me and that I was in therapy. He told her that he would bring a letter from my therapist to prove it. There was no therapist, but he got a letter from somewhere, maybe he forged it himself, and that was it. No one believed me, and what I got for reaching out were more beatings."

When Wendy chanced a glance at Vlad, his hand was over his mouth, and his eyes were closed.

It was just as she'd feared. He was disgusted by her and thought that she'd somehow earned the punishments.

Nothing new there.

People always blamed the victim for courting the abuse. They couldn't understand why a sane person would beat up a child, or a spouse, or rape someone. That's why she'd stopped even hinting at it and had perpetuated the monster's pretense of a loving father who was raising his daughter alone to the best of his ability.

Appearing normal had made it much easier to have friends.

Vlad

Vlad was in trouble. His damn fangs were fully elongated, ready to tear into Wendy's father and cut him to pieces, and his eyes were glowing.

She'd just bared her soul to him, and he couldn't even answer her without scaring the shit out of her.

"I need a moment," he mumbled into his hand. "I'll be right back."

Vlad turned around and broke into a jog. He wasn't going to leave Wendy alone. He was just going to run in circles around her until he got himself under control. Not that she was in any danger.

With the amount of aggression that he was emitting, no predator would dare to come close.

Wendy must think that he'd gone nuts.

No wonder she'd thought the paranormal program was her salvation. No one had ever offered her a helping hand before.

How could a teacher ignore her plea for help? Weren't teachers obligated to report each instance of suspected abuse?

Her father must be very charismatic, or maybe even possess some compulsion ability. Somehow, he'd managed to convince the teacher to keep quiet.

And what's more, Vlad had the gnawing suspicion that Wendy's mother hadn't left voluntarily. The bastard might have murdered his wife and then told everyone a story about her running away to do drugs. Keeping Wendy around and pretending to be a loving father was a good cover. No one suspected him of murdering the mother.

But maybe Wendy's mom was still alive, and he could call Roni and ask him to search the internet for her. She might have changed her name, but if they got ahold of an old picture of her, maybe they could find her using William's face-recognition software.

Except, he had a feeling that they wouldn't find anything because the woman was dead.

Should he share his suspicions with Wendy?

On the one hand, it would shatter any hopes she might still harbor of her mother resurfacing. But on the other hand, she would no longer think that her mother had abandoned her.

When he finally had his fangs under control, Vlad slowed down and walked up to Wendy. While he'd run in circles like a madman, she'd sat down on a boulder and waited for him.

"Sorry about that." He crouched next to her. "I was so angry, and I needed to calm down."

She lifted a pair of teary eyes to him. "I thought that you were disgusted with me."

"Why the hell would I be? I was disgusted with your father, and I wanted to tear him apart with my bare hands, but my anger was never directed at you."

When she still seemed doubtful, he took her hand and placed it over his heart. "What do you feel?"

She closed her eyes. "You are still angry, but not at me. You are also afraid." She opened them and looked at him. "Why?"

He was afraid that his damn fangs would elongate again, but he couldn't tell her that.

"I'm afraid for you."

She frowned. "Why? He can't find me. And anyway, I'm an adult now. If he gets near me, I can call the police or get a restraining order."

"I have a bad feeling that your mother didn't leave voluntarily. I think he killed her."

Wendy's eyes widened. "What makes you think that?"

"It's a gut feeling. Someone who abuses a child is capable of murder. I'll ask a friend of mine to investigate. You don't happen to have her picture, do you?"

Perhaps he could also talk to Eva. Maybe the former private detective would be willing to do some digging for Wendy's mother as well.

Wendy shook her head. "He destroyed all of them. There was nothing of her left. No albums, no home videos, nothing. He wouldn't even tell me her name. But Director Simmons told me. Her name was Margaret." Wendy took a deep breath. "There is one more thing that I need to tell you. Director Simmons is my uncle, my mother's brother." She cringed. "Do you hate me now?"

"Hate you? No, I don't hate you. But it makes things much clearer. How come he didn't help you when you needed him?"

"He and my mother were estranged. He didn't know about me, and he didn't know my mother had left my father."

"How convenient for him. Are you sure he is really your uncle? Maybe he just said he was so you would come with him?"

Wendy frowned. "Maybe he did that so my father would let me go. But with half my pay going to him, he would have allowed it anyway. Besides, I'm an adult. I didn't need his permission."

"Did your father know about him?"

"No."

"So, you have no way of knowing whether he told you the truth."

Wendy closed her eyes. "Yes, I do. He lusted after me, I could feel it, but he never made a move because I was his niece." She shivered. "He's old enough to be my grandfather, and getting that vibe from him grossed me out. He's a disgusting man to have such thoughts about someone my age and even more so a relative. And he's married."

Vlad gaped at her. "And you wanted to go back to that?"

Wendy shrugged. "As I said, he never made a move, and improper thoughts are not a crime." Her tone was far from convincing. "He offered me a safe haven and a future that I couldn't even dream of before."

"Do you still want to go back?"

She shook her head. "No, I really don't. I want the bright future that you, Jin, and Vanessa dangled in front of me." She lifted her eyes to him. "Am I making a mistake?"

"You are not." Vlad wrapped his arms around Wendy, lifted her off the boulder, and sat on the ground with her on his lap. "You've just made the best decision of your life." He dipped his head and kissed her.

Kalugal

"Aren't we late?" Jacki stepped out of the car and adjusted her wig.

"Kian told us yesterday that today the summit will start at ten, remember?"

"That's right. I forgot."

He took her hand. "Which was good since I had things that I needed to do this morning."

She smiled. "Stock market?"

"Among other things."

The market had been volatile lately, but Kalugal knew how to navigate his investments even without the help of insider information. After so many years, he could feel the market's ebb and tide in his bones, and making money had become nearly effortless. It didn't matter if the trend was down or up, there were always opportunities to make money.

He opened the door to the conference room and motioned for Jacki to go ahead.

"Good morning, everyone." She took the chair Lokan pulled out for her.

For some reason, Kian had a big grin on his face when Kalugal opened the door, but it turned into a frown when he saw Jacki.

What was the deal with that?

Then when Kian and Turner exchanged glances, Kalugal knew for sure that something was going on.

"Syssi was hoping that you would come up to the suite," Kian told Jacki.

"We need Jacki here." Kalugal pulled out a chair for himself. "I want to finalize the plan today, and we can do that faster with her here. She can supply details that we might otherwise overlook."

Turner nodded. "I agree."

"It's probably a good idea," Kian conceded. "But before we begin, I want to thank Kalugal for being a good sport and showing his goodwill time and again."

Finally, his cousin was starting to show appreciation for all the concessions he'd been making.

"I'm glad you noticed."

"I have, and it was also pointed out to me by several people." Kian pulled the cuff out of his pocket. "That's why I suggest that you put it on and then all of us will remove our earpieces. I think that's good enough as a safety measure. Besides, I'm sick of hearing the damn computer voice in my ears instead of all of your voices."

That wasn't much, but it was better than nothing. And anyway, Kalugal would have had to put it on later to escort Jacki to see her friends. "Very well." He reached for the cuff, put it on his wrist, and snapped it closed. "Proceed."

Kian pulled out his earpieces. "That's much better." He shook his head as if he was trying to pop his ears.

Then his and Lokan's bodyguards did the same.

Turner and Lokan hadn't had any to start with.

"Thank you." Kalugal dipped his head. "This signals a new stage in our relationship. I'm glad that you are finally willing to trust me." Not really, he still had the damn cuff on his wrist, but it was all part of the dance he and Kian were doing.

"To an extent," Kian said.

"Shouldn't we drink to that?" Anandur asked.

"Maybe later." Kian poured water into his glass instead of whiskey. "It's already late in the day, and I want to get down to business."

"I concur." Kalugal reached for the pitcher and poured water into his and Jacki's glasses.

Kian waited until he was done. "We ended our last meeting talking about infecting the program's computers with a virus. I talked with my hacker last night, and he has an idea. He can design the bug, but instead of launching it himself, he can have a hacker from another country do it. He likes the idea of sending it from China. To make sure that our involvement is not discovered, you will compel that hacker remotely into silence."

"I can do that," Lokan said.

"I know." Kian cast him an apologetic smile. "But your brother is more powerful, and in this case, I would like to use the best weapon I have for the task."

"How soon can this be done?" Kalugal asked.

"It will take months to develop a bug that will corrupt only the data pertinent to us. As I said before, I don't want to cause damage that might weaken this wonderful country we live in. I'm very fond of the United States of America, and I want it to continue to thrive."

"We don't have months," Kalugal said. "We need to get the trainees out now."

"What's the rush?" Turner asked. "Everyone is busy with the damn virus. No one is searching for immortals."

"Which makes it the perfect time to strike." Kalugal tapped his fingers on the conference table. "Perhaps we could tamper with the power? Cause a blackout? The bio scanners need electricity to work. And since everything is controlled by computers, we can use your Chinese hacker idea to take the power down. That's a very specific system, and it will not affect anything else. I need one hour tops to get the trainees out."

Kian regarded him with a smile curving his lips. "Maybe we don't need to take the power out. We can bring our secret weapon. Sylvia."

"Who is Sylvia? Or rather what can she do?" Kalugal asked.

"Sylvia has a unique talent. She can cause electronic equipment to malfunction."

"Is she a Guardian?"

"Sylvia is a civilian, but she helped us on missions before. I'm not sure she can handle something as sophisticated as bio scanners, though. We will have to run some tests first."

The clan seemed to have an assortment of talented people, and Kalugal wondered whether immortals with interesting special abilities like that had been born to the Brotherhood since he had left.

Lokan should know.

He turned to his brother. "Does Navuh have anyone like Sylvia?"

Lokan shook his head. "I think our father's discrimination against females is biting him in the ass. It seems to me that the clan's females lead in the special talent department."

Jacki

Jacki stifled the urge to pump her fist in the air. As the only female in this group of all males, she felt it was her job to represent her entire gender and show the guys that they were not the only ones who could come up with strategy plans.

"I think that it would be best to utilize an old-fashioned power outage and Sylvia's talent." With all eyes on her, Jacki felt a little uneasy. "The complex has backup in case the main generator goes out, and we will have to take out both. But there is a chance that the bio scanners and surveillance cameras also have battery backup, and if that's the case, we will need Sylvia to do her thing."

"Good thinking," Kian said. "I can have Roni start working on infecting the power generation software and redirect it through a hacker in a foreign country."

"Once the power is down, I will go in shrouded as either Simmons or Roberts or even the recruiter," Kalugal said. "Do you have pictures of her?"

Kian chuckled. "We do, but you are too tall to pull it off."

"Why? Is she short?"

"No, but she is at least four inches shorter than you, and when you talk, your voice will seem to originate from the top of your head."

Kalugal glanced at Jacki. "How tall is Simmons?"

"About Marisol's height."

"Roberts?"

"Even shorter."

Kalugal shrugged. "I'll just have to slouch."

"This is not the right time to do it," Turner said. "I bet the entire base is quarantined because of the virus, and there is limited traffic going in or out. They have many projects going on in there that they don't want to get interrupted because people are getting sick."

"Is there a way to check?" Jacki asked.

"I can make a few phone calls to old friends who are still part of the system and ask them how things are going." Turner scribbled something on his yellow pad.

"Do you have someone you know in that facility?" Kian asked.

"No, but the military is pragmatic and systematic. A decision is made, and the same procedures are implemented across the board."

"Simmons and Roberts are old," Jacki said. "And they are not actually part of the military. They might have gone home to ride this thing out."

"We need to check that." Turner scribbled another note. "If they are, it would make things easier. It wouldn't look suspicious if one of them decided to show up for work."

It suddenly occurred to Jacki that they were overcomplicating things and that there might be a much simpler solution.

"I have an idea." She looked at Kalugal. "But it will have to wait for after this freaking virus is over. We can get to Roberts when he's at home, you can compel him to tell us when and where the next trainee outing is going to be, and then you can thrall him to forget that he told anyone about it."

"What if the outings were canceled after your escape?" Kian asked.

"I'm sure they are not going to keep the trainees cooped up in the facility indefinitely. Both Simmons and Roberts kept talking about how important the outings were for morale, and they were right. Without those mall excursions, we would have felt like prisoners. The outings gave us an illusion of normalcy."

"Are you sure that Roberts is not immune?" Turner asked.

"He never said that he was, but he never subjected himself to our talents either. But if he is immune, you can torture the information out of him and then use the same drugs you used on Marisol to make him forget."

"I like it," Kian said. "Good thinking, Jacki."

Under the table, Kalugal took her hand and gave it an encouraging squeeze. "I don't like to wait, but it seems like Jacki's idea is the least complicated and therefore has the most chance of success."

"True," Turner said. "But I thought that your main objective was to shut the program down. I'm not sure that stealing the trainees will be enough. We need to get rid of Simmons and Roberts. That should buy us enough time to work on the virus."

Jacki cringed. "Kian said that no one is getting offed."

Kalugal lifted her hand and kissed the back of it. "I can compel Roberts to give Simmons a one-way ride to hell. That doesn't count as offing."

"Do you mean, have him drive off a cliff?"

"Something to that effect, yes."

"It's still murder."

"Let's solve one problem at a time," Kian interjected. "Perhaps stealing the trainees will be enough to get those two fired or retired."

Kian

Kian raked his fingers through his hair. "When I originally decided against taking the other trainees, I had good reasons for it, and not much has changed since then. Some might not be happy about losing the income, and we would have to take them against their will, and some are minors who need to be returned to their families. The only justification for doing it is the potential threat they pose to our secret existence, and I'm not sure that's a good enough reason."

"What about the compulsion and the breeding program?" Jacki asked. "That's immoral, and I doubt any of them would have signed up for it if they knew. Once we tell them about it, they will be happy we rescued them."

"I hope so."

"It's not much different from rescuing victims of trafficking," Anandur said. "Some of the victims are terrified of us when we get them out, and we often need to thrall them to calm down before we can transport them to the sanctuary. The traffickers manipulate the victims, threatening that if they don't cooperate, their families will pay the price. Then they promise them that a portion of the money they will earn from prostitution will be sent to support their loved ones. Because of that, some of the victims are not happy about getting rescued, but we do it anyway because it's the right thing to do."

Jacki nodded. "I agree with Anandur. The trainees are just promised good pay, and they are compelled to believe that they are hooking up with their classmates out of their own free will."

Kian had had the same thoughts, but doubt had chipped away at his conviction. He was well aware of his tendency to think with his heart first and his brain second, and to get all riled up over what he believed was unjust and unfair. Usually, Turner was the voice of reason who put things in proper perspective, but it was good to hear the same sentiment from Jacki, who'd been part of the program, and from Anandur, who'd made a valid argument that the program was nearly as morally abhorrent as trafficking.

"Then it's settled. We are doing it the way Jacki suggested, and if that doesn't work for some reason, we will use the power outage as plan B. Now I just need to figure out what to do with the trainees once we get them out."

"What did you do with the other two you picked up?" Kalugal asked.

"We're keeping them at a secret location with Guardians to watch over them. We introduced a fine young man to Wendy, and if he decides that she is the one for him, he will tell her about her potential dormancy, and they'll take it from there. Richard is also a work in progress. We are still trying to match him with someone."

"Poor Richard," Jacki said. "He's not that bad. I don't know why he's so unlucky in love."

Kalugal smiled at her lovingly. "He just hasn't met the right female yet." He turned to Kian. "If he and the girl are not immune, you should've brought them into your community and exposed them to more of your people. The Fates you believe in will have a much easier job matching them with the right person."

"I didn't do that because I suspected one or more might be a mole, and I was right."

"And yet you are giving the girl a second chance. How come?"

Kalugal seemed genuinely puzzled rather than critical of Kian's decision.

"Potential Dormants are not easy to come by, and I didn't want to lose Wendy if there was a chance of redemption for her. The clan's therapist convinced me that there was. Wendy is only nineteen, and her betrayal was fueled by fear, but that doesn't mean that I'm a hundred percent sure that I made the right decision. It might still bite me in the ass even if she turns. In fact, she would be more dangerous to us then. While she's still human, we can thrall her to forget about us, or have Lokan compel her if too much time has elapsed. Once she turns immortal, she will become immune to thralling."

"But not to my compulsion. I'll make sure that she can never mention you, the clan, or immortals in general to any human."

"Thank you. That's a good idea."

"Are you going to put the other trainees in the same underground facility you put us in?" Jacki asked.

Kian nodded.

"Do you have enough room in there?"

"I'll have to convert more cells into bedrooms."

Kalugal eyed him with fascination. "You have a dungeon?"

"I do, but it's much nicer than the cell you originally stuck Jacki and Arwel in."

"I have only one cell, not a dungeon, and it's deliberately dreary because I use it for disciplinary measures when needed. Locking up an insubordinate warrior in a nice apartment would be a reward, not a punishment."

"Your men are very well behaved," Jacki said.

"That's because passing by those bars every day reminds them of the consequences of defying my orders."

Glancing at Rufsur and then Kalugal's other two men, Kian noted that their expressions didn't show resentment, and Rufsur even smiled and nodded in agreement.

The way Kalugal's men regarded their leader was another point in his favor.

In truth, the only point against him was his incredible power over other immortals, but then he'd just offered to use it for the clan's benefit.

"Maybe you can use Kalugal's compulsion services with the new trainees?" Jacki suggested. "He is right about the better chances they'll have of bonding with someone if they have a larger selection."

Kalugal nodded. "I'll gladly assist in any way I can."

"That could be very helpful. I kept Wendy and Richard in a separate location because there is a limit to how many memories can be erased without causing brain damage. Wendy might not bond with Vlad, and we might have to introduce her to someone else, and Richard's situation is even worse because he doesn't have anyone at the moment. It could take weeks or even months before they bond with someone, and after that, they will still have to attempt transition."

Kalugal tilted his head. "How did you do that with the other Dormants?"

"The circumstances were different in each case, but most of those Dormants weren't hiding from anyone, so it wasn't urgent to bring them in. They bonded with my people first, and it was only then that I allowed them into our community. After that, it was a matter of them either transitioning or not, which normally takes up to two weeks. Luckily, they have all transitioned successfully, so there was no need to erase anyone's memories."

Kalugal

"Perhaps Kalugal and his men should move into the village," Lokan suggested. "Compulsion is different than thralling. Thralling is very effective at erasing recent memories, and they usually don't come back. If they do, they are so hazy that people think that they dreamt them. Compulsion affects behavior, and it needs to be reinforced from time to time. You will need Kalugal to do that at least once a month."

Both Kian and Kalugal shook their heads.

"I like my independence," Kalugal said. "I'm willing to visit once a month to reinforce the compulsion, or you can have them brought to me." It was a good opportunity to promote his own agenda, and since he'd been very generous with Kian, Kalugal expected his cousin to reciprocate. "And when you do, you can have several females escort them, so they can meet my men."

Kian frowned. "If the compulsion is not permanent, I can't bring the trainees into the village. Those who do not transition would have to be released. And if they have accumulated too many memories for thralling to be safe, and compulsion needs periodic reinforcement, we will have a big problem. I'll have to keep them in a different location and tell them the same story I told Jacki and her friends."

"I wish you had a place for them that wasn't underground," Jacki said.

"I have an idea." Anandur raised his finger. "What if we bring them to our village but segregate them? We can build a fence around part of the new phase and use the virus as an excuse for the quarantine. We can then have people visit them who are supposedly recovered, and therefore can't contract the virus again."

Kian shook his head. "We have to wait with the extraction until the virus is gone. There will be no mall excursions for the trainees for the foreseeable future."

Kalugal let out an exasperated breath. "I would have said to hell with that, and let's just go for the blackout plus Sylvia plan, but that's not feasible at this time either. There is so little air traffic going on that it would be impossible to cover up our escape tracks."

"That's not such an insurmountable obstacle," Turner said. "I can probably come up with an evacuation plan even under these unusual circumstances. I just need enough time to plan and organize it."

Kian looked skeptical. "I'd rather wait and not act under less than optimal conditions. But just in case we have no other choice, go ahead and formulate a plan." He looked at Kalugal. "My mother is a big proponent of listening to gut feelings, and you seem convinced that we should act sooner rather than later."

"I am, and it really is a gut feeling more than anything logical. That's why I didn't press the issue too forcefully."

Raking his fingers through his hair, Kian let out a breath. "Let's assume for a moment that we act now, bring the trainees to the village, and quarantine them. What are we going to do about the kids? We can't keep them until they are old enough to find a mate, and we can't quarantine them until then either."

"They will be safer among immortals," Jacki said. "If you send them back to their families now, they might get infected. Also, Marisol or another recruiter will just get them back."

Kalugal nodded. "I think that after a two-week quarantine, it will be safe to thrall them to forget who rescued them and deliver them to their families. Hopefully, by then the program will have shut down, and there will be no risk of them getting picked up again."

Jacki glared at him. "Because the director and Roberts will be dead?"

"Dead or discredited. Whatever works."

"Discredited. I don't want us to murder anyone."

"We shall see," Kian said. "Turner, since you are not overly busy right now, can I count on you to come up with the two alternative plans?"

"I will have the outline ready in a week. We can go over it then and make adjustments as needed. After that, I'll need another week to work out the details and the exact timeline."

Kian turned to Kalugal. "Is that okay with you? Or would you like to work on it together with Turner?"

"I'm fine with leaving it in Turner's capable hands." He took Jacki's hand. "Right now, I have more important things on my mind. Have you decided whether you and your people will be joining us for our happy occasion?"

Kian glanced at Turner, who nodded his approval.

"We will come."

"Thank you." Jacki clapped her hands. "It means a lot to me. Can I invite Jin and Arwel as well?"

"Certainly. And since we are going to need Yamanu to shroud the event and the drones overhead, you can invite Mey also."

"Awesome." Jacki grinned.

"I suggest that we pause the summit for tomorrow and Wednesday," Kian said. "Kalugal needs time to make everything ready for the wedding, and you can come here and have the ladies fuss over you. Tradition says that the happy couple shouldn't see each other before the wedding."

"No way." Kalugal squeezed Jacki's hand. "I'm not letting you out of my sight. I've made enough concessions already."

Jacki leaned and kissed his cheek. "I'm not letting you out of my sight either."

Kian affected a dramatic sigh. "Then I guess you have to come up to our suite now and try on your wedding dress."

Jacki's breath hitched. "Is it here?"

"My sister brought it." He lifted his phone. "I've been getting non-stop texts demanding that I let you go so you could come up and try it on, but you were instrumental to our discussion, so I kept ignoring them." He smiled sheepishly. "I'm sure that I'm going to pay for that."

Syssi

"Hello, darlings." Amanda strode into the suite holding a garment bag.

Right behind her was Dalhu, who carried a big suitcase.

Smiling, Syssi rushed to pull her sister-in-law into a tight embrace. "I'm so glad you are here." She then hugged Dalhu too, but he didn't seem happy about it.

The guy still had trouble with physical shows of affection.

Amanda lifted a brow. "Me or the dress?"

"Both." Syssi took the garment bag. "Did you get it altered?"

"Vivian did it. The woman is a genius. She added a two-inch strip of lace to the bottom, and it looks like the dress was designed that way. Beautiful job."

"I want to see."

"Me too." Wonder pushed to her feet and glanced at Callie and Carol. "Are you coming?"

"I've seen Syssi in the dress," Carol said.

Callie got up. "I didn't."

Syssi chuckled. "I'm not going to put it on. I just want to see Vivian's craftsmanship."

"Where should I put the suitcase?" Dalhu asked. "It's more stuff for the wedding."

"Follow me." Syssi headed to her and Kian's bedroom. "I assume you have the bridesmaids' dresses in there?"

"Among other things. I got a bunch of long-sleeved shirts for you to wear under the saris. It's still damn cold outside."

Syssi opened the door. "What do you mean us? Aren't you going to join us?"

Dalhu put the suitcase next to the door and made a hasty retreat.

"I'm coming to the party." Amanda sat down on the bed. "But I'm not going to be a bridesmaid."

"Why not?"

"I want to use the opportunity to check out Kalugal's men and see who I can match to whom." She winked. "I'm planning to snap discreet photos of the men so I can show them to the ladies."

Syssi chuckled. "Does Kian know about your plan?"

"Not yet."

Unzipping the garment bag, Syssi pulled the dress out and laid it on the bed next to Amanda.

"It's beautiful," Wonder said. "Jacki is going to look amazing in it."

Callie nodded. "And the lace at the bottom looks perfect. Kudos to Vivian."

Amanda got up and opened the suitcase. "You might as well try the saris on. I also brought sandals in different sizes and some jewelry to go with them." She handed a green one to Wonder. "This will look great with your coloring."

"I like the blue." Callie pointed.

"Then it's yours." Amanda handed it to her. "Which one do you like, Syssi?"

"Do you think the purple will look good on me?"

"Why not? Try it on." Amanda took out the rest of the saris and spread them over the bed. "By the way, has Kian made a decision yet? We might have gone to all this trouble for nothing."

Syssi leaned closer to her sister-in-law. "He was supposed to test Kalugal today, but given that they are still talking, nothing happened, and it's a go."

"What kind of test?"

"He and the others were supposed to take their earpieces out and see if Kalugal would make a move.

Just in case, Brundar was somehow supposed to keep his in and only pretend to remove them. If Kalugal made a move, he would have turned him into a shish kebab with his throwing knives. Except, Kalugal brought Jacki along, so I'm sure he was on his best behavior."

"How is he with her?" Amanda asked. "Does he love her? Or is he marrying her only because she is a possible Dormant?"

"He loves her." Syssi moved one of the saris aside and sat next to Amanda. "He has that adoring look in his eyes every time he glances her way."

Wonder nodded. "He is respectful and attentive. I didn't expect it from an ex-Doomer. Their opinions of women are disgusting."

"Lokan is also respectful and attentive." Carol walked into the room. "Robert and Dalhu are as well. It depends on the person."

Wonder shook her head. "I know, which is also surprising. Attitudes are learned, not inborn. How could it be that some of them are decent males and others are terrible?"

Amanda tapped her finger over her lips. "I wondered the same thing when I was just getting to know Dalhu. I figured that it depends on the women who raised them. Dalhu's mother loved him and cared for him and his sister despite the way her children were conceived. I guess Robert's mother loved him too. Lokan and Kalugal were raised by nannies, but Navuh probably chose the best ones for his sons."

Carol nodded. "Lokan remembers the Dormant who raised him fondly, but I don't think he felt loved by her."

"Did she take good care of him?"

"Obviously. He also had the best tutors, and Navuh kept checking on his progress. Compared to the other Doomers, Lokan was raised like a pampered prince."

"Figures." Syssi chuckled. "I like both Lokan and Kalugal, but they are a little too full of themselves."

Carol shrugged. "They are Doomer royalty. Lokan and Kalugal are the sons of a goddess and the most powerful immortal ever born." She fluffed her curls. "Does being mated to Lokan make me a princess?"

Kian

"How many more?" Jacki sounded short of breath. "I lost count."

Climbing seven floors wasn't easy for a human, even a young and healthy one like Jacki. Especially since Kalugal wasn't letting her touch the railing.

The guy was taking paranoid to a whole new level, but it was kind of touching to see how much he cared for her.

"One more," Kian said.

"Hallelujah."

Kalugal and Jacki were behind him on the stairwell, with the others closing the procession. Just like yesterday, Kalugal had sent his men home and Kian had dismissed the three other Guardians that were supposed to belong to Lokan.

Perhaps it was time to end the charade. Kalugal was well aware that the men weren't really Lokan's guards.

"Is your sister staying in your suite?" Kalugal asked.

Kian paused his climb and turned to look over his shoulder. "She and Dalhu are staying in their own. Why?"

"Just making small talk." Kalugal had his arm wrapped around Jacki, helping her climb.

"I'm so excited," Jacki said. "I can't wait to see the dress." She looked at Kalugal. "But you are not allowed to come with me when I'm trying it on. You can't see me in the dress until the ceremony."

"That's fine. I'm willing to let you go as far as the next room. But no further than that."

Kian turned around and kept climbing.

Jacki and Kalugal were getting along like an old couple, which reinforced his belief that their mating had been fated. He remembered it being the same way with Syssi. The first time he'd looked into her eyes, he'd felt as if he was coming home. At the time, he'd thought himself a fool, but he knew better now.

The other mated couples who'd come after him and Syssi had reported similar feelings.

When he opened the door to the suite, Kian found only Bridget and Dalhu there. "Where is everybody?"

"In your bedroom," Bridget said. "Don't go in there. I think they are trying the bridesmaids' saris on."

"Can I go in?" Jacki asked.

The door opened, and Syssi came out of the bedroom. "Finally. We thought you were never going to bring Jacki over." She walked up to Kian, gave him a quick peck on the cheek, and then ushered Jacki and Kalugal into the suite's living room. "Let me introduce you to Dalhu."

"Hello." Amanda walked out of the bedroom and gave Kalugal a once-over before doing the same to Jacki. "You look amazing." She pulled Jacki into a quick hug and then did the same to the surprised Kalugal. "I'm glad to see that you are taking good care of our Jacki."

"Of course. But she is *my* Jacki now."

Kalugal looked at Dalhu, who was doing his best to melt into the wallpaper and failing. At six foot eight, the guy couldn't make himself disappear no matter how hard he tried. "And you must be the Brother turned artist." He offered Dalhu his hand.

Reluctantly, Dalhu pushed away from the wall and walked up to Kalugal. "The name is Dalhu. It's an honor to meet you, sir." He shook Kalugal's hand.

"The honor is all mine, and please call me Kalugal."

Dalhu nodded.

"I would love to see your artwork. Is there a chance that you brought some samples with you?"

"He is too modest for that." Amanda threaded her arm through Kalugal's and led him to a couch. "But, I'm not." She pulled out her phone and handed it to him. "You can scroll through them."

Both Jacki and Kalugal oohed and aahed and paid Dalhu one compliment after another, and by the time Kalugal handed the phone back to Amanda, the ice was broken, and Dalhu had relaxed.

"If you'd like, I could paint Jacki and you a portrait," Dalhu said. "It would be Amanda's and my wedding present to you. But I won't be able to finish it by tomorrow."

"That would be lovely." Kalugal wrapped his arm around Jacki. "But don't we need to pose for it?"

"I can snap several photos of you two in different poses. You'll choose which one you like the best, and I'll paint it."

"Then let's do it." Kalugal pushed to his feet and pulled Jacki up. "Where do you want us to sit?"

"Give me a moment."

Dalhu grabbed an armchair and repositioned it this way and that until he was happy with the lighting falling on it. "Please, take a seat." He gestured.

Kalugal sat down and pulled Jacki to sit on one of his thighs. "Is that good?"

"Excellent." Dalhu snapped a photo, repositioned them, snapped another one, and another and another until Jacki groaned.

"Can I go see the dress now?"

"Just a couple more." Dalhu had her sit in the armchair and Kalugal stand behind it with his hand on her shoulder. "Now you can go," he said after snapping a few more photos.

"Come." Syssi took Jacki's hand and started walking toward their bedroom, then looked at Amanda. "Are you coming?"

"In a moment. I want to discuss the party arrangements with Kalugal."

"Okay, but don't be long. We need your hair-styling expertise."

"Give me ten minutes."

Kalugal

Kian's sister was a striking beauty. She was regal, confident, a real princess who had mated a simple soldier.

Kalugal had to admit that Dalhu was an impressive male specimen, and he was a talented artist as well, but he was still a simple man who didn't feel comfortable being part of the royal family.

And yet, they treated him as one of their own, and Kalugal hadn't detected an ounce of hostility toward the former Brother.

He had many questions that he wanted to ask Dalhu, but not in front of Kian and his people. The problem was catching the guy alone so they could talk privately. Perhaps he would have a chance to do that at the wedding.

"When can I come to see your house?" Amanda asked.

It took Kalugal a moment to realize that she was talking to him. "Whenever you want."

"You'll see it tomorrow at the wedding," Kian grumbled.

Amanda put her hands on her hips and struck a defiant pose. "I rushed over here because you said that Kalugal needs my help to organize a wedding."

"That was when I thought we were going to have it here in the hotel, but he wants all his men to be there and to hold it in his backyard."

"Then I'll help organize it over there."

Sensing that Kian was about to blow up at his sister, Kalugal intervened. "Thank you for your kind offer, but everything is taken care of. My men have it under control, and it's going to be a beautiful party. We're even going to have flowers on the tables." He looked at Kian. "And thanks to your brother, we will have an air show for entertainment. Perhaps you can have the drones write congratulations or some other lovely message with smoke?"

Kian chuckled. "I don't think the drones can do that, but maybe we can have them fly in formation. What do you think, Turner?"

The guy shook his head. "They have a different job to do."

Turner might be a brilliant strategist, but he lacked a sense of humor.

"Well, if I'm not going to help with the party, I can at least make sure that the bride has everything she needs." Amanda waved her hand at them and then ducked into the bedroom.

"Anyone want a beer?" Anandur asked.

"Bring them out," Kian said. "I'm going out to the terrace to smoke."

That was Kalugal's chance to catch a few words with Dalhu. The doctor had gone with the ladies to the bedroom, Brundar had followed his boss out to the terrace, and the only one left in the room was Lokan, who Kalugal didn't mind listening to his conversation with Dalhu.

He sidled up to the guy. "I was wondering how you made the transition from a warrior to an artist. Have you always wanted to paint?"

Artistic talent was not encouraged in the Brotherhood, and it had occurred to Kalugal that Dalhu might have crossed over to the clan not only because he'd fallen for Amanda, although that was motivation enough, but also because he wanted to pursue his dream of becoming a painter.

Anandur came out of the kitchen and tossed one beer to Dalhu and another one to Kalugal. Then he went back to get some more.

Dalhu popped the cap and took a sip. "I knew that I could draw, but I only used it to illustrate locations or provide crude portraits of adversaries before photos were invented. When Kian put me in a cell, I offered to draw the portraits of Navuh's sons, and to prove I could do that, I made a sketch of Amanda. He was impressed by it and told Anandur to get me art supplies. That's how it started. At first, I only used charcoals and pencils because I didn't have any training. Later on, I started experimenting with acrylics and oil paintings."

"You are very good, and I'm glad that you found your passion." Kalugal took a sip of his beer. "There is another thing I want to ask you. Kian said that your bond with his sister allowed you to free yourself from the compulsory loyalty to my father." He assumed an innocent smile. "Can you expand a little on that? As you can imagine, I don't know much about the supposed bond between immortal mates."

"It's real, not supposed. And once it binds you and Jacki, you will recognize it. It's more powerful than any loyalty you've ever felt. It will override everything. You'll do anything to keep her safe."

"Maybe it's just the power of love?"

Dalhu shook his head. "Not every pair is fated, but when it is, the connection is stronger than love. Humans fall in and out of love. Immortals mate for life."

"When did you know that you'd bonded with Amanda?"

"When her brother and his people came to rescue her, and I didn't kill them because I knew she didn't want them dead."

Jacki

"It's gorgeous." Jacki lifted Syssi's wedding dress and held it in front of her.

It looked even better in person than in the picture Syssi had shown her.

Jacki had never wasted energy imagining her wedding dress. Her wistful fantasies had revolved around the kind of man she hoped to one day start a family with. But life was full of surprises, and the man who'd found her wasn't even a man but a demigod, and he exceeded all of her expectations and then some.

"What are all those?" She pointed to the colorful shawls neatly folded and stacked next to the dress.

"Bridesmaids' saris," Wonder said.

Jacki's heart fluttered happily. "I'm going to have bridesmaids?"

"All of us except for Amanda," Callie said. "She wants to check out Kalugal's men."

Jacki frowned. "Aren't she and Dalhu married?"

Syssi laughed. "She wants to check them out as potential mates for other clan females. And as to your question, Dalhu and Amanda are not officially married, but they are mated, which means so much more than a human marriage. Immortals mate for life."

"Not all immortals," Bridget corrected. "Only the fated ones."

The door opened, and Amanda walked in. "Kian wouldn't let me help Kalugal with the party."

"It's okay," Jacki said. "His men can handle it. You've already done so much. Thank you."

Amanda waved a hand in dismissal. "You're welcome, but it was no trouble. Vivian did all the work altering the dress. Try it on." She shooed her toward the bathroom.

Syssi pushed to her feet. "I'll help you put it on. This is the last chance to make alterations. I'm not great at this, but I can handle a needle and thread."

"If you lock the door, I can change in here. I'm not shy."

Syssi chuckled. "I remember. You had no problem stripping naked in the van."

"I wasn't naked, just topless."

Amanda turned around and locked the door. "I hope you know that a locked door is no barrier to an immortal."

"I know." Jacki started on the buttons of her blouse. "Kalugal and I share the master bathroom because the office he converted into a bedroom for me doesn't have its own bath. It has access to the master, though, and when I get in, I lock the one to his bedroom. He told me it was only good as a signal for him not to come in."

It took her a moment to realize that everyone in the room was gaping at her. "What?"

Amanda shook her head. "Do you want to tell me that you haven't had sex with him yet?"

"I haven't."

"Why the hell not?"

Jacki shrugged. "I'm old-fashioned."

"Oh boy." Amanda smoothed her hand over her short hair. "That's why you are rushing to get married, but you are making a mistake."

"Amanda!" Syssi glared at her sister-in-law. "How can you say something like that to Jacki a day before the wedding?"

"Because it needs to be said." Amanda took the wedding dress, put it over the dresser, and then motioned for Jacki to sit on the bed with her.

"I don't need a lecture about the birds and the bees. I'm inexperienced but not naive."

"There are some things that you don't know and should." Amanda patted the spot next to her. "Sit."

Jacki shrugged her blouse back on, sat down, and closed one button. She had a bra on, but it would have felt awkward to have a sex talk in a state of half undress.

"How much did Kalugal tell you about sex immortal style?"

"I know all about the bite and the fantastic orgasms it's supposed to deliver. I'm still scared, but I figured that if all of you are okay with that, it can't be too bad."

Callie chuckled. "That's the understatement of the century. It's an earth-shattering, mind-altering experience."

"I'll take your word for it." Jacki turned to Amanda. "Anything else?"

"The bite combined with unprotected sex might trigger the start of your transition. So, if you want to wait with that, use condoms, and if you want to prevent pregnancy, you need to go on the pill or get a contraceptive shot."

"Bridget had already explained all that, and she also said that the chances of Kalugal getting me pregnant are very low."

"That's true. But there are exceptions. Eva got pregnant her first time with Bhathian, and they were both immortal, which should have lowered the chances of pregnancy to almost nothing."

Jacki felt a surge of hope. "I hope Kalugal and I will be that lucky. I don't mind getting pregnant right away."

Amanda rolled her eyes. "You've known the guy for one week, haven't had sex with him yet, and you want to make a baby with him?"

"I love Kalugal, and I know that he is the one for me."

"I can't believe that Kalugal went along with the no sex before the wedding nonsense," Carol said. "Immortal males are hornier than bunnies in heat."

Jacki grimaced. "That's an unflattering analogy. Kalugal is a gentleman and he respects my wishes. He also feels that I'm the one for him, and we don't need sex to confirm that."

"That's where you're wrong," Amanda said. "To bond with an immortal, you need to have sex with him. That's how it works. And if the bond doesn't form, then he might not be the one for you. But it's probably too late to test it now. The bond doesn't happen overnight."

"It did for Lokan and me," Carol said.

"That's because you were already an immortal. It takes longer when one of the partners is still human."

"Both you and Dalhu were immortal when you met," Carol said. "Did it happen immediately for you?"

"It must have, but I didn't know that until I tried to distance myself from Dalhu. I realized very quickly that I couldn't live without him, and that I had to fight for us or never have sex with anyone for the rest of my life." She turned to Jacki. "That's another thing you should know. When you bond with an immortal male, you become addicted to him and crave only him. No other male will appeal to you."

"That's not a problem. But does it work the same for him?"

"Yes, but for males, the addiction takes longer to set in. Don't worry about Kalugal straying, though. The bond is powerful enough to hold him tied to you without the addiction. He will never desire another female again."

Jacki lifted a brow. "Forever? What if I die?"

"If Fates forbid you or he dies, the bond will disintegrate, and only the addiction will linger, but not forever. Eventually, it would be possible for you or him to have sex again."

"What about love?"

Amanda shook her head. "I'm not sure about that. We are not supposed to get more than one fated mate, and even one is a rare blessing."

Lokan

Kian leaned against the balcony's railing and took another puff of his cigarillo. "If we get rid of the director and his lackey, there is no guarantee that they will shut down the program."

With the ladies gone, Lokan wasn't surprised that the men had started talking shop again, and he was quite sick of hearing about the paranormal program and his brother's peculiar obsession with taking it down as soon as possible.

He didn't know Kalugal well, but it just didn't make sense.

When Kian had decided not to take the other trainees, it had been after he'd consulted with Turner. And if Turner hadn't been worried about the potential threat the program posed to immortals everywhere, then Kalugal was probably blowing the problem out of proportion.

Turner was cautious, smart, and thorough. There was no way he hadn't considered all the ramifications.

Lokan had a feeling that Kalugal was plotting something, but he couldn't say so without causing a rift between them before they even had a chance to reconnect. Besides, he had no idea what Kalugal might be scheming. If he could only get him alone for a few moments, he might be able to coax it out of him, or at least get a sense of something.

On the face of it, Kalugal was too good to be true.

He claimed to have no aspirations for the island, he was much more accommodating than Kian, willing to make concessions in the name of cooperation that Kian was not. And he was winning everyone over with his charm and finesse.

"What I'm worried about is the safety of our locations," Turner said. "Kalugal's home is the most vulnerable. The keep has over a hundred residences that are occupied by humans, so I'm not worried about the director knowing that address. The village is invisible thanks to William's ingenuity, and no one can enter the tunnel without us knowing about it."

Maybe that was Kalugal's impetus for shutting down the paranormal program as soon as possible. Jacki was no longer emitting a signal, but her location had been marked.

"You'll have to move, buddy." Kian released a puff of smoke into the air. "Even if we get rid of Simmons, your address is noted somewhere in their database. It's not safe."

Kalugal waved a dismissive hand. "Why do you think I'm pressing so hard for corrupting their data? I like my house and my bunker. I don't want to move."

"You should consider relocating, at least temporarily, until we deal with the problem."

"I can deal with whoever they send." Kalugal leaned against the railing next to Kian. "Can I have one of those cigars you seem so fond of?"

"Cigarillos." Kian pulled out the pack and offered it to Kalugal. "My wife acquired them for me." He chuckled. "She didn't like the smell of cigarettes, so I tried to smoke cigars, but those take too long, and I don't have the patience for it."

Kalugal pulled one out and sniffed it. "It smells good."

Kian handed him the lighter. "The clan owns many hotels all over the world, and as you can imagine, occupancy is low right now. I'll gladly host you and your men until this is done." He took a puff and watched Kalugal light up his cigarillo. "In fact, our property in Hawaii is the perfect honeymoon spot. You and Jacki can take a couple of weeks off. Consider it my wedding gift to you." Kian took another puff. "And that includes your men as well."

Kalugal shook his head. "I'm not taking Jacki anywhere near other humans. Not while the virus is still spreading, and Jacki is still human. But after she transitions, I might take you up on your offer."

"Right." Kian tapped the small cigar. "I keep forgetting that she's not immortal yet. I also worry about Jin. She still hasn't transitioned."

"How long does it usually take?" Kalugal asked.

"It has been eight days since Arwel and Jin started working on her transition, and it usually takes no longer than two weeks. But the strep throat infection she had might have weakened her body, and we know from experience that transition doesn't start unless the body is in perfect condition."

"Then it's doubly crucial that I keep Jacki isolated from other humans. She could catch the flu or a cold and her transition would be delayed."

Kian cast Kalugal an empathetic smile. "You need to prepare yourself mentally for the possibility that she is not a Dormant."

"I'm aware of that. But as you've said, it seems like the Fates had something to do with Jacki and me finding each other. And that makes me hopeful."

"It's okay to hope, but you also need to prepare for disappointment. What will you do if she doesn't transition?"

"I'll keep her and enjoy my time with her for as long as she lives."

Kian's eyes were filled with sorrow. "I wish you all the happiness you can have, but I have to warn you. One day you will have to watch the woman you love die, and the pain of it is going to crush you."

"I know."

"Then you're a brave man."

Or one who was head over heels in love. Except, Kalugal didn't seem like the type. His brother was in perfect control of his emotions, and Lokan was sure that he wouldn't let himself fall for Jacki until she transitioned.

"Not at all," Kalugal said. "Letting Jacki go now is a much scarier prospect."

"You are only delaying the inevitable," Turner said. "Compared to your lifespan, hers will be gone in the blink of an eye."

"Perhaps. But I'm a young immortal, and I haven't lived for so long that the passage of time has lost all meaning to me. Fifty or sixty years still seem like a lot."

Jacki

"It fits perfectly." Amanda motioned for Jacki to turn in a circle.

Jacki turned and faked a smile, but her heart wasn't in it.

The dress was perfect, but after the bomb that Amanda had tossed at her feet, Jacki couldn't bring herself to care.

Amanda had made it sound as if sex was the ultimate compatibility test, and that marrying Kalugal before they formed a bond was a mistake.

None of the others had refuted Amanda's claim, which meant that it wasn't just her opinion but something everyone agreed upon.

Should she seduce Kalugal tonight?

It wouldn't be difficult, and Jacki didn't care that they were not married yet, but what difference would one night make?

The only one for whom it had happened the first time was Carol, and she was already an immortal and definitely not a virgin. From the other ladies' teasing, it was obvious that Carol had had a lot of experience in the sensual arts before meeting Lokan, and Amanda had been quite active herself.

Bridget had stayed out of it, reading news about the virus's spread on her phone, frowning and shaking her head, so it wasn't clear what her experience had been before meeting Turner.

"I brought you shoes." Amanda opened the suitcase and pulled out a pair with spiky heels at least four inches high. "We wear the same shoe size, and these are brand new. I bought them in several colors and haven't had the chance to wear the white ones yet."

"I don't think I can walk in those. I have white shoes with a comfortable heel."

"Don't be silly." Amanda put the pair on the floor. "Those are Louboutins. They are very comfortable despite the high heel."

Bracing with her hand on the dresser, Jacki stepped into one shoe and then the other. "I feel like a giraffe." She walked from one end of the room to the other. "They are pretty comfortable, but the wedding is outside in the yard. The heels will get stuck in the grass."

Amanda grimaced. "I hadn't thought of that. I'll have to sit this entire wedding out or wear flip flops, which I'm not going to do no matter what."

Syssi chuckled. "You can have Dalhu carry you around."

"I'll figure something out." She looked Jacki up and down. "I don't think any last-minute alterations are needed. You can take the dress off, and we will tackle your hair."

It was scary to let an amateur mess with it a day before the wedding, but the hotel's salon was closed because of the virus. They were lucky that the entire hotel hadn't shut down. But maybe the immortals had something to do with that, like thralling the management to keep it open.

After stripping out of the dress, Jacki handed it to Syssi, who put it back inside the garment bag it had arrived in.

"I have a question." Jacki pulled her slacks back on. "Do you think that I should seduce Kalugal tonight? Or should I wait one more day for after the wedding?"

Amanda smirked. "You can seduce him tonight, and tomorrow night, and every night after that. Why waste time?"

Pulling the blouse on, Jacki looked at Syssi. "What do you think?"

"I think that one night is not going to make a difference, and if you always wanted your first time to be with your husband, you shouldn't compromise. The bond is not likely to form after one time."

"I agree with Syssi," Callie said.

"Did you wait before you got married?" Jacki asked.

Callie snorted. "I was married before I met Brundar, and the only reason I got married in the first place was that I got pregnant." Callie's eyes saddened. "I lost the baby." She shook herself. "But that belongs in the past. Anyway, when I met Brundar, he played hard to get, and it took serious effort on my part to seduce him. We are not married yet, and I don't know if we ever will be, but we are mated for life, with or without a ceremony."

"The ceremony is not just for you," Syssi said. "It's so all the people you care about can join in your happiness for one evening. That's a lesson Kian taught me. When Annani pressed for a quick wedding, he was all for it while I was freaking out. Do you know how he convinced me?"

"I do," Amanda said. "But the others probably don't."

"He said that this would be the first wedding ceremony in the history of the clan and that it would signal a new beginning and renew hope for the future. The celebration was more for the clan than it was for us. We didn't need an official stamp of approval." She looked at Amanda pointedly. "It's about time that you and Dalhu celebrated your union in front of the entire clan too. It's especially important now that we have a bunch of immortal bachelors available for our clanswomen. Seeing you and Dalhu tie the knot in an official ceremony, with the goddess blessing your union, will send the message that it's okay to give the former Doomers a chance."

Amanda huffed out a breath. "Everyone knows that I'm mated to a former Doomer. I don't see why we need anything official."

"Dalhu hardly ever leaves his studio, and not many people know him. He is an enigma, and only your close friends know how much he adores you and how happy you are together." Syssi smiled. "What's the big deal? You are the queen of organizing fabulous parties. You could put together the most elaborate celebration the clan has ever known." She snapped her fingers. "Like that."

"Tonight and tomorrow are all about Jacki, and then we need to wait for the damn virus to be gone, and after that, we have to celebrate Kian's birthday. It will be a long time until I can even start thinking about a wedding party for Dalhu and me."

It seemed like the only married couple in Kian's party were Syssi and Kian, and the reason for that was more political than personal.

The more Jacki thought about it, the more convinced she became that there was no more reason to wait. She was going to seduce Kalugal tonight.

Jin

"I can't believe that the wedding is tomorrow." Jin wiped a hand over her sweaty forehead. "Are we driving or flying?"

Arwel pulled her on top of him and kissed her chin. "We can fly if you don't want to take the motorhome. Kian wants Yamanu to shroud the mansion and the drones flying overhead, so he and Mey are taking the clan's jet, and we can join them. But they are leaving early, so we will have to be at the airstrip at seven in the morning, and it's a two-hour drive to get there. If we take the motorhome, we can leave later, and we won't have to even change clothes. You can stay dressed in your birthday suit." He kissed her neck.

"I'd rather fly." Arwel was quite fond of the freaking motorhome, but Jin was sick of it. "Are we going to take this monster to the airstrip? Perhaps we can leave it for the Guardians and borrow Bowen's or Leon's car?"

"We can do that."

Jin rolled off Arwel's chest and snuggled up to his side. "I don't have anything nice to wear for the wedding. I only brought casual stuff with me."

"You can call Mey and ask her to bring you some of hers."

"Yeah, that's what I planned to do." She smiled. "I always borrow from her when I need something fancier. Why waste money on clothes that I'm not going to wear more than once, right?"

He turned to his side and wrapped her in his arms. "I love how practical you are. But now that you are my mate, you can buy whatever you want. I have loads of money saved up."

"That doesn't mean we should spend it on frivolous things. You can invest in *Tall and Fabulous*."

"Is that the name you and Mey have settled on?"

"For now. We are still tossing ideas around." Jin reached for her phone. "I need to call her before I forget."

"I'm going to hit the shower." Arwel slid out of bed.

"Are you going to shower in the cabin or here?"

"In the cabin. I don't want to deplete the hot water for you."

"Thank you."

The motorhome had sounded like a good idea in theory, but it wasn't as fun as she'd thought it would be. The water heater was tiny, the bed was uncomfortable, and Jin discovered that she was somewhat claustrophobic, and small spaces made her antsy.

Except, everything was annoying her lately, most likely because she wasn't transitioning. There was also the virus to worry about, and Vlad's mom bailing out on Richard had been an unexpected and upsetting setback.

The good news was that Wendy and Vlad seemed to be getting closer, and the best news was, of course, the wedding.

It still made her head spin to think that Jacki was actually marrying Kalugal. Jin wasn't sure whether she should be happy for her friend or worried.

Kalugal was larger than life, a freaking demigod, so it was no wonder that Jacki had fallen for him. But had he fallen for Jacki? Or did he want her only because she was a Dormant, and he could make immortal babies with her?

Jin sighed. The only thing she could do was hope that everything would turn out okay, and that the freaking Fates knew what they were doing when they'd put those two together.

Selecting Mey's number from her favorites list, Jin pushed up on the pillows and pulled the comforter up to her chin. The other thing she disliked about the motorhome was how cold it got inside.

"What's up, Jin?" Mey sounded breathless.

"Did I interrupt something?"

"Yeah, my belly dancing practice."

"Are you still at it? I thought you gave it up."

"I need some form of exercise, and Yamanu loves it when I dance for him."

"Aha. So it's a double whammy. You get a workout during and after."

"Precisely."

Jin laughed. "By the way, Arwel and I are joining you and Yamanu tomorrow on the flight to San Francisco."

"That's awesome. I thought you were taking the motorhome."

"We were, until I heard that you are flying over there. I need you to do me a favor. I don't have anything nice to wear. Can you bring me something? And shoes too?"

"Didn't Jacki tell you? The bridesmaids are going to wear saris."

"She must have forgotten. But why saris? Kalugal is not Indian, and neither is Jacki."

"They are from Eva's wedding, and since saris don't need to be fitted, they are a good solution when there is no time to prepare."

"Yeah, but it's freaking cold. We are going to freeze in them."

"I'll bring you pantyhose and a long-sleeved shirt to wear under it."

"Can you also bring me a nice dress? Just in case I don't like the sari."

"I can do that."

"And a cardigan to put over it."

"You sound like you are cold."

"I am. The damn motorhome is not well insulated, and it's cold up here."

"Why don't you turn the heater on?"

"Because it smells iffy in here when we do, and then it gets too hot when Arwel and I get busy under the covers. I'm so ready to sleep in a comfortable bed in a nice hotel room."

"Are you excited about the wedding?"

"I am. But I'm also worried. What if Kalugal is marrying Jacki only because she can give him immortal children?"

"Yeah, the thought has crossed my mind once or twice. Jacki is beautiful, and I like her as a person, but I can't see her with someone like Kalugal. You said that he was a stuck-up snob, and she is so down to earth."

"Maybe that's the attraction." Jin shifted to a more comfortable position. "Their differences make them interesting to each other."

Mey sighed. "For now, when everything is still new and exciting. But what happens a year from now when they realize that they have nothing in common?"

"Who knows? Maybe they do. We will find out more tomorrow."

Jacki

When they got home, Kalugal escorted Jacki upstairs, kissed her cheek, and handed her the garment bag with the dress and the other bag with the shoes. "I need to check on a few things, but it won't take more than an hour. After I'm done, would you like to meet me in the library for a cup of coffee or a drink?"

Amanda's words still reverberating through Jacki's brain, she swallowed to moisten her dry throat. "I would love to. But maybe we can do that in the master's sitting area instead?"

Kalugal smiled like a Cheshire Cat. "Of course. I'll come to get you when I'm done." He kissed her cheek again, opened the door to her room for her, and closed it behind her.

Letting out a breath, Jacki walked over to the bed, draped the wedding dress across it and sat down.

What should she do?

Should she wear the sexy nightgown and robe he'd bought for her? Let the robe part so the outline of her nude body would overpower Kalugal's self-restraint?

Or should she just wait until tomorrow night like they had both agreed to do?

Except, now that Amanda had planted the seed of doubt in her mind, Jacki would be stressing over it throughout the ceremony and wouldn't be able to enjoy herself.

What if they weren't sexually compatible?

What if that elusive bond would never form between them?

Damn.

She had an amazing wedding dress, a brand new hairdo that looked awesome on her, and instead of floating in a bubble of excited happiness, she was anxious and worried.

Did that happen to all brides to be?

A wedding was a happy event, but it was also stressful, and she probably wasn't the only one freaking out and questioning her decision. Except, she was probably the only bride aside from the deeply religious ones who was stressing about sex because she was still a virgin.

Jacki got up, opened the doors to the balcony, and stepped outside. As she lifted her face to the sky, hoping for a shooting star to give her a sign, the crisp night air was a welcome reprieve on her heated skin.

Perhaps instead of agonizing over whether she should make love with Kalugal tonight or wait, she should start working on her pledge to him. The few attempts she'd made so far had ended up in the bin, and she was running out of time.

What should she say?

If she went with what was in her heart, she would say that Kalugal was changing before her eyes. He seemed happier, more hopeful for the future. He was blossoming, but men didn't like being compared to flowers.

It wasn't manly enough.

Maybe she could say that she was happier and more hopeful than she'd ever dared to be? But that had been true before Amanda had scared her with her talk about bonds and compatibility.

With anxiety dampening her excitement, Jacki's happiness had dimmed together with her hopefulness, and the right words eluded her.

Perhaps instead of reinventing the wheel, she could just go with the traditional words.

I, Jacki, take you, Kalugal, to be my wedded husband, and I promise in front of God and these witnesses to have and to hold you from this day forward, for better, for worse, for richer, for poorer, in joy and in sorrow, in sickness and in health, until death do us part. I will love, cherish, and honor you all the days of my life.

She could take out the part about sickness and health and be done with it. The traditional vow was probably better than anything she could come up with.

Maybe she should take out God as their witness too?

Jacki didn't follow any particular religion, and Kalugal was probably an atheist. Back home, his people worshiped their murderous ancestor, but he obviously didn't, and following his example, his men probably didn't either.

Was there anything she could add? Or would that do?

For a moment, she contemplated emailing Jin and asking for her help, but she then discarded the idea. If she was about to use someone else's words in her vows, she might as well use those that had withstood the test of time.

With that major source of stress eliminated, Jacki returned to the other one.

To seduce Kalugal tonight, or to wait until after the ceremony?

Lifting her face to the sky, she searched for a sign, but when no shooting star appeared, she looked down at the backyard and imagined it set up for the party.

Would there be music?

Right now, all she heard were the sounds of crickets and a muted television show from one of the neighbors' houses.

When an owl hooted and was answered by another, Jacki wondered if that could be the sign she'd been waiting for. But were owls considered a good or bad omen?

Damn. This was so stupid. What the hell was she doing standing out on the balcony and waiting for a sign?

That wasn't like her. Usually, Jacki was much more decisive.

The root of the problem was that she was scared and didn't want to admit it even to herself. A twenty-two-year-old should not be afraid of making love with her future husband for the first time, she should be eager for it.

Kalugal

After trying on the wedding dress and getting a beautiful new hairdo, Jacki should have been excited. Instead, she seemed perturbed.

Kalugal berated himself for joining the men on the terrace instead of staying in the living room and eavesdropping on the ladies' conversation in the bedroom.

Someone must have said something to Jacki that had upset her.

But what?

Had Kian sent his sister to try to talk Jacki out of going through with the ceremony?

That was a ridiculous thought.

Kian had been surprisingly supportive of their decision to get married, and his cousin was not a good enough actor to fake it.

His sister, on the other hand, was star material, and not only because she was gorgeous. Amanda had an innate dramatic flair, and he had taken an immediate liking to her.

He could see a lot of himself in Kian's sister. She was extroverted, confident, stylish, and had a good sense of humor. And on top of that, she was also a professor of neuroscience.

Quite impressive.

What Kalugal found odd, though, was that the goddess's daughter had given Jacki a haircut and even styled it for her. How had she even learned to do that?

Apparently, Amanda had many talents.

If he hadn't met Jacki first, and if Amanda was single, he would have courted her like there was no tomorrow. Not only was she perfect in every regard, but their union could have also united their people.

But the Fates had different plans, and now that he had Jacki, he wouldn't trade her even for Annani's daughter.

Besides, they were cousins, so there was that.

Maybe that was what had upset Jacki? Perhaps the same kind of thoughts had gone through her head?

It made sense. He still remembered Jacki's freak-out when she found out that his mother was a goddess.

And Jacki had described herself on several occasions as a nobody.

Besides, Amanda was so over the top in everything that she could intimidate a queen, let alone a girl who grew up in foster homes and had no higher education. She might have inadvertently made Jacki feel inferior.

As he headed upstairs, Kalugal resolved to pay Jacki numerous compliments to shore up her confidence.

Knocking on her door, he waited patiently until she opened up.

"Hello, gorgeous." He pulled her into his arms and dipped his nose into her hair. "You smell absolutely fantastic."

She tilted her head up and frowned. "It's the perfume you got for me, and I've been using it every day."

"It must be the shampoo then." He wrapped his arm around her waist and led her to the master bedroom's sitting area.

Shamash had already brewed coffee, and a tray with cookies, fruit, and nuts waited for them on the table.

It wasn't a romantic setup, but it was cozy.

For tomorrow, he would have to come up with something more exciting. Perhaps he should scatter flower petals all over? Or light scented candles? And he definitely planned to put on soft classical music to enhance the romantic atmosphere.

The preparations would have to be delegated to Shamash, so everything would be ready for their first night together.

"What's that smirk about?" Jacki asked.

He hadn't been aware of smiling. "I'm just happy." He took her hand and kissed the back of it. "Tomorrow, you will be my wife, or mate. Which term do you prefer?"

"I like mate because it's gender-neutral."

He smiled again. "I guess it's more politically correct than the terms husband and wife, but it doesn't work well in a ceremony. If we had someone officiate over our wedding, he or she would have said, I pronounce you as mates. You may now kiss the mate."

Jacki chuckled. "It sounds funny. I think 'you may kiss the bride' should stay."

Kalugal pulled her closer against his side. "If it pleases you, I can ask Kian to officiate."

"No, I like the idea of us pledging ourselves to each other." She looked down at her engagement ring. "That's what's important, right? The promise we make to each other."

He'd managed to lift her mood for a few moments, but now her anxiety spiked again.

"What troubles you, my Jacqueline?"

She smiled. "Is it so obvious?"

"To me, it is. Has someone said something to upset you? Talk to me."

Taking in a deep breath, she looked him in the eyes. "I don't want to wait until tomorrow."

As his shaft sprang to attention, Kalugal opened his mouth to respond, but Jacki wasn't done.

Squeezing his hand, she smiled excitedly, and the cloud that had been hanging over her head dissipated, turning into a halo of sunshine. "Let's pledge ourselves to each other right now, just you and I." She turned her face heavenward. "With fate or God or whatever higher power brought us together as our witness."

Jacki

As the words left Jacki's mouth, a sense of rightness enveloped her.

Her and Kalugal's union was first and foremost a covenant between them. She might have needed the reassurance of having witnesses a few days ago, but that was no longer the case.

Kalugal loved her, she felt it with every fiber of her being, but it was time for both of them to stop playing chicken and lay it all out.

Except, her man, who was usually so eloquent, seemed lost for words and looked like he needed help to breathe.

Jacki squeezed his hand. "Did I shock you?"

He shook his head. "I don't have my pledge ready." He looked in the direction of the bedroom. "I have nothing ready. I wanted to make it perfect for you, with flower petals, and wine, scented candles, and soft music."

Jacki smiled. It seemed that Kalugal had been anxious as well, and he'd put a lot of thought into planning the perfect wedding night for her.

This was just as much uncharted territory for him as it was for her, and thinking about preparations had eased the weight of expectations that by now had reached monumental proportions.

It was kind of funny that she'd had the guts to say that she was ready, but the great Kalugal didn't have the guts to admit that he wasn't.

"If you want to wait until tomorrow, that's fine. You made all those beautiful plans, and I don't want to short-change them because suddenly I don't feel like waiting anymore."

With the glow in his eyes telling a different story than the excuses he'd just given her, Jacki had a feeling that her proposal was about to get accepted.

"What prompted this?"

"A gut feeling."

He lifted a brow.

"All right." Jacki let out a breath. They were supposed to lay it all out. "So, Amanda said something about a bond between immortals that can only form when they become intimate with one another. But the bond doesn't happen for everyone, only for those fated to be together. And I got scared that maybe it's not going to happen for us, and then I thought that we need to be brave and just admit that we love each other and that this is it for both of us, and that we don't need witnesses to validate how we feel about each other." She sucked in a breath. "Sorry. I always talk too fast when I'm nervous."

Kalugal smiled. "I love you." Wrapping his arms around her, he lifted her onto his lap. "Tell me that you love me."

"I love you."

"Now, kiss me."

Smashing her lips over Kalugal's and winding her arms around his neck at the same time, Jacki plastered herself to him and held on tight.

When she came up for a breath, she pulled back a little and looked into his eyes. "I'm never letting you go. You are mine."

"And you are mine, and I'm never letting go of you. That will do as far as our pledges to one another. We can embellish on them tomorrow." Holding on to her, he pushed to his feet and started walking toward his bedroom.

Correction, their bedroom.

The bed was only thirty feet or so away, but it was enough time for Jacki to pepper Kalugal's face and neck with soft kisses. "I love your smell." She buried her face in the crook of his neck. "Not the cologne, but the natural smell of your skin. I can lick you all over."

The glow in his eyes intensified, and his fangs elongated. "Careful, my love. I'm in no state for teasing. Your best defense is to appear virginal and a little scared."

She chuckled nervously. "I don't need to try too hard. This is precisely how I feel."

Somehow, he managed to hold her up with one arm while flinging the comforter off with the other, and then he laid her down gently on the bed.

When she reached for him, he gripped her wrists, pulled her arms over her head, and then let go.

Jacki stayed exactly as he'd positioned her. She knew what he wanted, and why he wanted it like that, and she was fine with that.

Sitting on the bed beside her, Kalugal looked at her with glowing, predatory eyes, his fangs protruding slightly over his lower lip.

But she wasn't scared.

Kalugal was a predator, his cultured and sophisticated veneer skin deep. The only way he could summon the patience and softness she needed for her maiden voyage was if she offered him her complete submission.

Not a problem.

That was precisely what she craved.

Kalugal

The trust in Jacki's eyes was as precious to Kalugal as her declaration of love, and it coated his iron-clad determination with an added layer of graphene.

Even if it killed him, he was going to give her a maiden voyage that was all about pleasure and not an ounce of pain.

But Kalugal wasn't deluding himself. It would be extremely difficult to stifle his urges and give Jacki the tenderness and the attention she deserved.

The last time he'd been with a woman was the night Jin and Jacki had made their first attempt at tethering him, and that had been weeks ago. Making love to a virgin after the longest dry spell of his adult life was asking for trouble, but it wasn't as if he could have done anything about it. Regrettably, masturbation was not a viable solution for an immortal male, and slaking his need with another woman had been out of the question as well.

Perhaps that should have clued him in that he was in love with Jacki long before she'd coaxed the truth out of him.

As much as Kalugal had tried to keep his heart out of it until Jacki transitioned, he'd failed, and he'd been fooling himself for days.

He was in love with her.

"I love you." He encircled one slender ankle with his palm, lifted her foot, and took her shoe off, then did the same with the other.

Lowering himself by her side, he wrapped his arm around her middle and turned her toward him.

Despite her trusting expression, Jacki's muscles felt tensed, and her body was stiff in his arms.

"You are so beautiful, my Jacqueline."

Holding her gently, he kissed her slowly, softly, and as his tongue penetrated her mouth, Jacki moaned, and her body softened in his arms.

Pulling the blouse out of her pants, he slid his hand under the soft fabric and put it on her quivering belly. "Are you scared?"

"A little." She chuckled nervously. "Your fangs are really long."

So that was the problem. She trusted him but feared his fangs.

"I promise that they will bring you only pleasure." He slid his hand upward and cupped one bra-covered breast.

"Oh, God." Jacki arched up.

He chuckled. "Yes?"

That brought a smile to her face. "Why does your hand on my breast feel so much better than mine?"

"No one has ever touched you here?" He circled his thumb around her nipple.

Her smile wilted. "Not like this."

A growl started low in his throat. "Tell me who was the bastard that groped you, and I'll tear him apart with my bare fangs."

"Please, I don't want to think about anything other than you and me, right here, right now."

Jacki was right. The last thing he needed was to add aggression to his lust. This was about her and her pleasure and nothing else.

Starting on the blouse's bottom button, Kalugal concentrated on slowly opening one at a time and kissing every inch of skin he exposed. By the time he reached the top one, he was back in full control of himself.

But as the silk parted, sliding down to the sides and exposing Jacki's bra-covered breasts, that control wavered again.

"Gorgeous." He dipped his head and kissed her nipple through the sheer fabric of her bra. Resisting the urge to suckle and lick, he moved to the other one and kissed it softly as well. "Let's get rid of this?"

As Jacki nodded and lifted her back, he removed her blouse, opened the bra clasp, and then slid the shoulder straps down her arms.

After tossing both garments on the floor, he leaned back and gazed at her beautiful breasts. Her pink nipples were so erect that he knew they must be aching, waiting for his lips and tongue to provide them with relief.

"Perfection."

Damn. Taking it slow was going to be the most challenging thing he'd ever done, but he was determined to succeed. Rubbing his hand over his mouth, Kalugal cleared a drop of venom from his lips.

Jacki's eyes were glazed with passion, her panting breaths the best invitation to give her more.

Lowering his head slowly, deliberately, he circled one turgid nipple with his lips and suckled. As Jacki gasped and arched up, he laid his arm across her chest to hold her down and kept suckling, flicking his tongue gently over the heated point and teasing more sexy moans out of her.

She didn't sound or act like any of the other women he'd been with. There were innocence and wonder in her eyes, in her soft, throaty moans, and in the way she moved.

Through Jacki, Kalugal got to experience the marvel of discovery as if it was his first time as well.

Moving to her other breast, he drew her nipple into his hot mouth, but he didn't neglect the one he'd just left, cupping, plumping, and thumbing the wet, turgid peak.

Jacki

The sensations bombarding Jacki's body were making her delirious.

Was sex like that for everyone?

If it was, then no wonder people were so obsessed with it. But Jacki suspected that it wouldn't have been nearly as intense with anyone other than Kalugal.

After all, she'd experimented with self-pleasuring. She'd cupped her own breasts, tweaked her own nipples, and massaged that little bundle of nerves at the apex of her feminine center. But although the sensations had been pleasant, they had been a weak echo of what Kalugal was doing to her body.

She was on fire, and the more he sucked and licked and even gently pinched, the more she craved. Her core tightened, frustrated that it had nothing to clutch around, and that little bundle of nerves pulsated and throbbed urgently, seeking relief in any sort of friction she could provide it.

Tilting her hips, Jacki rubbed against the leg he'd draped over her to hold her in place, but the angle was wrong and the relief only marginal.

As Kalugal released her nipple, Jacki mourned the loss of the wet heat of his mouth, but he quickly replaced it with his other hand, cupping both breasts, and started a line of tender kisses and small licks down her belly.

Except, when he reached a barrier, he let go of her breasts, rose onto his knees, and pulled her pants down her legs.

The predatory fanged smile he flashed her was both charming as hell and a little scary. He looked like a tiger eyeing a tasty treat a moment before devouring it.

"Oh, my beautiful Jacqueline, how absolutely perfect you are."

Still fully dressed, Kalugal hooked his thumbs in her panties and dragged them slowly down her hips, leaving her completely bare for him.

If not for the hungry look in his eyes, Jacki would have felt shy, but the approval in his words and his expression made her feel beautiful, sexy, and desired.

God, she wanted him so much.

Tossing her panties to the floor, Kalugal bent forward and dipped his head between her spread thighs, so his mouth was aligned with her mound. For a long moment, he just stared, and Jacki fought the urge to close her legs.

But then he kissed the very top, so softly and gently that if she weren't so aroused, she probably wouldn't have felt it, and then he lifted his head to look at her as if asking permission to continue.

Priceless.

Jacki knew what Kalugal was about to do and why, and she loved him all the more for it. He was being so selfless, thinking only of her pleasure and denying himself for as long as he could.

The restraint required would have tested the self-control of any male, let alone an immortal with a ferocious sex appetite who she knew for a fact hadn't slaked it with anyone for a very long time.

Jacki nodded.

With a sabretooth smile, he parted her wet folds with his thumbs and pressed his tongue against her throbbing clitoris.

Crying out, she arched into his mouth.

With a groan, he slid his hands under her buttocks and lifted her, opening her up for his expert ministrations.

Using just the very tip of his tongue, he probed her entrance with gentle flicks that were designed to accustom her to the sensation rather than penetrate, but Jacki wished that he would hurry up and relieve the aching emptiness inside her.

Instead, that talented tongue of his slid up through her folds, flicked at her clit, once, twice, and then his lips encircled the little nub, and he sucked.

Jacki cried out, and if not for Kalugal's tight grip on her butt cheeks, she would have surged up like a rocket.

His fingers digging into the soft flesh, he held on and suckled rhythmically, causing her core to clench with each gentle tug.

The orgasm building up inside of her was gaining momentum with every pull of his lips, and Jacki was desperate for it to reach its culmination.

Except, too many of her self-pleasuring attempts had reached this point only to fizzle out and never peak.

This time was going to be different, though. Kalugal played her body as if it was a musical instrument that he had complete mastery over.

His lips still encircling the most sensitive spot on her body, he lowered her bottom to the bed and pulled his hands out. Parting her folds with his fingers, he gently penetrated her with just a tip of his pointer.

"More," she groaned impatiently.

He lifted his head. "Patience, my Jacqueline. You are very tight."

Reluctantly, she nodded.

Dipping back down, he replaced the finger with his tongue, pushing the tip inside as far as it would go, which wasn't far at all.

He withdrew and thrust again, and this time it went a tiny bit deeper.

Reaching with his hands, he palmed her breasts, adding to the barrage of sensations already scrambling her brain.

Her hips gyrating, her throat emitting sounds she hadn't known she was capable of, Jacki should have been embarrassed by the display of wantonness, but she was beyond caring.

Hovering at the precipice, she was missing the final push that would catapult her over it.

As if reading her mind, Kalugal thrust his tongue inside her and at the same time pinched her nipples.

Lights exploding behind her closed lids, the orgasm tore through her like a class F5 tornado, the whirlwind and physical and emotional sensations catapulting her onto a euphoric cloud.

Kalugal

As Jacki soared on orgasmic wings, Kalugal slid up her body and held her tightly against his chest, thanking the Fates or whatever higher power that had brought this about.

Jacki's climax was magnificent, and the only reason Kalugal hadn't exploded in his pants or bitten her inner thigh was his huge ego. He was a conceited son-of-a-gun who prided himself on his extraordinary self-control.

Under similar circumstances, Kalugal had no doubt that no other immortal male could have exercised such incredible restraint.

The truth was that he'd almost bitten Jacki, not because he needed the release, but because it would have saved her the pain of losing her virginity.

The problem was that she would have been out of it and would have missed the experience when he joined them. If it were him, Kalugal would have preferred to suffer through a few moments of pain rather than miss out on that.

Except, he refused to accept that even a small amount of pain was necessary. He would do everything in his power so there was none even without the help of venom.

With a contented sigh, Jacki opened her eyes and wrapped her arms around him. "This was just, wow. I have no words." She kissed his chest over his shirt. "Why are you still dressed?"

Kalugal chuckled. "Indeed."

For the first time, he didn't throttle his immortal speed as he got rid of his clothes in front of a woman. And the liberty to do so added unexpected satisfaction to what was already the best night of his life.

The speed had another advantage. He'd gotten naked and on top of Jacki before she had a chance to get a glimpse of his shaft. He wasn't enormous, but to a virgin, even an average-sized member might seem so, and he wasn't average.

Jacki parted her legs to cradle him between them and wound her arms around his neck. "I love you."

Cupping her cheeks, he pressed a soft kiss to her lips. "I love you too. If at any moment it becomes too much, tell me, and I'll pull out."

The only other virgin he'd been with was Eva, and she'd gritted her teeth through the pain, urging him to continue. He hadn't enjoyed that and was adamant about providing Jacki with a much better experience.

Positioning himself, he pushed just the very tip past her tight entrance and stopped when she cringed. "There is no rush, love. I'll wait as long as it takes."

It was going to kill him, but at least he would die knowing that he hadn't hurt the woman he loved.

When she relaxed under him, he kissed her again, careful with his fangs. "Are you okay?"

"Yes." She touched his cheek. "The glow from your eyes is so beautiful." She arched up and kissed him lightly. "You are magnificent."

"And so are you." He retreated and pushed a little deeper. "Okay?"

Jacki nodded. "More."

Even though she was still drenched from her orgasm, he wanted her even wetter. Reaching between their bodies, he pressed his thumb to her clitoris and rubbed gently.

Jacki rolled her hips, impaling herself another inch on his shaft.

Retreating, he kissed her and then pushed a little deeper. When she didn't cringe, he did it again, and again, until he was two-thirds in.

Kalugal lifted his head and looked into Jacki's passion-glazed eyes. "Okay?"

"Never been better." Her hands tightened on his buttocks, and she arched up.

As he surged the rest of the way in, they both groaned.

He hadn't felt her hymen tear, or even stretch, but she was very tight, which must be uncomfortable if not painful.

Except, Jacki didn't grimace, or cringe. Her expression was full of wonder, gratitude, and adoration.

For him.

This was the best reward Kalugal could've ever hoped for.

The restraint he'd forced upon himself had stretched his willpower to the utmost limit, but it hadn't been wasted. It seemed that Jacki had experienced almost no pain.

"I love you," he whispered before kissing her softly.

For a long moment, he stayed still, waiting for Jacki's sheath to stretch until it could accommodate his shaft comfortably.

She started moving first, rolling her hips and spurring him on, making it obvious that he no longer needed to ask whether she was okay.

Looking into her eyes, he retreated and then slid back in, and when she rolled her hips again, he knew he could finally slacken the tight leash he'd wrapped around himself.

Not by much, though.

Jacki was still an untried human, and he was too strong and too hungry to let go.

Swiveling his hips, Kalugal plunged back inside her, retreated, and plunged again, but he wasn't going nearly as fast or as hard as he would have if Jacki were an immortal.

He didn't mind. Soon, she would become one, and they would have the rest of their lives to make love immortal style.

Fates willing.

Jacki

If Jacki wasn't immune, she would have thought that Kalugal had used his mental tricks on her to minimize her pain.

Heck, there had been none.

She'd experienced a moment of discomfort as her sheath stretched to accommodate his girth, but he'd been so patient with her, so thoughtful, that in no time, she felt nothing but intense pleasure.

But it was more than that.

To be fully joined with the man she loved felt incredible. The intimacy, the sense of being one with another and no longer alone.

It was pure magic

Was that the bond Amanda had been talking about?

It sure felt like it.

Looking into Kalugal's glowing eyes, Jacki was suffused with love and adoration for the incredible man who had chosen her to be his life partner.

Not a man. A demigod.

Except, Kalugal's godly genealogy had little to do with how she felt about him. Her love for him had flamed into an inferno because of the way he was with her.

She'd expected desire, but what she'd gotten was so much more. Jacki felt cherished, loved, and adored by this incredible man. It was all in his eyes and the way he touched her.

Looking up into Kalugal's handsome face, she found him beautiful and charming, even with the huge fangs that were protruding over his lush, lower lip.

And the way he filled her was just perfect. They were made for each other.

Arching up, she whispered, "More," but what she actually meant was faster and harder.

He was still holding back, sweat dripping from his forehead, and every muscle of his incredible body straining with the effort to go slow.

As much as Jacki appreciated Kalugal's sacrifice, she didn't want their first time to be all about her. She wanted him to remember it not as the pinnacle of his self-control, but as the first time that he'd made love to his eternal mate.

God willing, this was an amazing start to the rest of their lives together.

"I'm in no rush." He pulled nearly all the way out and then slowly pushed back in. "This is our one and only first time, and I want it to last."

Jacki wanted that as well, but the fire raging inside her demanded a culmination.

Wrapping her legs around his thighs, she pushed her heels into his ass cheeks and arched up, spurring him on.

"Naughty girl." He gripped her hands and brought them over her head. "You want more?"

"Please."

His hands pinning hers to the mattress, he pulled back and plunged in deep, then withdrew and immediately surged in again. The tempo and force were no longer gentle, but they weren't brutal either. Kalugal was giving her what she wanted and yet still holding back.

The man was incredible.

Jacki was awed by his willpower, but even he couldn't last like that indefinitely.

As a powerful climax washed over her, her core contracting around his pistoning shaft, Kalugal threw his head back and roared.

Feeling his hot seed jetting into her, Jacki instinctively spread her legs even wider and tilted her head to the side, exposing her neck.

It was the ultimate display of surrender, and it had been fully earned. Kalugal had conquered her, body, heart, and soul, and there was nothing she wanted more than to belong to him from this day forward.

Closing her eyes tightly, she waited apprehensively for his fangs to pierce her skin, but she should have known by now that Kalugal would keep his promise.

Even as far gone as he was, he kissed and licked the spot in preparation, and when his fangs penetrated her neck, it felt more like pressure than pain.

A moment later, another climax rocked her body, and the world as she knew it disintegrated. Euphoria suffusing her, Jacki soared on a cloud, drifting to a place where angels sang, and countless rainbows intersected to form magnificent ethereal cities.

Was she dead?

Was this heaven?

Kalugal

His arms wrapped around his mate, Kalugal shifted them both to their sides. For a long moment, he just stared at Jacki's blissful expression.

Impossibly, she was even more beautiful like that. Gone were the subtle lines of worry that had creased her forehead, and her flushed cheeks were the most adorable shade of peach. He kissed one softly and then the other, but Jacki didn't even flutter her eyelashes.

She was out, and from experience, he knew that it might take a few hours until she floated down from the euphoric cloud.

By the looks of her, Jacki's excursion to the fantasy realms was most pleasant, and even though Kalugal wanted her to come back to him, he didn't want to shorten her stay in there. He hadn't experienced it himself, but his past partners had reported that it was the closest a person could get to checking out what heaven was like without dying.

Regretfully, he'd had to erase those wonderful memories from their minds, but not anymore. Jacki would not only keep hers, but she would also share with him her impressions from many more heavenly visits.

Carefully sliding out, he shifted his legs over the side of the bed and padded to the bathroom.

After giving himself a quick wash in the sink, he wetted several washcloths with warm water, wrung them out, and brought them back to the bedroom.

Kalugal found Jacki in the same position he'd left her, with the same angelic expression spread over her beautiful face.

Cleaning her and the mess they'd made as best he could, he tossed the used washcloths on the floor and got back in bed.

From now on, he would never sleep alone again, and the room Jacki had occupied would be turned back into an office for her to administer the new charity he'd put her in charge of.

Or better yet, he could move things around in his downstairs office and make room for another desk for Jacki. That way, he could look at his beautiful wife all day long as they worked side by side.

That was his own version of heaven. Forget about rainbows and cotton-candy clouds. Having Jacki with him twenty-four-seven was it for Kalugal.

He would find another use for the upstairs office, like a nursery. It was way too premature to be thinking about children, but a guy could hope.

Except, this location wasn't safe enough to raise his children in. As long as he was home, the government could send whoever they wanted, and he would deal with them. But he wasn't going to always be there, and that was unsafe for Jacki.

Eventually, he would have to go out to meetings, and he also had no intention of giving up his archeological digs just because the government was sniffing around his home. Naturally, he would take Jacki with him on his trips abroad, but once they were blessed with a child, he would have to halt those until he or she was old enough to transition. He wouldn't risk a trip with a kid that was still a fragile human.

Bottom line, as much as he loved his house and his bunker, he would have to move to keep Jacki and their future children safe.

Where to, though?

Kian's village seemed like the perfect place to raise their children. They would be safe, enjoy the company of other kids like them, and he could even take Jacki on trips and leave the children behind with friends to watch over them.

Except, Kalugal didn't want to give up his independence or his plans for taking over the world.

There were so many things that needed fixing, and he was the only one who was capable of doing that. Regrettably, on their own, and even with the best of guidance, humans would never achieve the utopia he envisioned for them.

It just wasn't in their nature.

Besides, the village was not the answer because Kian was not about to invite him and his men into his community.

He had to find another solution.

Once Jacki transitioned, her immortal body would expel the invisible signal emitting tracer, so that would no longer be a problem.

Perhaps he should start looking for a new home in Hillsborough. It wasn't rated as highly as Atherton, but it was still a very nice neighborhood. He could find a large house, expand it so there were enough rooms for his men, and build a new bunker.

Or even better, he could build a brand new house that would have two separate wings. A family wing for him and Jacki and their future children, and a separate one for his men.

With various layouts for a future mansion swirling around in his head, Kalugal drifted off with a smile on his face and a heart full of hope.

Director Simmons

Elijah Roberts struggled with the safety belt as he tried to fit it under his large belly. "We are both batshit crazy for doing this." He finally snapped it closed and leaned back in his seat. "We have no recon, and we are going in blind with guns blazing, or in our case, long-range acoustic device blasting."

Director Simmons smiled at his old friend. "Who said that we don't have recon? I sent my guy to snoop around the mansion again."

"I thought that he was compromised."

"I told him to use a different car, and I had to give him the address again. He kept insisting that I had it wrong and that the signal was coming from another location. They really did a good job on him. I would love to put my hands on their compeller. With two of them, we can double our recruiting efforts."

Elijah waved a dismissive hand. "Most of the stuff the bots pick up is crap. We barely have enough good leads for Marisol, aka Eleanor, aka Gina." He huffed out a breath. "At my age, it's hard to keep track of all her names."

"How about you just call her the recruiter. That's easy to remember."

"I think I'll do that." Elijah shifted in the seat and tugged on the belt, trying to loosen it. "Did you notice that they make everything for young people? Like these damn safety belts. Or like the small print on labels that I can't read without a magnifying glass. Old people are discriminated against."

Simmons chuckled. "They think that we are obsolete, but we are going to show them that we are not. These two old men are still kicking ass."

Roberts didn't seem to concur. "So what did your guy report?"

"We are very lucky, my friend. Apparently, they are planning a big party at the house. He saw a delivery truck arrive with tables and chairs and carts full of serve ware."

Elijah frowned. "They are violating the quarantine."

"Precisely. Which gives us the perfect excuse to come knocking on their gates. On top of that, they are setting it up in the backyard, which will make our job much easier. I'm telling you, this is fate at work. Not only are we going to get all of the runaways back, we will also bring in a large crop of other paranormal talents."

"What makes you think that the invited guests are all paranormals?"

"Who else could be organizing a party at a time like this? I bet that the entire independent organization of paranormal talents will be there. But that's not a problem. Once we activate the LRAD, they will all drop like flies no matter what talents they possess or how strong those talents are. Their eardrums are still the same as everyone else's."

Elijah grinned. "We will just swoop in and pick them up off the ground. How many men is your guy bringing with him?"

Simmons sighed. "Only eight, ex-Marines from his old unit. That's the best he could do. But they will arrive with seven vans, and each van can seat eleven people. My guy counted sixty chairs, so that should be enough to get all the talents out. I don't want to leave anyone behind."

"And what then? This plane isn't big enough for so many. We originally estimated that there were no more than twenty people at that house."

"I know, but once I heard the news, I knew that it's a golden opportunity, and it was too late to get another plane. I'll pay the men to drive the cargo home." He patted his leather briefcase. "I printed documents to cover their asses if they happen to get stopped on the way. The story is that they are collecting deserters."

Elijah shook his head. "You should have called me as soon as you knew. We will need to drug the talents to keep them from yelling murder, and I didn't bring enough with me. Also, we will have to ride back with them. I don't want to risk any of the talents dying of overdose."

"Don't worry." Simmons patted his friend's arm. "I got it covered. I brought enough to knock out a herd of elephants."

JACKI & KALUGAL'S STORY CULMINATES
The Children of the Gods Book 40
Dark Overlord's Clan

Turn the page to read the excerpt—>

Join the VIP Club
To find out what's included in your free membership, flip to the last page.

Dark Overlord's Clan

As Jacki and Kalugal prepare to celebrate their union, Kian takes every precaution to safeguard his people. Except, Kalugal and his men are not his only potential adversaries, and compulsion is not the only power he should fear.

Kalugal

Kalugal opened his eyes and glanced at the brightening sky through the bedroom's open window. The rising sun was painting the dark blue canvas with pink and orange hues, blending them into soft peaches and purples. The sight was magnificent to behold, but its beauty paled in comparison to the one sleeping peacefully next to him.

Jacki.

His mate.

His love.

His life.

With her arm draped over his middle, her leg thrown over his thighs, and her nose buried in the crook of his neck, Jacki had claimed him as hers, and he couldn't be happier about it.

His heart overflowing with gratitude and love, Kalugal caressed her back and leaned to kiss her forehead.

Precious.

He hadn't expected the connection to be so strong. Love had always seemed like a soft emotion to him, but the power of that softness was nearly overwhelming.

The metaphysical sphere that contained who he was had grown, and Jacki had become an integral part of it. Kalugal's self-definition had changed. He was no longer an individual but a part of a greater whole.

Except, he hadn't lost any of himself in the process. He'd gained a new dimension of feeling, of thinking, of being.

Was that how his mother felt about his father?

No wonder Areana stayed with Navuh. She loved him despite who he was and what he did. Perhaps she didn't know the full extent of his evil deeds, but she must be aware of at least some of it. If what Areana felt toward his father was as strong as what Kalugal was feeling towards Jacki, then leaving Navuh was simply impossible.

Was that the powerful bond between immortal mates that Kian and Amanda had been talking about?

But how could it have already formed? Jacki was still human, and it wasn't supposed to happen so fast.

Or was it just the beginning, and the bond hadn't even reached its full strength yet?

How much stronger could it possibly get?

Already, Kalugal couldn't fathom one hour without Jacki, let alone his life without her.

Leaning, he nuzzled her lush hair and inhaled deeply. Her scent was intoxicating, and it wasn't the perfume he'd bought for her or the shampoo she used, it was just her.

His woman.

With a sigh, Kalugal kissed the top of Jacki's head and contemplated the best way to sneak out of bed without waking her up.

As much as he would have loved to stay and just hold her, duty called. His mother should hear the good news about his upcoming wedding from him and not from Annani, which meant that he had to beat his aunt to it.

The discovery of his real heritage still made Kalugal's head spin.

Not only was he the son of a goddess, but he was also the nephew of the formidable head of the clan. Annani and Areana were only half-sisters, but since they were the last goddesses on the planet, the half was irrelevant in the grand scheme of things.

Jacki kept referring to him as a demigod, but despite Kalugal's natural arrogance, he hadn't internalized it yet. In his mind, he'd always been and still was the second most powerful immortal ever born, and he was good with that.

Demigod seemed like too much.

He didn't deserve the title, at least not yet. Perhaps when he took over control of the entire world, he would be more comfortable with it.

Carefully untangling himself from Jacki's arms and legs, Kalugal slid out of bed and took his phone with him to the bathroom.

Regrettably, Tuesday wasn't his turn for Areana's daily call, but he hoped that given the occasion, Annani would allow him to switch days with her. The problem was that he couldn't contact the goddess directly and had to arrange it through Kian.

It was six-fifteen in the morning, and hopefully, his cousin was up already. The guy was grumpy even when fully rested. If Kalugal woke him up, Kian might refuse to arrange the call.

Making as little noise as possible, he finished up in the bathroom and then ducked into the walk-in closet for a robe.

After quietly closing the door between the bedroom and the master sitting room, Kalugal loaded the coffeemaker, sat on the couch, and typed up a text to Kian.

Good morning. My apologies for the early text. I wish to share the happy news about my upcoming wedding with my mother, and I was wondering whether Annani would be willing to switch days with me. Please let me know if that can be arranged.

Long minutes passed as Kalugal waited for Kian to answer, but the time wasn't wasted. The coffee had finished brewing, and when Kian's return text finally arrived, Kalugal was sipping on his second cup.

No problem. Annani sends her congratulations and regrets not officiating over your wedding. When Areana's call comes in, I'll have William patch it through to you.

Kalugal typed back. *Thank you. And thank the goddess for me.*

A quick glance at the time revealed that it was six-thirty. Areana's daily call came at precisely seven every morning, which meant that he had half an hour to plan how he was going to condense everything he wanted to tell his mother into a ten-minute conversation.

Except, Kalugal's thoughts kept wandering in other directions.

He was practically already mated to Jacki, and by tonight it would be official, but he still hadn't shared his plans and aspirations with her.

Kalugal feared that she would find them objectionable.

It wasn't necessary to have that conversation today, but eventually he wanted to share everything with Jacki, even things that he wasn't sure would ever come to fruition.

Right now, Kalugal's world domination ideas seemed far removed from him, and if he didn't believe wholeheartedly that his rule would improve the lives of billions and secure the future of humans and immortals alike, he would have shrugged it off.

Why shoulder such a monumental undertaking?

Let someone else save the world.

Except, there was no one else.

Annani and Kian's hearts were in the right place, but they were going about it the wrong way. They believed in gentle nudges, supplying ideology and technology and hoping that humans would take it from there.

But that was not going to happen, or rather not happen soon enough. Humanity would destroy itself in one way or another long before it reached enlightenment, and it would take immortals down with it.

He'd thought that he had more time, but things were moving faster than he'd anticipated.

Technology was a double-edged sword.

In the right hands it was a blessing, but the problem was that it didn't discriminate, serving both benevolent and malevolent masters equally well.

When his phone rang, Kalugal shook himself out of his morbid reveries and planted a smile on his face. He wanted his mother to hear how happy he was, and that required his expression to match the sentiment.

"I'm patching you through," William said.

A moment later, Areana came on the line. "Kalugal? Is everything all right?"

"Hello, Mother. I have exciting news that I want to share with you. I'm getting married tonight."

Areana gasped. "Are you doing it to secure the alliance? Who is the bride? Someone important in Annani's clan? One of her daughters, perhaps?"

His mother sounded so hopeful and excited.

He should have expected that. Naturally, Areana thought that the rushed wedding had something to do with the summit. The truth was that if Annani had unmated daughters, that would have been a good move despite them being cousins. In that, Areana and Annani being only half-sisters was beneficial, and marriage between their children wasn't genetically problematic.

On the contrary, a child born to him and Annani's daughter would be extremely powerful. But Kalugal had met Jacki first, and she was the one for him.

Leaning back, he crossed his legs and smiled. "Jacqueline is not part of the clan, and at the moment, she is still human. But not for long."

"She is a Dormant?"

"Indeed. She is also an immune, which means that I can't compel her or thrall her or influence her mind in any way. I can just love and cherish her and hope that's enough."

Areana laughed, the otherworldly sound sending goosebumps up his arms. "I can see the appeal. She is a challenge."

"In more ways than one. She is also smart, direct, beautiful, and the least demanding female I've ever encountered."

Except when it came to commitment, but Kalugal didn't want to share that with his mother, lest she think that Jacki had manipulated him to marry her.

Jacki didn't want his money, and she wasn't interested in a cushy life as a rich man's wife either. She wanted to earn her keep, and she was willing to work hard for it.

The one thing she refused to compromise on was his soul. Jacki demanded his love, devotion, and loyalty.

Others though, and that included his mother, might think that she was after his money, or after the immortality he could give her, and that she'd maneuvered him into marrying her.

The opposite was true.

His soul might be priceless, but it wasn't an asset Jacki could or would ever sell, and in exchange, she'd given him hers.

In Kalugal's opinion, the bargain was skewed in his favor.

He was getting much more than he was giving away.

Jacki

As the cobwebs of sleep dissipated, the first thing that Jacki became aware of was the muscular chest her nose was pressed against, and the second was the steady heartbeat within it.

Kalugal.

Her fiancé, the love of her life, her first and last lover.

Or was he her husband now?

They'd already exchanged pledges last night, had consummated those pledges with mind-blowing lovemaking, and tonight they were going to make it official.

Jacki was a virgin no more, and as far as she was concerned, waiting for the right man had been one of the best decisions she'd ever made. The other one had been ditching the government program despite the fabulous salary.

Both had brought her to where she was now. In bed with the best man on the planet.

Not a man, a demigod.

Were they now Mr. and Mrs. Demigod?

With a soft chuckle, Jacki threw her arm around Kalugal and pulled him on top of her.

Naturally, he helped. "Good morning, my love." He dipped his head and kissed her. "Did you sleep well?"

"Best night of my life." She ran her hands over his muscled back. "You've been keeping secrets from me."

He cocked a brow. "Like what?"

"Like the fabulous physique that you were hiding under those cashmere sweaters and suit jackets. The entire time I've been here, I haven't seen you working out even once, and yet there isn't an ounce of fat on you, and every muscle is defined as if it was sculpted by an artist." Jacki pretended to narrow her eyes at him. "Were you sneaking out to the gym in the middle of the night?"

"I'm afraid not." Kalugal affected an apologetic expression. "I've been neglecting that aspect of my daily routine, and if I don't resume it soon, I might become flabby, and you won't want my body anymore." Swiveling his hips, he rubbed his erection against her center.

Jacki's laugh was deep and throaty. "I'll always want you. Besides, you probably don't need to do anything to look like that." She squeezed his bottom and arched up. "Demigods don't get fat."

"Says who?" He smoothed his hand up her ribcage and cupped her breast.

She stifled a moan. "In every myth and legend, gods and demigods are flawless, seducing unsuspecting maidens left and right. Training is never mentioned."

"Unfortunately, that's not true." He thumbed her nipple. "I can get away with doing very little to maintain my fabulous physique, but if I try really hard, I can get fat." He assumed a frown. "I will if that's what you desire." No longer bracing on his forearms, he let her feel the full weight of his athletic body.

Jacki wasn't a small woman, but even though Kalugal was slim, all those muscles were heavy. The weight on top of her was more than she'd expected, and yet it was just right.

"Don't you dare gain or lose an ounce. You are perfect the way you are." She squeezed his muscled bottom again.

Smiling, Kalugal exposed his fangs, which had elongated significantly since they had started their mutual teasing. "Is this an invitation, my Jacqueline?"

As if she needed to answer that.

Just the sight of those fangs was enough to trigger a gush of moisture that he could surely feel as well as smell.

After last night, she would never again look upon his fangs with fear. In fact, she would probably get wet every time Kalugal flashed them at her.

Just as he'd promised, the bite had left no mark on her, and if she hadn't just seen his fangs again this morning, she would have thought the bite hadn't happened and she'd dreamt it.

Jacki wasn't sore either, which was most likely thanks to the healing properties of the venom as well.

Which reminded her that she hadn't seen Kalugal's manhood yet. She'd definitely felt it, though, and the fit had been perfect. But she wanted to see, and touch, and lick, and suck...

The images triggered another outpouring of wetness.

"What do you think?" She arched up a little, rubbing her center against his hard shaft.

His smile turned into a fanged smirk. "I think that it's a yes." He dipped his head and kissed her.

She was already so wet that he could have penetrated her right away, but Kalugal had other ideas. Kissing a trail down her neck, he lingered a moment over the spot he'd bitten last night, licked it, and then sucked the skin in.

Jacki giggled. "There is no trace of your bite, so you want to mark me with a hickey?"

"I wish I could." He kissed the spot. "But nothing will be left of it after I bite you again." His voice dropped an octave.

"I can't wait," she whispered and turned her head sideways.

"Not yet, my love." He chuckled. "First, I need to worship at my goddess's temple." He slid further down, his lips hovering a fraction of an inch over her straining nipple.

Grasping his hair, Jacki pulled his head down to her breast. "The temple awaits your tribute."

Kian

As Kian glanced around the conference table, he felt a stab of guilt for not including Lokan in the strategy meeting.

The truth was that the Guardian briefing had nothing to do with the summit, and therefore should be of no interest to Lokan, but his cousin might disagree. After all, he'd offered his help numerous times and had taken part in missions.

Except, Kian needed to finalize the details of securing his people during Jacki and Kalugal's wedding, and having Lokan there would have made everyone uncomfortable.

Or maybe just him.

He still didn't fully trust Lokan, especially with anything that had to do with Kalugal.

The brothers weren't close, and they interacted more like distant acquaintances than family members. But blood is thicker than water, and Kian had no doubt that when push came to shove, Lokan would side with Kalugal.

The problem was that when Lokan found out about the meeting, he would feel excluded, and that wasn't good either. If Kian wanted Lokan's loyalty, he needed to show the guy that he was part of the team.

Under different circumstances, Kian might have compromised in the name of diplomacy, but this time there was too much at stake to risk it. He was about to walk into Kalugal's compound with Syssi, Amanda, and some of his best friends.

Hell, who was he kidding. This entire thing was one big compromise in the name of diplomacy.

Agreeing to attend the fucking wedding had been a leap of faith on his part, and now it was giving him a mental ulcer.

Perhaps he could convince Syssi not to come?

She could use nausea as an excuse, or fatigue, or some other pregnancy-related syndrome, and bow out gracefully. He would be much less stressed if Syssi went home instead of attending the wedding in Kalugal's mansion.

Yeah, good luck with that.

"Good luck with what?" Yamanu asked.

Kian hadn't been aware of speaking out loud. "Convincing Syssi to go home instead of coming with us to the wedding."

He was answered with a collective murmur of agreement.

Apparently, every mated male in the room felt the same. None of them wanted to expose their mates to even a whiff of danger.

Yamanu clapped Kian on the back. "We are all nervous, but it's going to be okay. The Fates brought us to this fork in the road for a reason. We could have chosen to keep going alone, like we have done up till now, or to take a risk and walk toward a new beginning. As much as I would love for Mey to be safely back in the village, I don't regret bringing her with me."

Kian shook his head. "I wish I had your faith. Nevertheless, let's continue. How many drones do we have on hand?"

"Seven," Turner said. "We had five already, and I'm getting two more delivered. I figured seven would look better in formation."

Kian frowned. "Who is going to operate them?"

Flying drones was not easy, and since he'd promised Kalugal an air show, the operators needed to be skilled in more than the basics.

Turner smiled. "I decided that it would be best if all of them were operated from the village. I'm not taking chances with Kalugal and his compulsion. If he somehow manages to get the cuff off, I want the drone operators to be out of his mental reach. William sent a signal booster that we will put on the balcony of the rented house. He, Roni, and Charlie are going to handle the drones from the safety of the village, and in view mode only. No sound."

"Good. But that's three operators. We need seven."

"I thought so too, but William explained that all seven drones will be controlled by the computer, following a program that he wrote for the occasion. If something happens and the need to use the drones in attack mode arises, the three of them will take over. There is no need for all seven drones to attack at once. We are covering a backyard, not a city block."

Kian shook his head. "I don't like it. Tell William to get at least two more operators. I know it's overkill, but I'd rather err on the side of caution."

"You're the boss."

Kian turned to Magnus. "What about your men? We didn't decide yet where to station them. I'm debating whether to have you join us at the party. The advantage is that you and your men will be right there if I need you. The other option is having you patrol outside."

"Kalugal is not going to allow us to keep our weapons on his property," Magnus said. "I'd rather stay outside with the men and, if needed, rush in fully armed. We can wear earplugs and communicate via text like we did before. That way, if Kalugal somehow manages to pull a magic trick, get rid of the cuff, and command everyone to freeze, we won't be affected."

"Good plan." Kian rapped his fingers on the table. "Stay in the rented house. I don't want him to see you patrolling."

"Why not? He knows we're out there."

"Diplomacy, my friend. I want to pretend that I trust him. He will know it's a lie, but he'll pretend to believe it, and everyone will feel good about themselves. The houses are so close that you can get there in under a minute."

"That's true," Magnus conceded.

"I suggest that as an added precaution, Kian and Brundar should wear earpieces," Turner said. "You both have long hair, so they won't be conspicuous."

Kian grimaced. "It's going to be a pain to hear everyone sound the same, but you're right."

"I'll wear mine too," Anandur said. "I don't care if Kalugal sees them. I'm your bodyguard, and my job is to protect you."

"Aren't you all forgetting something?" Magnus asked.

Kian glanced at Turner, but the guy shrugged. "There is always something. What did we miss?"

"I might be wrong, but I was under the impression that Kalugal went home without the cuff. When are you going to put it on him?"

Kian shook his head. "I can't believe I forgot about that. I should have asked him to keep wearing it." He pulled out his phone. "He'll have to come here."

"On his wedding day?" Anandur huffed out a breath. "Magnus can meet Kalugal outside the gate and put the cuff on him." He looked at the Guardian. "Just wear your earplugs and take a couple of men with you."

Magnus nodded. "I have no problem with that."

"Let me check with Kalugal first," Kian said. "As Anandur pointed out, it's the guy's wedding day, and we should make an effort to accommodate him."

Anandur chuckled. "All in the name of diplomacy."

"That's right," Kian agreed. "But we are also doing this for Jacki."

Syssi

The squealing started as soon as Mey and Jin walked through the door. Actually, Jin was making most of the noise and hugging everyone as if she hadn't seen them for months, but Mey contributed a few more joyous sounds of her own.

When it was Syssi's turn to get crushed in Jin's arms, she was glad that the girl wasn't immortal yet. Jin was surprisingly strong for a human.

Chuckling, she hugged the girl back. "Welcome to our home away from home."

"I'm so happy." Jin released her and wiped tears from her eyes. "I missed you all so much."

Behind her, Arwel shook his head. "You saw everyone on Friday, and it's only Tuesday."

"I know. But Jacki is getting married, and it makes me emotional." Jin wiped away another tear. "I can't wait to see her. She is going to be such a beautiful bride. Thank you so much for loaning her your wedding dress. Last night, Jacki emailed me a picture of herself wearing it, and she looked absolutely gorgeous."

"It's my pleasure."

"Where is Yamanu?" Amanda asked.

"Downstairs at the briefing," Arwel said. "I should head there as well." He glanced at Jin. "You don't need me here, right?"

She pecked him on the cheek. "You can go."

The Guardian looked relieved, which wasn't surprising given that he was the only male in the room. Nevertheless, he hesitated. "You're safe up here. Kian had Roni hack into the hotel's surveillance cameras, and if any suspicious activity is spotted, we will take care of whoever they are before they can get up here."

"I'm not concerned." Jin kissed his cheek again. "Go, have fun with the boys."

As the door closed behind the Guardian, Amanda sauntered over to the sisters and put a hand on each of their shoulders. "Do you need to rest a little, or are you ready to try the saris on? We have a lot of work to do."

Syssi glanced at her watch. "It's eight-thirty in the morning. We have plenty of time."

The party was scheduled to start at nine in the evening, but they were going over there a couple of hours earlier than that to help Jacki get ready. And while the ladies fussed over the bride, the guys were going to throw the groom a mini bachelor party.

It had been Kian's idea to surprise Kalugal and his men with premium whiskey and fine cigars. Despite being wary of his cousin, Kian must have grown fond of him to come up with that. Or maybe it was just another attempt at diplomacy, which Kian had been experimenting with since the whole thing with Kalugal had started.

In either case, Syssi was sure that the gesture would be appreciated, and sharing in a pre-wedding celebration would further the spirit of cooperation between their people.

"We have a lot of work to do." Amanda repeated as she herded the ladies toward the bedroom.

"It won't take us that long to get ready." Syssi followed the procession. "Can I make you girls coffee? Something to eat?"

Mey waved a dismissive hand. "I'm good. I prepared breakfast to go, and we had coffee and sandwiches on the plane."

"I would like some tea if it's not too much trouble." Jin rubbed a hand over the front of her neck. "My throat feels scratchy, and tea helps."

"How long have you been having these symptoms?" Bridget asked.

Jin waved a hand. "Since Arwel and I went up to the mountains. I don't know if it's allergies or if it's the freaking motor home's fault. It was either too cold or too hot inside, and we couldn't get the temperature right."

"Do you have a fever? Are you coughing? Do you have a runny nose?

Jin smiled. "Relax. I don't have a fever, and I'm not coughing. It's just an allergy."

"Do you usually get allergies this time of year?"

"Sometimes, but only mildly. I guess it depends on where I am."

Bridget shook her head. "Just in case, let me take your temperature."

As the doctor left to bring the tools of her trade, Amanda unfolded the two remaining saris. "Everyone has already picked theirs, and these are the only ones left."

Jin reached for the pink one. "Are they all this gaudy?"

"They are beautiful." Mey patted her back. "A sari without the vibrant colors is not a sari. Besides, we are both lucky to have the right coloring to pull it off. Dark hair goes with everything."

Amanda handed Jin a pink, long-sleeved T-shirt. "You can use this instead of the tiny one that comes with the outfit. The wedding is outdoors, and it gets quite chilly here at night."

"Thank you." Jin put the shirt on the bed and whipped her blouse over her head. "Mey brought me a long-sleeved T-shirt too, but it's probably not electric pink." She pulled the shirt on and glanced at the mirror mounted over the dresser. "Good fit." She unfurled the sari and eyed it suspiciously. "How do you put this thing on?"

"I'll show you." Amanda took the long swathe of fabric and expertly wrapped it around Jin. "I also brought safety pins to hold it in place."

"I guess the yellow one is mine." Mey picked up the last sari. "Not my favorite color, but it will do."

"I can switch with you," Syssi offered. "Do you prefer purple?"

Mey looked at her hopefully. "After red, that's my favorite color. But are you sure? Yellow might be too pale for you."

"It has pink embroidery." Syssi took the sari from Mey. "It might work."

"You see?" Amanda waved a hand. "That's why we needed to start early. I also have to do everyone's makeup, and Callie has to do everyone's hair."

"You don't have to," Syssi said. "We can do it ourselves."

Amanda glanced at Wonder, who suddenly looked panicked. "Not everyone can, and if I'm doing it for one, I might as well do it for everybody." She grinned. "When I'm done, you are all going to look fabulous."

"Oh, boy." Syssi groaned. "Now I know why you need ten hours to get us ready."

ORDER DARK OVERLORD'S CLAN TODAY!

JOIN THE VIP CLUB
To find out what's included in your free membership, flip to the last page.

The Children of the Gods Series

Reading Order

THE CHILDREN OF THE GODS ORIGINS

1: Goddess's Choice

When gods and immortals still ruled the ancient world, one young goddess risked everything for love.

2: Goddess's Hope

Hungry for power and infatuated with the beautiful Areana, Navuh plots his father's demise. After all, by getting rid of the insane god he would be doing the world a favor. Except, when gods and immortals conspire against each other, humanity pays the price.

But things are not what they seem, and prophecies should not to be trusted...

THE CHILDREN OF THE GODS

Dark Stranger

1: Dark Stranger The Dream

2: Dark Stranger Revealed

3: Dark Stranger Immortal

Dark Enemy

4: Dark Enemy Taken

5: Dark Enemy Captive

6: Dark Enemy Redeemed

Kri & Michael's Story

6.5: My Dark Amazon

Dark Warrior

7: Dark Warrior Mine

8: Dark Warrior's Promise

9: Dark Warrior's Destiny

10: Dark Warrior's Legacy

Dark Guardian

11: Dark Guardian Found

12: Dark Guardian Craved

13: Dark Guardian's Mate

Dark Angel

14: Dark Angel's Obsession

15: Dark Angel's Seduction

16: Dark Angel's Surrender

Dark Operative

17: Dark Operative: A Shadow of Death

18: Dark Operative: A Glimmer of Hope

19: Dark Operative: The Dawn of Love

Dark Survivor

20: Dark Survivor Awakened

21: Dark Survivor Echoes of Love

22: Dark Survivor Reunited

Dark Widow

23: Dark Widow's Secret

24: Dark Widow's Curse

25: Dark Widow's Blessing

Dark Dream

26: Dark Dream's Temptation

27: Dark Dream's Unraveling

28: Dark Dream's Trap

Dark Prince

29: Dark Prince's Enigma

30: Dark Prince's Dilemma

31: Dark Prince's Agenda

Dark Queen

32: Dark Queen's Quest

33: Dark Queen's Knight

34: Dark Queen's Army

Dark Spy

35: Dark Spy Conscripted

36: Dark Spy's Mission

37: Dark Spy's Resolution

Dark Overlord

38: Dark Overlord New Horizon

39: Dark Overlord's Wife

40: Dark Overlord's Clan

Dark Choices

41: Dark Choices The Quandary

When Rufsur and Edna meet, the attraction is as unexpected as it is undeniable. Except, she's the clan's judge and councilwoman, and he's Kalugal's second-in-command. Will loyalty and duty to their people keep them apart?

42: Dark Choices Paradigm Shift

Edna and Rufsur are miserable without each other, and their two-week separation seems like an eternity. Long-distance relationships are difficult, but for immortal couples they are impossible. Unless one of them is willing to leave everything behind for the other, things are just going to get worse. Except, the cost of compromise is far greater than giving up their comfortable lives and hard-earned positions. The future of their people is on the line.

43: Dark Choices The Accord

The winds of change blowing over the village demand hard choices. For better or worse, Kian's decisions will alter the trajectory of the clan's future, and he is not ready to take the plunge. But as Edna and Rufsur's plight gains widespread support, his resistance slowly begins to erode.

Dark Secrets

44: Dark Secrets Resurgence

On a sabbatical from his Stanford teaching position, Professor David Levinson finally has time to write the sci-fi novel he's been thinking about for years.

The phenomena of past life memories and near-death

experiences are too controversial to include in his formal psychiatric research, while fiction is the perfect outlet for his esoteric ideas.

Hoping that a change of pace will provide the inspiration he needs, David accepts a friend's invitation to an old Scottish castle.

45: Dark Secrets Unveiled

When Professor David Levinson accepts a friend's invitation to an old Scottish castle, what he finds there is more fantastical than his most outlandish theories. The castle is home to a clan of immortals, their leader is a stunning demigoddess, and even more shockingly, it might be precisely where he belongs.

Except, the clan founder is hiding a secret that might cast a dark shadow on David's relationship with her daughter.

Nevertheless, when offered a chance at immortality, he agrees to undergo the dangerous induction process.

Will David survive his transition into immortality? And if he does, will his relationship with Sari survive the unveiling of her mother's secret?

46: Dark Secrets Absolved

Absolution.

David had given and received it.

The few short hours since he'd emerged from the coma had felt incredible. He'd finally been free of the guilt and pain, and for the first time since Jonah's death, he had felt truly happy and optimistic about the future.

He'd survived the transition into immortality, had been accepted into the clan, and was about to marry the best woman on the face of the planet, his true love mate, his salvation, his everything.

What could have possibly gone wrong?

Just about everything.

<u>Dark Haven</u>

47: Dark Haven Illusion

Welcome to Safe Haven, where not everything is what it seems.

On a quest to process personal pain, Anastasia joins the Safe Haven Spiritual Retreat.

Through meditation, self-reflection, and hard work, she hopes to make peace with the voices in her head.

This is where she belongs.

Except, membership comes with a hefty price, doubts are sacrilege, and leaving is not as easy as walking out the front gate.

Is living in utopia worth the sacrifice?

Anastasia believes so until the arrival of a new acolyte changes everything.

Apparently, the gods of old were not a myth, their immortal descendants share the planet with humans, and she might be a carrier of their genes.

48: <u>Dark Haven Unmasked</u>

As Anastasia leaves Safe Haven for a week-long romantic vacation with Leon, she hopes to explore her newly discovered passionate side, their budding relationship, and perhaps also solve the mystery of the voices in her head. What she discovers exceeds her wildest expectations.

In the meantime, Eleanor and Peter hope to solve another mystery. Who is Emmett Haderech, and what is he up to?

49: Dark Haven Found

Anastasia is growing suspicious, and Leon is running out of excuses.

Risking death for a chance at immortality should've been her choice to make. Will she ever forgive him for taking it away from her?

Dark Power

50: Dark Power Untamed

Attending a charity gala as the clan's figurehead, Onegus is ready for the pesky socialites he'll have a hard time keeping away. Instead, he encounters an intriguing beauty who won't give him the time of day.

Bad things happen when Cassandra gets all worked up, and given her fiery temper, the destructive power is difficult to tame. When she meets a gorgeous, cocky billionaire at a charity event, things just might start blowing up again.

51: Dark Power Unleashed

Cassandra's power is unpredictable, uncontrollable, and destructive. If she doesn't learn to harness it, people might get hurt.

Onegus's self-control is legendary. Even his fangs and venom glands obey his commands.

They say that opposites attract, and perhaps it's true, but are they any good for each other?

52: Dark Power Convergence

The threads of fate converge, mysteries unfold, and the clan's future is forever altered in the least expected way.

Dark Memories

53: Dark Memories Submerged

54: Dark Memories Emerge

55: Dark Memories Restored

Dark Hunter

56: Dark Hunter's Query

57: Dark Hunter's Prey

58: [Dark Hunter's Boon](#)

Dark God

59: Dark God's Avatar

60: Dark God's Reviviscence

61: Dark God Destinies Converge

Dark Whispers

62: Dark Whispers From The Past

63: Dark Whispers From Afar

64: Dark Whispers From Beyond

Dark Gambit

65: Dark Gambit The Pawn

66: Dark Gambit The Play

67: Dark Gambit Reliance

Dark Alliance

68: Dark Alliance Kindred Souls

69: Dark Alliance Turbulent Waters

70: Dark Alliance Perfect Storm

Dark Healing

71: Dark Healing Blind Justice

72: Dark Healing Blind Trust

73: Dark healing Blind Curve

Dark Encounters

74: Dark Encounters of the Close Kind

75: Dark Encounters of the Unexpected Kind

76: Dark Encounters of the Fated Kind

The Children of the Gods Series Sets

Books 1-3: Dark Stranger trilogy—Includes a bonus short story: **The Fates take a Vacation**

Books 4-6: Dark Enemy Trilogy —Includes a bonus short story—**The Fates' Post-Wedding Celebration**

Books 7-10: Dark Warrior Tetralogy

Books 11-13: Dark Guardian Trilogy

Books 14-16: Dark Angel Trilogy

Books 17-19: Dark Operative Trilogy

Books 20-22: Dark Survivor Trilogy

Books 23-25: Dark Widow Trilogy

Books 26-28: Dark Dream Trilogy

Books 29-31: Dark Prince Trilogy
Books 32-34: Dark Queen Trilogy
Books 35-37: Dark Spy Trilogy
Books 38-40: Dark Overlord Trilogy
Books 41-43: Dark Choices Trilogy
Books 44-46: Dark Secrets Trilogy
Books 47-49: Dark Haven Trilogy
Books 50-52: Dark Power Trilogy
Books 53-55: Dark Memories Trilogy
Books 56-58: Dark Hunter Trilogy
Books 59-61: Dark God Trilogy
Books 62-64: Dark Whispers Trilogy
Books 65-67: Dark Gambit Trilogy
Books 68-70: Dark Alliance Trilogy
Books 71-73: Dark healing Trilogy

MEGA SETS

INCLUDE CHARACTER LISTS

The Children of the Gods: Books 1-6
The Children of the Gods: Books 6.5-10

TRY THE SERIES ON

AUDIBLE

2 FREE audiobooks with your new Audible subscription!

PERFECT MATCH SERIES

Vampire's Consort

When Gabriel's company is ready to start beta testing, he invites his old crush to inspect its medical safety protocol.

Curious about the revolutionary technology of the *Perfect Match Virtual Fantasy-Fulfillment studios*, Brenna agrees.

Neither expects to end up partnering for its first fully immersive test run.

King's Chosen

When Lisa's nutty friends get her a gift certificate to *Perfect Match Virtual Fantasy Studios*, she has no intentions of using it. But since the only way to get a refund is if no partner can be found for her, she makes sure to request a fantasy so girly and over the top that no sane guy will pick it up.

Except, someone does.

> **Warning:** This fantasy contains a hot, domineering crown prince, sweet insta-love, steamy love scenes painted with light shades of gray, a wedding, and a HEA in both the virtual and real worlds.
>
> Intended for mature audience.

Captain's Conquest

Working as a Starbucks barista, Alicia fends off flirting all day long, but none of the guys are as charming and sexy as Gregg. His frequent visits are the highlight of her day, but since he's never asked her out, she assumes he's taken. Besides, between a day job and a budding music career, she has no time to start a new relationship.

That is until Gregg makes her an offer she can't refuse—a gift certificate to the virtual fantasy fulfillment service everyone is talking about. As a huge Star Trek fan, Alicia has a perfect match in mind—the captain of the Starship Enterprise.

The Thief Who Loved Me

When Marian splurges on a Perfect Match Virtual adventure as a world infamous jewel thief, she expects high-wire fun with a hot partner who she will never have to see again in real life.

A virtual encounter seems like the perfect answer to Marcus's string of dating disasters. No strings attached, no drama, and definitely no love. As a die-hard James Bond fan, he chooses as his avatar a dashing MI6 operative, and to complement his adventure, a dangerously seductive partner.

Neither expects to find their forever Perfect Match.

My Merman Prince

The beautiful architect working late on the twelfth floor of my building thinks that I'm just the maintenance guy. She's also under the impression that I'm not interested.

Nothing could be further from the truth.

I want her like I've never wanted a woman before, but I don't play where I work.

I don't need the complications.

When she tells me about living out her mermaid fantasy with a stranger in a Perfect Match virtual adventure, I decide to do everything possible to ensure that the stranger is me.

The Dragon King

To save his beloved kingdom from a devastating war, the Crown Prince of Trieste makes a deal with a witch that costs him half of his humanity and dooms him to an eternity of loneliness.

Now king, he's a fearsome cobalt-winged dragon by day and a short-tempered monarch by night. Not many are brave enough to serve in the palace of the brooding and volatile ruler, but Charlotte ignores the rumors and accepts a scribe position in court.

As the young scribe reawakens Bruce's frozen heart, all that stands in the way of their happiness is the witch's bargain. Outsmarting the evil hag will take cunning and courage, and Charlotte is just the right woman for the job.

My Werewolf Romeo

The father of my star student is a big-shot screenwriter and the patron of the drama department who thinks he can dictate what production I should put on. The principal makes it very clear that I need to cooperate with the opinionated asshat or walk away from my dream job at the exclusive private high school.

It doesn't help matters that the guy is single, hot, charming, creative, and seems to like me despite my thinly-veiled hostility.

When he invites me to a custom-tailored Perfect Match virtual adventure to prove that his screenplay is perfect for my production, I accept, intending to have fun while proving that messing with the classics is a foolish idea.

I don't expect to be wowed by his werewolf adaptation of Red Riding Hood mesh-up with Romeo and Juliet, and I certainly don't expect to fall in love with the virtual fantasy's leading man.

The Channeler's Companion

A treat for fans of *The Wheel of Time*.

When Erika hires Rand to assist in her pediatric clinic, she does so despite his good looks and irresistible charm, not because of them.

He's empathic, adores children, and has the patience of a saint.

He's also all she can think about, but he's off limits.

What's a doctor to do to scratch that irresistible itch without risking workplace complications?

A shared adventure in the Perfect Match Virtual Studios seems like the solution, but instead of letting the algorithm choose a partner for her, Erika can try to influence it to select the one she wants. Awarding Rand a gift certificate to the service will get him into their database, but unless Erika can tip the odds in her favor, getting paired with him is a long shot.

Hopefully, a virtual adventure based on her and Rand's favorite series will do the trick.

Note

Dear reader,

I hope my stories have added a little joy to your day. If you have a moment to add some to mine, you can help spread the word about the Children Of The Gods series by telling your friends and penning a review. Your recommendations are the most powerful way to inspire new readers to explore the series.

Thank you,

Isabell

FOR EXCLUSIVE PEEKS AT UPCOMING RELEASES & A FREE COMPANION BOOK

Join my *VIP Club* and gain access to the VIP portal at itlucas.com
To Join, go to:
http://eepurl.com/blMTpD

INCLUDED IN YOUR FREE MEMBERSHIP:

YOUR VIP PORTAL

- Read preview chapters of upcoming releases.
- Listen to Goddess's Choice narration by Charles Lawrence
- Exclusive content offered only to my VIPs.

FREE I.T. LUCAS COMPANION INCLUDES:

- Goddess's Choice Part 1
- Perfect Match: Vampire's Consort (A standalone Novella)
- Interview Q & A
- Character Charts

If you're already a subscriber, and you are not getting my emails, your provider is

SENDING THEM TO YOUR JUNK FOLDER, AND YOU ARE MISSING OUT ON **IMPORTANT UPDATES, SIDE CHARACTERS' PORTRAITS, ADDITIONAL CONTENT, AND OTHER GOODIES.** TO FIX THAT, ADD isabell@itlucas.com TO YOUR EMAIL CONTACTS OR YOUR EMAIL VIP LIST.

**Check out the specials at
https://www.itlucas.com/specials**

Printed in Great Britain
by Amazon